MYRRIDDIN

MYRRIDDIN

BOOK II OF THE MERLIN FACTOR

STEVEN MAINES

Purple Haze Press

MYRRIDDIN

BOOK II of THE MERLIN FACTOR

COPYRIGHT © 2008 by Steven Maines

Purple Haze Press books may be ordered through booksellers or by contacting:
Purple Haze Press
PBM 167 2430 Vanderbilt Beach Road, #108
Naples, FL 34109
www.PurpleHazePress.com

This is a work of fiction. All characters, names, incidents, organizations and dialogue in this novel are either the products of the author's imagination or are used fictitiously.

COVER DESIGN:
Jeffrey Bedrick

ISBN978-0-9773200-4-2

Library of Congress Control Number: 2008923188

Printed in the United States of America

1. New Age 2. Fiction 3. Historical Fiction

ACKNOWLEDGEMENTS

I wish to express my deepest appreciation to the following people:

Michele Genovese Maines, Vaishāli, Elliot Malach, Maxine Chavez & Purple Haze Press® for their profound love, support, wisdom & faith.

My son,
Liam Maines.
You are an inspiration.

Ann Maines. Sharon Maines. Chris, Daisy, Sean & Benjamin Maines. Jonathan Rose, Jeffrey Bedrick.

DEDICATION

I wish to dedicate this book to my father,
BARRY MAINES.
Though you are no longer here,
you are ever with me.
Thank you for your love
& guidance. I love you.

MYRRIDDIN

BOOK II of THE MERLIN FACTOR

Character Name Pronunciations

MYRRIDDIN — Méir-rĭ-dĭnn

MOSCASTAN —Mōz-káz-tăn

LEONI —Lee-ó-nee

BALDUA —Báll-doo-ah

IGRAINES — Eé-grān

KINDRIXER —Kĭnn-drícks-er

CRAMUSIN —Krămm-yóo-sun

TRASTONUS —Trăs-tóne-us

LORD CRECONIUS MAB —Kreck-ón-ee-us Mŏb

FATHER PRETORIUS —Prāy-tór-ee-us

NIMUE —Nímm-oo-wāy

TREMEL —Trĕ-méll

BISHOP ROZINUS —Rózz-ee-nŭs

GORLIS LOT —Gór-lĭss-lŏt

Characters Mentioned

UTHER PENDRAGON — Oó-ther Pén-drăg-ŭn

ARTURIUS —Ar-tóo-er-ee-ŭs

PROLOGUE

I could see nothing; darkness, emptiness was all there seemed to be. Floating. I felt light, without weight. Yes, I was floating. I remembered my name. It was Longinus, Centurion of Rome. Rather, that *had* been my name, my title. That person, that body, had been crucified in a place called Antioch. I was no longer that individual, but *I* continued to exist, continued to *be*. I had my full faculties in this apparent state of the spirit; could think, could feel, could . . . see . . .

Floating, still. Specific images became apparent before me. I was watching as if from above, hovering just slightly over . . . Irena. Yes, it was my Irena and, two small boys: my boys, Longinus' boys. They were beautiful. I felt emotion begin to well up at the sight of the three of them. But there were others there, too. There was an older man. Joseph. His name was Joseph of Arimathea. There were others as well: a woman and a small girl. Mary of Magdalene, friend and intimate of Jesu, and their daughter, Sara. They were all together—Irena, Longinus' sons, Jacobi Arturius and Joshua; Joseph, Mary and Sara. Several other people were with them, too, but I did not know them. They were all aboard a ship which was traveling to Gaul; a ship that flew the Wild Boar insignia.

I moved forward in time. The ship arrived in the southern part of Gaul. Mary and the girl, Sara, disembarked with an escort of men and women. Irena went off the ship briefly. She and Mary embraced, tearfully, no doubt reliving in an instant the past years together, and knowing full well they would probably never see each other again.

The images changed again: back on board the ship, cutting through the water, moving west toward the setting sun. Irena, the two boys, and Joseph stood at the bow, the ship's master, Ventrix, alongside them. To Britain, they sailed.

From the ship to the land. I now saw Irena, Jacobi Arturius, Joshua and Joseph of Arimathea making their way across land with a large cart being led by a raggedy horse. There was something in the cart that was covered by animal skin blankets. They continued on land, passing a large, ancient stone circle, and arriving at the edge of a large lake. An island lay in the middle of the lake. A flat barge greeted them, large enough for the four of them and their cart. They boarded the barge and made their way across the lake to the island.

A Temple. An ancient Temple not yet in complete ruins, but certainly no longer in its prime, adorned with symbols of the ancient Druids, was the destination. In the lower chamber of this place stood three Druid Brahmins in white robes, and three brown-robed Ascetics, followers of the Christ as evidenced by their robes and the wooden crucifix hanging around each of their necks. Irena and the boys were but a few feet away, observing. The three brown-robed Ascetics embraced Joseph, in turn, knowing him well. Joseph had come to this land previously and had established a group of Christ followers in this place called Britain, on this Isle of Mystery, in the middle of a lake.

On the ground before them was a large box—that which had been under the skins on the cart. It was rectangular and six feet in length, two-feet high and two-feet wide. Joseph opened the box slowly and revealed its contents for all present to see: three items, each individually wrapped in cloth coverings. Gently, he unwrapped the first item and held it up for inspection. It was a small wooden bowl. Reverently, he placed the bowl on a nearby rectangular stone slab. Next, he unwrapped a bundle of three pieces of old wood, each approximately two feet long and roughly squared. My spirit recognized them; they were pieces of the Rood—pieces of the Cross on which the Christ had been crucified. These, too, Joseph placed on the slab.

Then came the final item from the box; something my spirit remembered with great joy. It was the spear, my spear, Longinus' spear—the instrument that had pierced the side of the Christ while he hung on the cross. Joseph handled this item with the utmost reverence. It was widely known and believed that after the crucifixion, I, while Longinus incarnate, had performed great feats with the spear's aid. But, more importantly, for Joseph and the others, the spear's blade still had the blood of the Christ, Jesu, on it. After a moment, Joseph laid the spear on the slab, as well. They all bowed their heads and prayed before the items.

Joseph, tenderly, separately rewrapped the bowl, the Rood and the spear, and placed them once again in the wooden box. The slab on which the items had rested for a short time was now open, its top removed, the large stone covering leaning against the slab's side. The slab was actually a sarcophagus-type structure. Gently, two of the men, a Druid and an Ascetic, placed the wooden box within the stone sarcophagus. Once the box was inside its new stone housing, it took all three of the Druids, and all three of the Ascetics to lift the stone lid back on top of the sarcophagus, thus creating the look of a large stone slab again.

The image then faded from my sight. It was replaced by an image of Irena bidding Joseph farewell as he boarded the Boar ship once more. Irena and the boys would stay in Britain.

Floating. I was still floating, now surrounded by mists. After a moment, the mists began to fade. I felt a slight jolt, as if I had bumped into something. I was no longer floating, no longer seeing things from the abstract perspective of a spirit. Presently, I looked out from the eyes of a boy, my present life on this earth. I stood in the Temple's lower chamber or room, the same room where the sacred items had been entombed. But now, the Temple was in ruins. It had been three centuries since the items had been laid to rest here. The bowl and the Rood were not seen. Stolen or perhaps still there, but now buried deeply in the rubble, not to be found by anyone. Regardless, I knew nothing of those things, nor would I have cared even if I had known. I was only a boy, after all. The spear, though—that was different. I held the spear in my hand, having just found it in the crumbling sarcophagus. In this life, many called me Merlin. I preferred the ancient version of that name or title: Myrriddin.

ONE

The moon was high and full. Its silver light bathed the valley and road with a brightness that seemed more akin to midday than to midnight. I saw the road clearly through a nearby cluster of shrubbery. My *sight* was so clear, in fact, that it was as if I were actually there.

The traveling party approached on the road from the east, just as my Druidic Master had predicted. There were three wagons drawn by two horses each. The wagons were surrounded by horsemen; Romans, to be precise. They were a contingent of soldiers, perhaps two Decades strong, their Decurions leading the way. Seeing an escort of Roman soldiers was an increasingly rare sight in this place and time, but certainly not unheard of. Rome still had Britain in her grasp, though that grasp was becoming looser by the day.

"Well, boy, what do you see?" asked High Druid Master Moscastan. He was young for a High Druid Master. No more than forty-five summers.

Moscastan was a striking figure: over six-feet tall, broad of shoulder and thick of muscle. He had an exotically handsome face with eyes as black as coal, and skin as brown as baked bread. He had been born in the land of the Jews, but Hebrew he was not. He was Persian by paternity. Moscastan had come back with his mother to her homeland, the isles of Britain, when he was but a child.

His mother being a Britton explained Moscastan's shock of red hair. She had been taken as a slave by Rome when she'd been but a lass and sold to a wealthy Persian noble for his harem. She had been freed by her owner, Moscastan's Persian father, upon his death, as set forth by his posthumous wishes. She then made her way back to Britain, child in tow. "I ask again, Master Merlin, what do you see?" he repeated.

Master Moscastan knew that I preferred one of the ancient Gaelic spellings and pronunciations of my name, as opposed to the common one propagated by the Romans. But he used the latter when he wished to chide me. Merlin. *Merlin* had always been a title, a level of achievement within the Druidic ranks, and, therefore, a special word, even a sacred one. But as with so many of our ways, the Romans—and the new peoples calling themselves Christians—had destroyed, or at the very least, bastardized them; the old Celtic and Druidic traditions. The title, or word, "Merlin", was one such example. The word Merlin had become almost more of a meaningless name now than anything else. But, there were many of us who knew that the old ways still existed, and hence their titles and words still held not only meaning, but power. Though I was given the name Merlin, I had too much respect for the title to use it as my name. Instead, I used Myrriddin, one of the more ancient and obscure spellings. This particular spelling also meant *the learner*, which I certainly was still, even at thirty summers and with my many years of study with the Druids.

"I see three wagons and a Roman escort," I finally replied.

"Look within the wagons," commanded Moscastan.

"What?"

"Do it!" he ordered.

I peered through the shrubs again just as the wagons were passing in front of my view. I concentrated on the wagons, commanding my inner eye to *see* their contents. Indeed, after a moment, I could perceive the parts of Roman war machines beneath the wagon's canvas covering.

"Siege engines!" I shouted.

As I did so, one of the Decurions on the road reined in his mount and looked in my direction.

He could not have heard me, I thought. After all, I wasn't actually there.

But then the Decurion, the leader of one of the groups of Ten, nudged his mount toward me; toward what was my viewing position.

As the Roman officer did this, I jumped back with a start and bumped hard into Moscastan. My surroundings were no longer the moonlit valley and road and shrub, but Moscastan's sparse, dank, underground dwelling. Though its floor was dry, hard-packed earth, its walls always seemed to be damp; they were made of dark, soft clay. The whole dwelling only measured about ten-feet by ten-feet.

It was dug out of the earth by Moscastan, himself, many years prior, and had a five-foot high, thirteen-foot long tunnel leading to the surface on a semi-gradual incline as the only way in or out. Three holes, a foot each in diameter, were scattered around the dwelling. They were ventilation ducts that led to the surface.

I stepped forward once again and cautiously peered back into the waters of the large scrying bowl through which I had been remotely viewing the moonlit valley and Roman-escorted wagons. The image I had been viewing and the scene I had been living was gone.

"I could swear an oath that one of the Roman officers saw me," I said, disappointment and embarrassment at having lost the images seeping into my voice.

"Not *saw* you, *sensed* you. Outbursts of emotion project your essence. Those whom you are viewing will sometimes sense your . . . presence, so to speak, if they are sensitive enough," Moscastan explained. "But you know this already, do you not?"

His half-smile was mocking, though not unkindly so. He was right. I knew that control of emotion in this instance—indeed, in most instances—was paramount to a successful viewing. More specifically, in the case of remote viewing, it was the control of one's thoughts that counted the most. An emotional outburst signaled the loss of this control, even if it was for only an instant.

"Yes, yes," I said. Though I wanted to try the remote viewing again, it was late and I was tired.

"The night is nearly gone, Myrriddin," said Moscastan in an echo of my thoughts. "We've seen what we needed to. The Romans come again."

"I admit I was surprised to see the siege engine parts in the wagons, but I'd hardly call twenty some-odd soldiers and three wagons another coming of Rome, even if they do carry war implements." I replied. "Perhaps they're leaving for good," I added, sardonically.

"Hmm," said Moscastan, noncommittally.

"Well, I should be off," I said, after a moment of silence. "Must be on the drilling field at dawn."

"Then you'd best be gone. The sun appears again in but four hours," replied the Master Druid.

"Peace be yours, Master," I said.

"And with you, lad."

With that, I headed up the tunnel and into the night air.

Luna went to slumber quickly, the sun birthing again much sooner than I had wanted it to. I had not yet developed the ability to gain a full night's replenishing sleep on a half-night's (or less) turbulent rest. Only a Druid Master like Moscastan was capable of such a feat. Though I had been a student of Master Moscastan's for many summers, twelve thus far, I was far from being a Deryddon—a full-fledged Druid; a full- fledged Magi or Magician. I had moments when I felt connected to this caste of Druid, the Magi, but not very often. There were actually three castes of Druids and I felt more a part of the other two than I did the Master Druid caste. The other two castes were known as the Bard, which was the historian or poet caste, and the Vates, which was the caste of the Prophet. It was especially this latter one that I felt most connected to because, more often than not, and more often than the average person, I would have prophetic visions during my sleep.

Yet, this was probably due not so much to my Druidic studies as it was to two other facts: The fact that I slept nightly on wattles from the rowan tree, which were known to quite often produce visionary experiences in one who slept on them, and the fact that I also slept with my staff, which was formed from a Roman spear I found in the ruins of a nearby ancient Druid Temple when I was a lad. It was barely still recognizable as a spear. Its blade now cradled a *Druid Egg*, a rough, apple-sized crystal. The blade itself was straight and intact, not bent to cradle the crystal, though I had tried to bend it by heating the metal. No matter how hot it became, the blade would not bow. Nor would the hot flames cause any discoloration to the metal, or cause any of the corrosive stains that had been there for centuries to burn away. There was one cluster of stains on the blade that was definitely not corrosion. I was convinced that it was blood; it had the color and thickness of dried blood. But if it was blood, why could I not clean it off or burn it away?

On more than one occasion, the spear-staff had vibrated or become warm in my hands for no apparent reason, and seemed to convey something from the Otherworld. Exactly what that something was I still could not decipher, but I knew, felt, that it was something important and profound. I was not frightened by these occurrences.

When the blade wouldn't bend to cradle the crystal, I created a small, oval-shaped binding wicker cage made of oak and rowan sticks. It is called binding, for as one makes the cage, one speaks and thinks his desire and intent for it, thus binding it to those intents and desires. In this case, the intent was to protect and conceal the spear. I then secured it to the base of the blade, keeping the blade with it. Before securing it completely around the blade I placed within the cage, resting against the blade itself, the Druid Egg. This was not only to further aid in the protection and concealment of the spear's identity, but a Druid Egg, being a conduit of energy, also served to amplify the spear's power. Or so I chose to believe. I secured the cage and Druid Egg with leather thongs. The whole thing was impressive, a true Merlin's staff. Why didn't I just keep it as a spear? I was more of a wizard than a warrior, to be sure—though I enjoyed my youthful daily warrior training. But the spear, I knew beyond dreamy, idle wishing, was something special and was not to be paraded forth—at least, not as a spear.

Having the knowledge that the spear was something special, however, sometimes made me feel unworthy of it. Yet, as I said, occasionally when I touched it, it seemed to communicate with me, not in words, but with a small vibration or warmth. I almost felt that it was alive or even that something divine could come through it, though that had not yet happened. Other times, however, and in fact, most of the time, I knew that the spear, my staff, was meant for me and me alone. On the two occasions I had let friends handle it, they both had burned their hands quite severely when they touched the shaft. The warmth that *I* felt when touching it was more of a loving caress channeled from the Otherworld. It was a warmth that never exceeded the temperature of comfort. In addition to this, there was one other very important reason why I knew this spear was meant for me: it had *always* been mine. Not just in the life I now led as Myrriddin, but in a previous life as a Roman centurion, had this very spear belonged to me, this soul.

The combination of sleeping on the power-laced wattles and next to the spear would, on occasion, produce in my mind the vivid images and experiences of this man of the Empire from over three centuries prior. Yet, it was more than just the images and experiences of this centurion, whose name had been revealed to me as being Gaius Cassius Longinus that impinged themselves on my mind during my nocturnal sojourns. It was also the certain knowledge that I had been *him* in that very life; that my soul and his soul were one-in-the-same soul. Even more, was that according to Moscastan, I, Myrriddin, was related to Longinus, the man, by blood! This he had yet to explain to my satisfaction. But, he had assured me that it was so, and that he would explain it all to me in due time.

"It is enough for now that you have the spear, and that it speaks to you. Guard it well," he had said to me on the day that I had revealed my treasure to him, and the fact that it communicated with me. Guard it well, I did. No one knew that my Merlin's staff, my Magi's wand, was the spear of Longinus, Roman centurion. I had disguised it well.

As the sun crested the hills to the east, I left my small, round, thatched dwelling on the western outskirts of the village with staff in hand, and made my way to the cooking fires at the center of the village. There were a few people at the fires breaking their fast of the previous night. A bit odd, that was. Usually, there were many more on hand at that time for the morning meal.

"Ach, Master Merlin," came Leoni's familiar, deep, husky voice. I had assumed since my childhood that her deep voice was due to her hefty girth, and that its raspiness was from years spent in the smoke of the cooking fires. She had been with me since I was a tot. Her plump face and black hair had been the first images my eyes saw. My parents—having been told by the then High Druid Aberdinus that my coming had been foretold, that I was to be a great Druid—had given me up at birth for rearing by the community on the island of Avalon, the Isle of Mystery, at the High Druid's insistence. Avalon, a small island in the middle of the Lake Essex, was where all prospective Derwyddons and Dryadesses, Druids and Druidesses, and all manner and levels thereto, were trained and housed. Many, such as myself, arrived not long after birth, if, that is, they had been chosen for it. And, one could only be accepted into the Mystery School on the island if chosen, as I had been.

Once the choosing had taken place, all ties to one's actual parents were severed for fifteen summers or so, at least. One did not actually begin formal Druidic studies until the age of eight. Before that, in addition to being allowed to just enjoy childhood, the little one was groomed for his or her future education in many ways; being taught to recognize the Spirit, the God, in all things, was one example. When I had first arrived on the island as a babe, Leoni had been a caretaker in the community's nursery. She had already achieved the status of a low-level priestess, but chose to go no further with her Druidic studies. "You must recognize your pattern," she had said to me once. "Know your meaning. Mine is to serve the younglings of this place and beyond." Leoni had been the one to call me from the ruins the day I had found the spear. I had taken it with me that day, removed it from its place of rest, concealed, wrapped in its rotting cloth. She had looked askance at me as I came out of the ruins of the Temple, silently asking, *What is that you carry?* But she never actually asked, never mentioned it. Now, even here, in our village off the island, she is with me still, not in the same way as when she was my caretaker, of course, but seeing her daily at the village's cooking fires reassured me that all was right with the world.

"Ach, forgive me, Master Myrriddin, I mean," Leoni corrected herself. "You did not join this morning's Sun birth rite."

"No," I replied. "I was with Master Moscastan until quite late last evening."

"And yet, Master Moscastan was there. Hmm," she said with mock bewilderment, bordering on reproach.

I said nothing. She could still disarm me as if I were naught but a very young lad.

She smiled broadly, a clean, dimpled smile. She still had most of her teeth. "Ah well," she said. "I'm just glad you're still at the study, even if it is a private tutelage with Master Moscastan. Concerned, we were, when you announced your leaving the Mystery School all those summers ago. We thought, 'Why? Why would the lad do this?' We all said, 'What with only half his years of study done . . . ?'"

She continued rambling to herself as she resumed her duties at the cooking fire, poking the embers while reliving the events as she remembered them, all but forgetting my presence. I quickly took advantage of the moment, grabbing two oatcakes hot off the fire pan, a small wedge of cheese, and a cup of mead. "I'm off to the drill field, Leoni. Blessed day to you!" I called as I trotted away, all the while trying desperately to balance my mead, oatcakes, cheese and staff.

"And you, Myrriddin," Leoni called back to me. I hadn't thought she heard my goodbye. "You'd best be quick," she continued. "There're things swirling in the wind."

TWO

Whatever Leoni meant by her last statement, I hadn't a notion so I did not attempt to understand it. I made my way to the drill field, stuffing my face as I went.

My staff, mead and oatcakes were not the only things I carried. Tucked under my tunic in my leather belt strap was my sword. It was an old Roman gladius, refurbished, polished and honed to a deadly sharpness. I found it the day after I had found the spear in the Temple ruins. The gladius, however, I found in another set of ruins altogether. These ruins were near the village of the Ruthernus clan. They were not as dramatic as the Temple ruins where I'd found the spear, my staff; not by any means. That place had been a sacred stone Temple built by the *Antewonc*, the *Ancient Ones*, or more accurately, my ancestors. The exact function of the place in ancient times was now only known to the oldest of our Druids, although I suspected Moscastan held the knowledge, as well. Still, the place was considered hallowed ground. No doubt, I would have been severely reprimanded had the fact that I'd removed an artifact from the place become common knowledge. Yet, I knew my secret to be safe with the two besides myself who held the awareness of my possession.

I found the gladius, however, in a not so sacred place: a dilapidated Roman fort long since abandoned. I had also found a legionnaire's shield; three, actually, and two helms, also common legionnaire issue—the helms each had the tell-tale ring atop, not the cresting plum of an officer. I kept one of those along with the sword, but gave away the other items. I might as well have given away the helm, too. I never touched it after that day—no *real* Celtic warrior would ever use a helmet, after all.

Staff in hand, gladius tucked away under my tunic, I arrived at the drill field just as I finished stuffing food into my mouth. I thought I would be early. Yet, the field was already packed with many, young and old. Leoni had said to be quick; that there were things *swirling on the wind*. Indeed, I now understood at least part of what she had said; there was something on the wind, an air of tension wafting on the breeze. It appeared that most of the village was in attendance, as well as many from other villages around the area. No one was in drill formation. In fact, most everyone was cloistered about in groups, talking and whispering in anticipatory, if not anxious, tones.

As I approached the first group, I saw that it was made up of villagers and clan members, around my own age. They, too, were chattering excitedly like a flock of geese. Among them was my good friend Baldua. He was a mixture of the small, dark Hill People and Saxon: short, stocky and dark of skin, but yellow of hair and light of eyes. Though we were the exact same age, he was a good foot shorter than I. "Baldua," I said as I approached.

"Merline, mihi amice!" (Merlin, my friend!) he said in perfect Latin.

Though most in the region knew Latin, we mostly spoke in our native Gaelic. I loved my friend Baldua: we had always shared everything—from the same nurse-maid as infants, to the same lovers as grown lads—but he was a pretentious sort. For example, he preferred to speak mainly in Latin, convinced he was, or so he claimed, that it was the language of the future. For the sake of friendship, I let him get away with it while most others ridiculed him for it.

"Myrriddin, you sod," I said in Gaelic.

"As you wish," he replied in our native tongue, to my surprise.

"What is happening?" I asked.

"Horse Master Kindrixer says we must ready for battle. The Picts come from the north and Saxons from the northeast. They are fighting together. Apparently, they have one leader," he said excitedly.

"They're one force?" I asked, dumbfounded. No such thing had ever happened before. The Romans had, for the most part, kept the region free of the raiding Picts and Scotts, as well as the Saxons. But lately, Rome seemed to have abandoned her charge, leaving us open and susceptible once again to these brutal raiders. I often wondered which was worse, the oppressive yoke of Rome, or the bloody and frequent skirmishes with our natural enemies and neighbors. One question that had been on my mind seemed to have been answered right then and there. The vision in the scrying bowl from the previous evening had shown

Roman soldiers and their war machine on the move. They had been leaving us, I was now sure.

The rumble of pounding hooves sounded from behind. I turned to see a contingent of horsemen, among them, Horse Master Kindrixer—a half-Roman, half-British bear of a man. Tall, even in the saddle of his giant steed, he had dark hair and blue eyes. His face had the handsome features of a man in the *classic Roman sense*, as Leoni had crooned, whatever that meant. Her description must have been accurate for the reaction from women was the same everywhere the man went; a ridiculous swooning and faint glassing of the eyes, as if the female, upon laying eyes upon the man, had suddenly been rendered under a glam of love and lust. Even some of the males had the same reaction when they gazed at Kindrixer.

Aside from, or perhaps because of, his amorous affect on the lasses, and some of the lads, he was also a wonderful and charismatic leader. He had retired from the Roman military at the ripe age of thirty summers, having served his con-scripted service of fifteen years. He had worked his way up to and through the ranks of the Roman military machine to the unprecedented level of Horse Master, a rank one was traditionally born into. Yet, as I've pointed out, much about the Empire and her might was changing almost daily.

Horse Master Kindrixer and his party halted now, his large brown bay neigh-ing loudly at the hard yank on her bit from her Master. Kindrixer looked over the assembly, seemingly eyeing every one of us. "To the east!" he commanded in his deepest, authoritative voice. The urgency was unmistakable. "We leave now!" With that, he spun his mount and led the way off the drill field, followed by the rest of his mounted party.

The spear, my staff, began to vibrate quietly in my hand. Whether as a portent or not, I could not tell. It stopped as quickly as it had started. Then, almost as one, the throng that was assembled on the field moved to follow Kindrixer, not a one of us knowing our destination, let alone what awaited us at day's end.

My village must have been nearly empty, as with the surrounding villages. Everyone, it seemed, had answered the call to assemble with arms on the drill field outside our clan's village—the call that runners had apparently yelled throughout the villages after the morning's sun-birth rite. Obviously, the morning's ritual was not the only thing I'd missed.

"Form up!" someone shouted. The mass of people that followed Kindrixer attempted to do as ordered. There were more than a few clan members among us who had served in the legions of Rome. These men brought their experience and knowledge of Roman warfare and military back home with them. Some of them became leaders of our village's fighting army and even those of other villages. A given village's *army*, though, was probably a misnomer; my village's so-called *army*, for example. At first, we drilled in secret because of the Roman presence. But as more and more time went by, less and less of Rome was seen in the area. Gradually, our fighting group became bigger and a little better, drilling and training more in the open.

But two things became apparent quite soon. The first: though our group became bigger, no one really took the organized body of fighters seriously, especially the fighters themselves. It was thought to be too Roman. Celts fought as individuals within a group, not together as a unit. No matter how much we trained—no matter how much discipline was imposed on us by our actual battle experienced—Roman-trained brothers and fellow clan members, we were still Celts; group discipline was a foreign thing. Yet, that discipline is in part what had made Rome so great militarily. She could put thousands and thousands on a field of battle, and those thousands and thousands would fight as one; cohesive and deadly in the execution of its duty, efficient and precise in the carrying out of its objective. The forces of Rome had inspired awe and fear across the world. With that, however, she also left in her wake experience and knowledge of her techniques in the ways of war. Yet, those of us who tried to emulate the techniques for our own purposes often found ourselves ensnared by our own cultural habits and fighting techniques, or lack thereof. We were nothing like Rome. Thus, these exercises were more sport than anything else.

The second thing that became apparent was that although we used real weapons for our sparring—sharp swords, daggers and spears—most of us had never seen actual battle. Oh, there were certainly injuries from these practice battles, such as deep cuts from blades, broken teeth, bruised and bloodied bodies and body parts, but in the end, it was all just that; practice, not the real thing. Most of us had never seen any real fighting because for as long as I could remember, at least, we had always been a subjugated people; Rome had always been here. And, of course, we had never had an army of our own. But Rome's time among us was ending. So, threatened with raids and warring parties from other regions, other peoples, we tried to stand an army of our own.

Such was the case on this morning's march behind Horse Master Kindrixer. Our acting centurions formed us up into the tight rows of a legionnaire force.

Though we numbered far less than any legion—a few hundred as opposed to a few thousand—we looked liked a formidable Roman force, minus the matching tunics and leather carassi of a real legion. And, for a while, we actually marched as one small army, comprised of many small centuries, behind the Horse Master and his mounted men. As the morning wore on, however, the whole of our large group lost interest in being one force and walked as individuals once again; without formation, laughing and talking, and carrying on almost as children.

Toward the end of the morning, we stopped for a short rest. We had marched out of our valley, through a dense forest of small oaks and maples, and across a meadow plain of poppies and grass; then into another larger forest, this one comprised of ancient and sacred oaks and willows and dubbed by some the Dark Forest.

Though over time, this forest had become a place of mystery and even fear to many—indeed, more than one child had wandered in never to be heard from again—its name, *Dark Forest*, was originally derived from the fact that its trees were so tall and its canopy so dense that barely any sunlight slipped through to the forest floor. Still, many maintained that it was a place of spirits and hauntings. It was no wonder, then, that we made it through the Dark Forest in tight formations. Well, as tight as could be managed while dodging and darting around the mighty, sacred oaks. Finally, when we were nearly through to the other side of the forest, we stopped for a rest.

The respite was short-lived, however, and we were rudely summoned back to the task of marching. "Come now!" shouted Cramusin, a dark haired, short tyrant of a would-be centurion, whose only real skill, militarily or otherwise, was constantly annoying the general population of the clan—and everyone else with whom he came into contact—with his empty arrogance. "Form up. I order you!"

"Shut yer yap, Cramusin, or I'll kick ya like the mut ye be," replied an older clansman named Trastonus, who had served as a conscripted legionnaire for some twenty-five years.

"I am your centurion," cowed Cramusin in a whiny, nasally tone.

"Yer nothing, I say," answered Trastonus as he rose off his seat on a fallen tree. Trastonus, though around fifty-five summers in age, had the dried, leathery skin of one who had been exposed to the elements for a century of seasons. "We only follow you at times cuz Kindrixer, for his own odd reasons, likes ye, Cramusin. Make no mistake, lad."

Several of the others in our *century*—more a couple of dozen; our little group was no more a century than Cramusin a centurion—began to grumble their agreement with Trastonus. Trastonus and Cramusin had served together for one year under a brutal Roman commander. According to the older clansman, Cramusin was a coward, usually hiding behind a shield on the battle field. He excelled in the field ranks of the legionnaire and was granted certain privileges in rank and title because of particular *favors* he gave the Roman general, much to everyone's consternation. Those privileges seemed to have carried over to his service under Kindrixer.

"Be-s-sides, we've not be-een told wh-where we are going," stuttered a slight lass of about nineteen summers, by the name of Igraines. She was quite thin and pale, with emerald-colored eyes and chestnut shaded hair that hung in ringlets down to her underdeveloped breasts.

But her breasts and slight body were the only things underdeveloped about her. Beneath her chest beat the heart of an old soul and truly-tried champion. I had first met her on the Isle of Mystery when she was very young, where she had come to study for what turned out to be a short time. Once back in the general population, and still a wee lass, she had taken much teasing and abuse over her stammering way of speech. She finally snapped two winters past when two lads, one sixteen, the other seventeen, had cornered her in the horse paddock to tease and torment the girl. Their fun turned violent, though, when some of Igraines's clothes were torn. It became clear that the young men were interested in more that a malicious game of mockery.

In short, Igraines smashed one of the lad's balls with the heel of her foot and cracked open the skull of the other with her bare fist, gouging out one of his eyes in the process. Once the lads had recovered from their injuries, they were banished from the clan and vanished from the village. No one ever dared mock Igraines again. She further proved her fighting prowess on the drill field. Her combat-sparring abilities were so impressive that most of the boys and many of the men voiced openly that they would not at all mind having her next to them in a fight.

While she was a good fighter, I was also of the mind that adding to the sentiment of wanting her next to them in a fight was the fact that Igraines was budding into a beautiful young woman, as well. I had heard as much on more than one occasion while the drink of mead went around an evening's cooking fire, after the women had gone, of course. Many of my fellow clansmen had commented on the girl's impending womanhood. And, I admit that I, too, was enamored with her. It was obvious that in a short time, she would be ripping out the hearts of men, young and old, in more ways than one.

I smiled. Yes, I was charmed by her. She may have had a stutter, but to me, her voice had the same sweetness of sound as the good fairy folks did, or, I imagined, as the angel folks. The latter I'd heard about through the *new religion* people—the *Christians,* as they called themselves. "Yes," I heard myself agreeing with the lass while staring into her lovely eyes. I then turned my gaze to Cramusin. "The point is made. Where are we going?"

THREE

"East," said the brick-headed Cramusin, once again donning a false mantle of authority.

"That don't tell us nothin' we've not heard yet," countered Trastonus.

"Well, that's all you get," replied Cramusin, again cowering under the older man's gaze, yet holding in his tone; a haughtiness which was clearly meant to imply that *he* knew more about where we were going than the rest of us. But it rang false.

"Cuz that's a-a-all *you* know," observed Igraines, garnering a round of laughter from those within the hearing of it. She had simply voiced what the rest of us had been thinking.

Bested, Cramusin said not a word more. He turned and made his way back to join the larger group assembling in the nearby clearing.

"All right, then," Trastonus declared to the rest of us after a moment. "I s'pose we should join 'em, eh? We'll see soon enough where we go." We gathered with all the others in the clearing and continued the trek *east*.

However, approximately three miles into the next leg of our march, the question of our destination was suddenly and brutally rendered irrelevant.

We had come away from the so-called Dark Forest and traveled through a valley for nearly two miles. We then passed through another forested region, though this one was much more sparse than the Dark one, and then into yet another valley after nearly a mile of the sparser forest. Baldua and I walked side by side, had done so for miles, when he suddenly said, "Here now, what's it doing?!"

I followed his gaze to my staff. The Druid's egg atop was glowing red, as if a fire had been lit from within it, the staff itself was beginning to get warm. Others around me began to mumble to each other in fear at seeing the red glowing orb, some even making the gesture to ward off evil. But I knew it for what it was: a warning, but a warning too late. Then all at once, its glowing stopped; its warmth ceased.

The sudden screams were guttural, primal and seemed to come from everywhere at once. Hundreds upon hundreds of them came pouring into the valley, swinging their weapons: battle axes, swords, spiked balls on chains, even long pikes with iron nails sticking out horizontally and curling upward at the tip beneath the blade; one and all of them screaming a blood-curdling cry of battle, and heading straight for us.

For an instant we froze; indeed, all time seemed to freeze. Only the voice of Kindrixer snapped us out of our reverie of disbelief. "Tight formations, now!" bellowed Kindrixer. Most obeyed, drawing their weapons and bumping into each other as we tried to form ten tight rows as we did on the drill field.

Unfortunately, there were a few who panicked, young and inexperienced in the ways of war—as I was myself, but there was no panic in my bones this day—who dropped their weapons and ran. But the handful that did this—lads between ten and fifteen summers—ran straight into the enemies' blades, for the Saxons and Picts were everywhere. Those that ran were cut down instantly, mercilessly. In the future, their deaths would be remembered for more than they were worth that day. A Celt does not run from battle. But the runners were the first to die in battle on that day, and they would be remembered in song for it.

"Shields up, first rank down!" ordered Kindrixer from his mount.

Many of us had no shield so we doubled up with those who did. Little good it availed, however, for the enemy, whose number seemed to swell with each passing moment, pinched us from all sides like the claw of a giant raven. Yellow-haired Saxons from the eastern shores; dark, squat Picts from the northern regions, engulfed us. The noise was deafening; hundreds and hundreds of men, and none-too-few women, yelling at the peak of their lungs; some in the crazed ecstasy of battle frenzy, some in the horrifying agony of unimaginable pain, as weapons found their marks on the bodies of my people. Added to the din was the clash of weapons, metal upon metal, sword to sword. What shields we had were either made of wood and split at the first violent stroke from the enemy, or were old Roman left-behinds and crumpled in the fight from mere age and corrosion.

Baldua and I were near crushed in the middle of the melee. The tight rows we Celts had started with had collapsed in on themselves, until we were nothing more than a tight onion ball. There were about seventy-six of us left layered in this ball, which the enemy was peeling back layer by bloody layer. Soon, there would be none of us left.

"What, by the Goddess, do we do?!" Baldua screamed above the din.

Dirt and dust kicked about by the crush and chaos of fighting filled my mouth, the stink of loosened bowels and fear filled my nostrils. I was being crushed and smashed from all sides. Looking down, I saw the face of Cramusin staring back at me, eyes wide open and vacant in death, his body broken underfoot. He had been trampled by his own people in the fighting.

I suddenly felt something violently shaking in my hand; it was the staff. I had not even had time to draw my sword. But I had held fast to the staff, always the staff. And then, I heard it. For the first time, I heard it! In my head, came the voice of my staff, the voice of the spear. "He returns," *it* whispered—I say *it*, for, indeed, it sounded like neither a man's nor a woman's voice, which spoke the words, "Leave here."

For a moment, within my own being, time stood still; all was silent. Though the battle and its din raged on, I heard it not. *What, who, was this voice?* I asked myself. Was it indeed the spear? A spirit? My own self? My imagination? Or all of those things? Images came to my mind, flashed inside my head: a crucifixion, a Roman soldier piercing the side of one being crucified with the very spear I held, my staff. He was an important person, the one being crucified. I felt it. And the Roman soldier, a centurion . . .

Pain was in my arm. Far off, I heard Baldua speaking in perfect Celt, his Latin abandoned for now, his hand roughly clenching my arm. "Myrridin!" he screamed.

The noise of battle, the crush of bodies, returned to me, or I to it.

"What's wrong with you?" Baldua yelled. "You became rigid, like a stone. We must do something!"

I nodded. Looking at the spear, I willed it to guide us. It seemed to tug me, pulling me in one direction. Perhaps *I* was causing it to do this. But for the moment, it didn't matter; I followed the spear, my staff, and Baldua followed me. We squeezed our way through the mass of struggling bodies towards its perimeter, beyond which, on the side of the valley to which we were headed, I now remembered there being a stand of pungent smelling saplings nearby in which we might hide.

We had almost reached the edge of the fighting mass. I could see the stand of saplings, possible sanctuary within reach. And then I heard the voice—not the spear's voice this time, but a human voice thunderously projected from a man sitting atop the largest white horse I had ever seen. "Halt! Halt and heed!" the man bellowed.

I froze. For a horrifying instant, I actually thought he was yelling at me and Baldua. But as I turned and looked closer at the man, it became clear that he was yelling for everyone, all those fighting, to cease their combat.

The man raised a hand, palm opened, and called again, "Halt, I command it!" His voice boomed with such depth, volume and authority that one by one, all ceased their fight, disengaged the opponent and turned to face this imposing figure on the white horse.

He sat tall in the saddle: six-and-half feet tall when standing on his own feet, I guessed. Straight, glossy, black hair hung down to his chest. His deep-set eyes were a piercing light-gold and his nose was slightly hooked. All that, plus his slightly protruding rigid brow, gave him the look of a demon. I shivered for an instant with awe. And fear! This one projected evil; was evil. I could feel it emanating from his being as surely as I could feel my own breath.

He was clearly the leader of the Pict-Saxon horde, for all of them, to a man, looked to him now, stiff at attention. *Strange, that*, I thought. All my people— those left alive—stared at him, too. It was my people that the man now addressed.

"I . . . am Lord Creconius Mab," he declared.

My heart thudded, pounded. Though I was already sweating from the fight, even more began beading on my brow, my palms. A tingling of intense nervousness swept through my being. This man, this Lord Creconius, was an old and bitter enemy of mine. I felt it. I knew it. Though I, Myrriddin, had never laid eyes on him, Creconius and I had known each other before, many life-times before. As a Celt, I knew I had occupied a physical body before this one; in another life and in many a life. Being born again into a new body was a choice one's spirit made in the Otherworld. The Christian folk were trying to change that belief—called it pagan, they did. Some of our folk had abandoned the belief. But if ever there was confirmation on this side of the veil as to whether I had lived before, what I felt in that moment toward Creconius was it.

I studied him even closer. He wore dark riding breeches and a black cloak with matching black gloves. A gold torque studded with rubies adorned his neck.

I looked at his face again. Yes, his face was nearly as my mind remembered it, though it was decidedly more feminine. It also glowed softly, as if a glam or spell surrounded it. But, there was no mistaking whom this face belonged to or whom he had been in a previous life. "Draco!" I whispered, not knowing exactly where the name came from, but knowing beyond doubt that was this dark lord's name in a previous time.

"What?" Baldua whispered urgently. "Come, we can still make it to those trees there. 'Tis where you were leading us, yes?"

I nodded and continued pushing my way through the people and slipped out past the last man to a boulder lying in front on a tree. We hid for a moment behind the boulder. I looked back at all the people, now transfixed by the figure on the white steed.

"C-c'mon," came the familiar stutter.

Baldua and I looked to our right, and there, next to us behind the boulder, crouched Igraines, breeches torn at the knees, grey tunic splattered with dirt and mud, as was her face, but still in one piece.

"This is m-my spot!" she declared.

"Puella fatua! (Stupid girl!)," said Baldua finding his Latin tongue. "You'll be found if you stay here," he said in our native tongue.

"Yes," I added, and began crawling on my belly to the trees. Baldua followed. I looked back at Igraines. She hesitated, looked back at Creconius, then followed Baldua and me into the trees.

Rocks dug into my stomach as I crawled, dragged myself, along. Looking behind me again, I saw that both Baldua and Igraines were close behind me. Looking beyond them I saw Creconius on his mount. He was saying something about absolute surrender.

"Attack!" came the reply from someone in the crowd—Kindrixer, on foot, in the middle of those of my countrymen left alive.

I stopped.

Baldua nearly crawled over me, but stopped just short behind me. "Are you mad? Why'd you stop?"

"Kindrixer," was all I could manage to say. I was suddenly torn between continuing on to apparent safety and joining Kindrixer in fighting Creconius, the evil one I've known in one form or another for some time. Ancient, confusing animosity welled up within my being.

Someone was pulling on my shoulder, dragging me onward. "C'mon!" cried

Baldua. It was he who dragged me toward the safety of deeper cover in the trees. It was now Igraines alone who was behind me. I was unaware of it at the time, but Baldua had maneuvered around and ahead of me during my hesitation. "There's no use in fighting. There are too many of them."

"F-for once I agr-ree with Baldua," whispered Igraines.

A huge battle cry went up then from all the Celts present. Though surrounded and outnumbered, the Celts, with Kindrixer leading the way, began an assault, breaking the tight ball they had been in and attacking the enemy. I felt shame. As I said, Celts do not run. Yet, that is precisely what I was doing. I looked at my two companions. Baldua had no compunction about saving our skins, or more accurately, his own. In spite of what she had said, however, Igraines did. I saw reflected in her eyes a similar shade of shame to my own: dishonor. I was about to disengage from my friend, Baldua, and abandon our flight to safety, in order to join the fight instead. But then the slaughter began.

FOUR

Kindrixer was the first to fall, his head nearly severed from behind by a wickedly wielded battle axe, his assailant unseen in the throng and confusion of battle. I was shocked. All of us who saw him fall were shocked. Kindrixer had been the only cohesive element keeping the Celts in any semblance of a fighting unit. When he fell, many were easily cut down as they froze, startled at the sight of their leader killed. Others ran, some heading straight toward us.

"That's it then," Baldua said with finality. Obviously, he had read in my eyes the intent to stay and fight. "Come! Now!" He took the lead, crawling further into the bush before anyone could get even close to us. I followed, as did Igraines, as if in a daze.

The urgency of our plight shifted into a more desperate form. We could easily be revealed if those coming toward us overran us. So the three of us got to our feet and ran for our lives.

Deeper and deeper into the stand of trees we went. The further we went, the thicker the forest became. Deceiving that was. From the outside—from the clearing we had been ambushed in—it simply appeared that the stand of trees was deep, but thin. But here we were, trudging through a wooded area that was becoming thicker, denser and darker by the moment. The sound of the battle was receding quickly. I was not sure whether that was because of the distance we were putting between us and the fighting or because it had become such a rout that it was almost finished. I tried not to think of that, but kept moving.

In addition to the darker, denser forest we were now in, something else suddenly became clear: we had been making a steady climb; an ascent up a hillside. And, it was becoming steeper by the step.

Baldua stopped, hands on knees, head hanging low, panting to catch his breath. Igraines and I stopped as well. It was a strange respite in a mad day. "Where are w-we going?" asked Igraines, after a few moments.

Baldua looked at me.

"Well, don't ask me," I said. But it was not me that Baldua was asking with his eyes. His gaze drifted down to the spear, all but forgotten in our rush to escape. It vibrated again, slightly, its tip moving toward . . . what, I could not tell. No matter. It seemed as good a direction to go as any at that point. "This way, I guess," I said, my voice laced with uncertainty. My companions looked at each other, apparently none too pleased with my reply. "C'mon," I said more forcefully. "At this point, we've naught to lose."

We continued our trek, up the hill and through the dense forest.

We walked for hours, trudging uphill, then down, then up again, all the while surrounded by huge oaks and pines standing as sentinels. We no longer heard the noise of battle. Instead, the sounds of birds twittering and breeze-blown trees soughing, filled the air with a beauty that only the mother goddess could produce. I felt at peace as I walked along. But it was a brief and fleeting thing; a temporary false sense of security on a violent and terrifying day. The fact was that we were escaping from certain death. And, even if we survived, we would probably become refugees in our own lands, for I had no doubt Creconius would raze our village once he had finished off our so-called army. Such were my thoughts as we continued on our forced march. But then I realized something that was of a more immediate urgency. We were lost.

I believed we were heading west, toward home, or what was left of it by now. But it was difficult to tell for two reasons: the forest was getting denser and the light was fading. The light was fading because of the thick forest top, yes, but also because the sun was setting. Still, the spear, my staff, led us on with its insistent vibration and definite pull in a particular direction. It was acting as if it were a divining rod leading us to water. Yet, where it was actually leading us I knew not. No matter. Since it was getting dark, I would see to it that we stopped soon to make camp and find food. Traveling through an unfamiliar forest at night would be foolish at best. And our dinner would have to consist of scavenged nuts and edible roots. I would not risk being spotted by an enemy because of a cooking fire.

We would not hunt for meat this night. Igraines was the only one of us who had a water-skin. I could tell by its sloshing throughout the day that there was precious little of the liquid in it, but it would do for the night. She had already offered to share it earlier, but Baldua and I had declined at the time.

We reached a small clearing that had flat ground and was well protected. One side of it faced the hilled forest through which we had just marched; the other half faced rock outcroppings: large boulders that seemed to be at the base of a mountain. It was difficult to tell in the twilight how large it might be. *We will find out in the morning light*, I thought. "We should stop here," I said out loud.

"I agree," said Igraines, for once unstuttered.

I half expected Baldua to give a sardonic reply in Latin. But he said nothing. He simply plopped down on a rock, exhausted. This day had taken a toll on all of us.

"I s-saw f-ficob-berry bushes a quarter l-league back," Igraines said.

"Good. Just be careful," I said. "Anything else you can find, too – nuts, anything. No meat, though. No fires."

The look she gave me was incredulous. "Just because I stutter, does not mean I'm stupid," she said.

I looked away from her, blushing, I'm sure.

"Can I have some of that water now?" Baldua mumbled. "I'll only sip it, I promise."

Something was wrong. My friend was not just tired from our march. I looked at him closely. He was pale and he grimaced with every breath. Obviously, he was in pain, a lot of it. Then, for the first time, I noticed that he was intently clutching his right side. "Baldua?" I asked, concern grasping my throat.

He looked into my eyes, courage and sincere pleas dripping from his gaze. He lifted his tunic, with much difficulty at that movement, to reveal two grotesque lumps which had formed over the region of his right lower ribs. In addition to the lumps, there was a hideous discoloration; a dark purple had spread across the affected area. "I think they're broken, these two," he said, pointing to his two bottom ribs.

"You would n-not have been able to come this f-far if they were broken," Igraines declared as she knelt next to Baldua to examine the ribs. She gently traced the fingertips of her right hand back and forth over the lumpy, discolored region, finally letting them come to rest between the two lumps. Slowly, she began to push.

Baldua's face contorted in agony.

"W-well, say it hurts. Don't b-be an ass!" she said reprimanding him.

"All right! Stop, you wench. It hurts!"

"Fine. They're c-cracked. B-badly. But they're n-not broken," Igraines diag-nosed.

"Why didn't you say something?" I asked angrily.

Baldua simply shook his head. "Quorsum istuc?" (To what purpose?) he coun-tered. "We had to get out of there. I had taken someone's sword hilt in the side. Hurt like fire at the time. Didn't think it to be this bad, though."

"You n-need a moss and mistletoe poultice p-placed on it," Igraines said.

"Sure. I'll pull one out of my ass," Baldua replied.

"You are n-not doing anything," Igraines stated flatly, as a matter of fact. She was small in structure, but huge in stature, especially in moments such as this, when she was clearly in command.

"Is that all you need—moss and mistletoe?" I asked her.

Igraines nodded, then added, "But m-moss from the m-mighty oak's trunk only. Nowhere else."

"Very well," I said, and slipped out of the clearing in search of the medicinal items.

I walked for a while and found only saplings and pines. I should have gone back the way we had come, not further up the mountain. I remembered there being several ancient, sacred oaks about a half mile back from the clearing. But that was moot now. Presently, I was about three-quarters of a mile farther on from the clearing.

Finally, after nearly an hour of searching, I found two gigantic and clearly very ancient oaks. As I approached them, I found myself becoming reverent, as if I were approaching two sacred sentinels. The staff in my hand felt warm as if it, too, were solemn. The mighty oak has been a sacred entity and symbol to Celts for thousands of years. It was engrained in my mind and blood to respect and honor these trees. But for the first time, I was truly feeling a sacredness emanating from an oak—from both of them. Something tangible was occurring. The lower branches of both trees intertwined, though their trunks were some thirty-feet apart. The uppermost branches were not only intertwined, but in some places were grown together as one—not fused together, but grown as one, as if from one tree.

Then I touched the one closest to me. Emotion welled up within me; the staff began to chill in my hand. Sadness. I was astounded to feel sadness emanating from this mighty tree. I looked to the other tree and understood. I walked over to the second tree to touch it and had my thoughts confirmed; it was dying. Its bark was without moss, dry and brittle, its life and spirit nearly gone. These two trees had grown together, seen centuries of life together and intertwined in a marriage of oneness. And now, one of them was dying. Would the other be far behind?

After a moment, I snapped myself out of this reverie, remembering my purpose for being there. But I didn't just start searching the healthy oak's trunk for moss and the lower branches for mistletoe. Instead, I felt compelled to ask. I stepped back a few paces and looked at both trees, addressed both in a reverent manner.

"F-forgive my intrusion," I stammered, suddenly feeling as Igraines must have on occasion. "I am sorry for the state of your being, your partner's being, for both of you, and ask that the blessings of Dana be upon you," I found myself saying. On the Isle of Mystery, I had chanted and sung to mighty and sacred oaks in a large circular group of other initiates, but never alone. I had been with Moscastan on several occasions when he had addressed prayers to the earth Goddess, Dana, through the oaks, but those too had been in groups. Yet, here I was, alone and beseeching these living things. On the one hand, it felt strange. But on the other, it felt completely natural. "I seek your help. I need moss from your body and the healing of your mistletoe for my injured friend. With your permission, of course." I paused. Silence. A slight breeze rustled the branches. The sound of a small forest creature scurrying through the undergrowth came and went. Again, silence. *Fool,* I thought. *Did you expect them to speak?*

Then it happened: The staff, the spear, began to vibrate; to point to the healthy tree. I walked back to it, around to the other side of it and there, on its far side was a thick, moist blanket of moss. A rustling in a branch just above the moss blanket drew my attention. A beautiful cluster of mistletoe hung there. "Thank you," I said out loud, and began to gather the items for my friend's poultice. By the time I had gathered all I needed, it was almost completely dark. No matter. I could still make out the pseudo trail I'd used to come to this point. I would simply follow it back.

I left the two wondrous oaks and made my way back toward the clearing and my friends. But after a few minutes, the way became more and more difficult with each and every step. Darkness descended like a cloak over my eyes. I kept forging ahead, carefully, knowing Baldua needed what I carried, yet cursing myself for taking so long as to allow darkness to become a barrier. I silently asked the staff to help guide me, but silence was its only response.

Finally, I broke into the clearing which was adequately lit by a half-moon in a cloudless sky. But my heart dropped! This was not the right clearing. The surrounding rock formations were different, and, of course, my friends were not to be seen. I almost yelled for them. Foolish that would have been. I stood in the clearing and looked all around. *Now what?* I thought. My staff began to vibrate, tugging me in the direction to my right. I looked that way and saw in the distance through the trees, a glow. This was not the glow of a camp fire. It was larger, eerie, and at a constant, steady pulse. It was like something from the Otherworld. In spite of my better judgment, I found myself walking toward it. What I would find there, I knew not. But what I would discover there would change my life forever.

FIVE

I cautiously made my way through the undergrowth, quietly moving toward the glow. All the while, the staff vibrated harder in my hand. Usually, if the vibration were some sort of warning of danger, the staff would change its temperature, too. But there was no such temperature change this time; just the vibration which was more on the verge of becoming a shaking. In fact, if anything, I would say it was . . . excited—excited at the prospect of going to the source of the glow. I tried to dismiss that thought. It seemed ridiculous. But I could not dismiss it outright. It's what I was *feeling*, *sensing* from the staff, the spear.

I drew nearer the source of the glow, the pulsating light. It was emanating from a cave whose opening appeared small; perhaps four feet-high and five-feet wide. It was located on the side of a huge granite rock formation lodged in the mountainside. The light itself escaped from the cave's mouth in more of an undulating, intense rainbow, but washed out to appear bright white, especially from a distance. So bright it was that the little glen just outside the cave's opening was bright as day. There was no telling how deep into the mountainside the cave went. Because of the smallness of the cave's opening and the intensity of the light escaping from it, 'twas tempting to say that it was shallow. But I knew that both of those things were deceiving when it came to judging the cave's depth. My mind suddenly shifted back to my friends. *Baldua!* I thought. I must get these things back to Igraines so that she can help him. *But how? I was lost before, in the wrong clearing when I saw this glow. How will I find my way back? The staff!* I looked at the still-shaking staff in my hand. "I don't care about this place," I said aloud, speaking to the staff. "Find my friends!"

It continued its shaking, not altering it in the slightest. I turned to leave, still looking at the staff. After one step, it gave a last shudder and stopped, laying still in my hand. I stopped in my tracks and noticed that a cold was descending in the air and with it, a mist, thick and dense, enshrouding the immediate area completely. If someone had been standing fifty feet from me back up the path from where I had come, I had no doubt that they could not have seen me nor even the glow from the cave.

"What is this?" I asked out loud, suddenly feeling trapped and angry. But the sound of my voice was deadened by the mist. It was obvious that no one could hear me even if they were near and I yelled. *Something* was compelling me to the cave, to the pulsating light. I looked at the staff. "So this is the way of it?" I asked rhetorically.

Silence.

I turned back around and looked at the bright cave opening some forty feet away. "So be it," I said, and walked to the cave's mouth and entered.

I was momentarily blinded by the brightness as I ducked into the opening in the hillside. The light was intensely bright. Feeling my way along one side of a wall, I found I could stand upright. I stood there for a moment, shading my eyes with one hand as I stared at the ground, allowing my eyes to adjust. And listening. I just listened, trying to discern any sound but the silence that assaulted me. Then, out of the silence, very faintly, came the sounds of what could only be described as the very quiet tinkling of tiny glass bells. Yet, the sound was more pure than that, more crystalline. The smell of this place was unique, too. It smelled of fresh spring water and mint. The cleanest aroma I had ever experienced. Next, as my eyes adjusted, I truly noticed the ground that I'd been staring at. It sparkled. Even in the brightness of the space, it sparkled dazzlingly, as if a billion-and-one little stars were embedded at my feet. Slowly, I looked up, trying to peer through the brilliant light at the rest of my surroundings. My eyes adjusted further and the bright pulsating lights seemed to dim.

The cave's interior was vast, at least four times as large as any village's central lodge I had been in, which granted, in my whole life had only been two. The cave was large enough to hold several hundred people, perhaps a thousand. Its floor and walls were jagged rock-type formations and its ceiling was breathtakingly high. It seemed that this cavernous space touched the sky, or rather, was its own sky. Amazing! But what was even more astounding was the fact that the pulsating light seemed to be coming from millions and millions of crystals embedded, or rather growing from, the walls and stone formations everywhere in the cave. They were of every color. I then noticed that some, in fact most of the jagged rock formations I had seen a moment ago, were not comprised of plain rock with crystals growing out of them, but were themselves, in fact, huge crystal formations. I was awestruck.

"Twilight of the gods," a man's voice said.

I nearly dropped the staff and medicinal collection I carried. My heart pounding, I spun to my right to see the figure of what looked to be a very old man standing some fifty paces away at the opening to a passageway leading deeper into the mountain from within this main cavernous chamber. Though he was fifty or so paces away, his voice had sounded mere inches from my face.

"The domed shape of the cavern does magical things with sound," he explained, apparently reading my thoughts.

Looking up, I noticed that in addition to having some rock formations, the high ceiling to this place was indeed a curved dome shape. It was like being on the inside of a giant egg.

"Twilight of the gods," the old man repeated, resuming his initial line of speech, referring, I assumed, to the twinkling of all the crystals.

My heart still raced at the surprise of seeing someone else in there, let alone an old man. I took a breath to calm myself. The old man walked toward me. My first instinct was to duck out of the cave. But I held my ground for curiosity's sake, if for no other reason.

He appeared quite old: ninety summers at least, although that was probably not accurate. He was skin and bones. His skin was so wrinkled, it was as if it had been flayed from his bones, stretched and wadded, then placed back over his skeleton. His hair was white as snow with streaks of red. Surprisingly, he apparently still had all his teeth, all of which were also a snowy white. He smiled as he approached and that smile reflected the light in the room, as did the countenance of his whole being. He wore a cloak that looked fairly new. Black, it was, with little gold and silver stars all over it. *You're a strange old man*, I thought. He did not walk like an old man though. His gait was steady and sure. He stopped before me and I looked into his dark eyes.

"I've waited for you to find this place," he said.

"I don't . . . " I stammered. Then it hit me—the familiarity of his voice and eyes. "*Moscastan?*"

The old man's smile now beamed.

"You've known me by many a name," he said. "Presently, it has been Moscastan, yes."

I searched his eyes, his face. Beneath the aged surface, it was indeed my mentor. I was stunned beyond belief. "But how?"

He looked at me quizzically, even pityingly. "You have studied the Druid ways and the mysticism therein for many a year. Have you learned nothing, Master Myrriddin?" he asked.

I felt a flush of embarrassment. Of course, I had learned a great deal about the nature and workings of the world we live in and the greater universe as a whole: how to control various elements in the world around me by joining with them at the level of thought, for example. Higher Truths about the oneness of our world and the Otherworld are things that I learned, too. And, glamour—the ability to cast certain spells, if you will; to cloak oneself or his or her surroundings so that they appear as something different to others—is also something I learned. All of these things were simple applications of natural laws properly understood and utilized. But this! Was this how Moscastan actually appeared? Was his appearance as the younger Moscastan that I knew and loved naught but a glamour, or was this old man-persona before me the glamour?

"Ah, Myrriddin. Do not look so perplexed. Come," he said soothingly. It is time for you to venture deeper into this Crystal place." He gestured to the whole of the sparkling cavern. "And hence, deeper into your soul."

I looked at the mistletoe in my hand.

"Fear not. Baldua will be fine. Presently, he is on his way to feeling much better. Trust me," Moscastan said, reassuringly. "Leave all but the spear, your staff. The spear will aid you on the journey you are about to embark upon."

Reluctantly, I placed the medicinal items on the ground and clutched my staff, the spear. There was nothing to do but follow.

SIX

We entered a low passageway through which Moscastan had come into the large main chamber. He led the way back through it and it seemed to go on for a long while—five-hundred paces and more. We remained stooped the whole way. The light had not diminished at all, nor had the pleasant smell of spring water and mint. In fact, if anything, these smells became more pronounced the deeper we went.

We were indeed traveling deeper and deeper into the mountainside, going down at a slight angle, too, into the bowels of the earth. I wanted to ask where exactly we were going, but knew in my heart that trust was in order here. I trusted Moscastan implicitly. I always had. Not only that, I sensed that I was about to experience something beyond my comprehension. But I was not apprehensive in the least; Moscastan was with me; my spear was with me. That last thought struck me as odd when I caught it, but I also knew that old Moscastan was right when he had said the spear would aid me on this journey.

Presently, my staff, the spear, began to feel warm in my hand, soothingly warm. I felt that it was telling me we were close to our destination.

Finally, Moscastan halted. He turned to face me, still hunched over because of the low-ceilinged passageway, and motioned for me to enter an opening in the wall that was now between us and to my right. I had not noticed it until that very moment.

It was a round, roughly-honed hole in the rock and crystal wall that was only about three feet in diameter. The bottom portion was approximately a foot off the floor of the passageway. It appeared to have been made by the hand of men, not naturally formed. I did as the old man bade and stooped even lower as I entered the hole or entryway. Moscastan followed.

I entered another room, a fraction of the size of the main chamber I had been in earlier, but no less bright. The walls were ten-feet high and composed of solid crystal, reflecting a light that seemed to be generated from within. The room itself was oblong and only as big as a large sleeping chamber. In the middle was a solid, rectangular crystal slab that stood in the center of the space. It was just large enough for a fully grown man to lie on comfortably. The slab was a beautiful deep-blue in color. It looked like a solid block of the ocean set still in the middle of the room. I then noticed something that filled me with awe: the crystal slab had a glow at its center. It pulsated, the glow did, as if a heart of light beat within, as if it were alive.

"Please, Master Myrriddin," Moscastan said softly, reverently. "Lie on the Altar. Go within and attune with the Mind of All to know your Self, to know your purpose. It is time." He slowly retreated back out the small entryway and stood in front of it out in the passageway as if guarding it. What or who he could possibly have been guarding it from, I had no idea.

I looked at the Crystal *Altar* and felt my pulse quicken. I admit, however, that a part of me felt silly. How was this thing going to attune me with the Mind of All or tell me my purpose? Yet, another part of me already knew the answer to that: it wasn't the thing itself that would tell me about anything; it was simply a tool to help amplify my attunement with a higher nature within my being. I stepped up to it. Its flat top came up to my navel. I climbed on and lay on my back placing the spear at my left side close to my body. For a moment, I stared at the ceiling. It sparkled with crystals, each winking at me. I closed my eyes, breathed deeply, slowly and rhythmically, as I'd been taught to do on the Isle of Mystery when calling on the Natural Powers of the Universe. Thus, I began to go deep within my own mind, to my very soul. As I did this, the spear began to vibrate in a pulse that matched the rhythm of my breath.

Soon, I was floating. I felt no substance to my self, to my body. That was because I was no longer in my body. I knew that for sure. A mist surrounded my mind's eye. I could see nothing. Floating, floating, and floating still. Finally, I felt a slight jolt, as if I were entering something. Slowly, the mist began to clear.

I heard a woman—no, more than one woman—sobbing softly. I looked over to its source and saw three women shrouded in dark robes, on their knees consoling one another as they kept glancing up in my direction. But it was not me they were looking at, or so I thought. They were looking at the person in whom my consciousness had entered. In effect, though, they were looking at me, for I had entered into the body, the time, the moment, of my former self; the Roman Centurion Gaius Cassius Longinus. *How could this be?* I thought. My Myrriddin self or soul was that of Longinus, this I already knew. So, how could the same soul occupy the same space in two different times at the same time?! But then I realized what I was experiencing. Though *real* in every sense of the word, it was a moment in what we call "time" as stored in the Universal Mind. As such, it was quite easy to experience something that has already happened, or re-experience it, if one attunes to it properly. Many lives I had lived on the planet we call Earth. But for some reason, it was this one of Longinus that I needed to see now, relive now. But I wasn't the man himself, as I was then. Now, I was a witness, looking out from his eyes, but merely as Myrriddin, the observer, not the participant.

The women looked at me/Longinus with agonized, bloodshot eyes. A round of raucous laughter erupted from behind me. I turned to see several legionnaires kneeling on the ground, playing a game with dice. Their game table was a tattered and bloody cloak or robe spread on the ground. Looming over the soldiers, and standing between myself and them was a large wooden cross. And, hanging on this cross was a man. His body was badly beaten. His wrists and feet were the color of the dark iron nails that protruded from those areas, his blood having drained and stained his skin. On his head, he wore a hideous crown of thorns and blood. I knew who this man was. The world knew who this man was, or at least, it would know. He looked dead. But he wasn't.

I felt the indifference that I, and *"my host"* were feeling. He/I thought about joining the game going on under the cross. *Can't do that*, Longinus thought. *I am their commander. What is Irena doing right now?* he wondered. I sensed every one of his thoughts as if they were my own. They *had been* my own! Next, he thought about this man's death. The time had come. *Enough of this,* I heard him think. Longinus stepped up to the cross, and stood on the condemned one's right side. Longinus' left arm reached out and up. It was then that I saw it in his hand; the Spear, my spear! It looked new.

Slowly, as if in a bad dream, the spear's sharp tip inched toward the ribs of the man on the cross. "Jesu," my inner voice, Myrriddin's inner voice, whispered in recognition. The tip touched the skin in-between the condemned one's lower ribs. The skin beneath it stretched inward as the pressure was applied. Then the skin broke, tore, as the blade slid into the body. I heard a sickening sloshing and scraping sound as the blade rubbed against tissue and bone. For an instant, blood and body fluid spurted out of the wound, splattering a few drops on my face, Longinus' face. The initial spurt was quickly replaced by a slow flow of body fluid and blood which seeped out of the blade's entry point, oozing down the blade itself. Suddenly, the spear was yanked out of the body on the cross. The blood and body fluid then flowed freely from the wound.

I felt myself, both my Longinus self and my Myrriddin self—now virtually merged as one—recoil for an instant. *What have I done?* I thought. *You've simply done your duty*, came the next thought.

A rumbling sounded in the distance. It did not take long to realize that the rumbling emanated from both earth and sky. *A storm approaches*, came the thought. I felt the whole demeanor of my host, myself, harden. I looked at the one on the cross. *Jesu, is that what you're called? Or are you called by a different name, Simon, perhaps?* I knew not where that thought had come from. Surely this man was Jesu, and Longinus was simply in denial of what he/I had done in that moment.

The ground and sky rumbled again. The earth then shook, knocking three people, spectators, to the ground and nearly toppling one of the other crosses that were there, and its dangling occupant. It was then that I felt a small twinge of fear run through the body of Longinus.

Jesu made a sound, mumbling something seemingly to the sky. Then his head plopped on his chest. He was gone. Sheets of rain fell then—a torrent of tears from the heavens. The noise of it was deafening. "He's dead! Cut him down!" shouted Longinus. Two of the legionnaires nearby, who were playing the game on the robe, seemed frozen with fear and awe.

A third legionnaire yelled at them both: "Come on, you dogs. You heard the Centurion!" He slapped the soldier nearest him, knocking him out of his stupor. The other legionnaire followed suit, and they all ran to bring the Condemned One down.

I/Longinus began to back away. Suddenly, I looked down at the spear in my hand, at the blood on the blade's tip. I wanted to throw it to the ground, but could not. Then I heard it, The Voice: "What have you done, my son?"

Was it His voice, Jesu's?

I felt a yank on my mind, my soul, as if I were being violently pulled by a force beyond comprehension. Scene after scene began to rapidly play out before the eyes of my spirit; my life as Longinus after that fateful day. Irena. Friends Jacobi, Dosameenor and more. My sons. All were there. I lived that whole life over again in three heartbeats, up to and including my own upside-down crucifixion in Antioch. Then, it was done. In a flash of white light and a thud of hard landing, I was back in the bowels of the Crystal Cavern, lying on the still ocean slab, Myrriddin once again.

Slowly, I opened my eyes. The brightness was nearly unbearable. The light in the crystal room seemed even more intense than it had before.

"Ah, Master Myrriddin. You return," said Moscastan.

I sat up on the slab, my heart still pounding from my experience; my journey of mind, of spirit. I looked at my hands—yes, solid flesh, *my* flesh. Next, I inspected the staff, the spear.

"You have complete understanding, complete knowledge, do you not." Moscastan said this as a fact, not as a question.

I looked at my mentor. He was once again standing just inside the room. Then, I looked back to the staff. Perhaps it was time for it to just be *The Spear* again. I began to remove the leather thong that held the piece of crystal at the top against the blade.

"I believe it would be best to leave the spear in its disguise. For now, at least. There are forces arrayed against us all, and part of what they seek is what you hold," said Moscastan.

After all that had happened that day, I knew that Moscastan was right. I retied the thong I had loosened and swung my legs off the slab to face the old man before me. I saw in his eyes the man I'd known in that life so long ago. "Jacobi . . . ," I began.

"Moscastan, now, if you please," he replied.

"All right," I said, smiling with awe. "That was unbelievable! Have you . . . " I started, indicating the slab and the journey it seemed to induce. " . . . Of course, you have. Stupid question, that. Forgive me." My feeling of awe gave way to excitement. "I was there, really there! 'Twas no dream, Moscastan. I know it was real." I let this feeling of excitement wash through me for a moment. Soon, though, another feeling began to take hold: confusion. "But . . . why?" I asked. "You said a minute ago that now I 'completely understand.' I don't know if that's true. What am I supposed to do?"

"Do?"

"What am I supposed to do with this . . . knowledge or understanding?" I asked.

His brow crinkled in bewildered amusement. "Why, you are *supposed* to live your life," he said, laughing.

"You know what I mean," I countered. "Why show me all this without telling me what it means to my life now?"

"What you experienced was for you alone; to know your-Self completely, to know your greatness in the past, present and future," Moscastan replied.

Now it was my turn to laugh. "What I did in that life as Centurion Longinus, I don't think that everyone would call it greatness. They might call it evil . . . "

"The ignorant, perhaps. You simply played your part. Judgment is from fear and ignorance of *The Workings, The Law*."

"What does that mean . . . ?" I had always loved Moscastan. In addition to being a mentor, he was like a father to me. But there were times when he was vague, to say the least.

Still, I remembered much of certain natural laws we had used in Druidic training to manipulate natural phenomena with and in the mind. But I sensed that was not what he was talking about here. I sensed that he was referring to something much bigger, and yet at the same time, something which all else was a part of and subject to. " . . . 'The Workings, The Law'?" I asked more evenly, sincerely.

"Enough, for now. Let this day's events settle into your mind and soul," Moscastan said cryptically. "Come. Your friends await."

Yes, my friends. *How long had I been in here?* I wondered. And, *my friends: were they still back where I'd left them? Or, had they found their way here, as I had?* Something in Moscastan's tone just then made me believe that he knew they were near. But how?

"Come, and you'll find out," he said, as if reading my thoughts. With a snorting giggle, he ducked through the opening and back into the passageway.

I hopped off the slab and quickly followed.

SEVEN

I followed Moscastan back out into the main chamber of the crystal cave.

"Myrriddin!" came the familiar voice of Igraines, un-stuttered.

She stood just inside the cavern near the main entryway.

"How did you find this place?" I asked, as I ran to greet her.

"I started looking for you," she said.

"You should've stayed put," I retorted, feeling a tad guilty, defensive.

"When y-you didn't c-ome right back, I thought to quickly g-get the poultice myself and maybe look for you, too. You'd b-been gone for hours. Th-thought to find you eaten by wolves, I-I did." Igraines managed to say.

"And Baldua?" I asked.

"I left h-him. Was c-coming right back. Got lost, though. Like you, I g-guess," she said, sardonically. "An odd mist d-down . . . "

"I know."

Igraines looked away then. I think she felt as stupid as I had initially for getting *lost*. She peered at the walls and the ceiling, a look of wonder spreading across her face. "What is this place?"

I looked to Moscastan, but spoke to Igraines. "Good question."

"'Tis a place of knowledge, a place of learning, a place of initiation—"

"A place for the soul to soar!" I added.

Now a look of confusion crossed Igraines' face.

"I'll explain later," I said, picking up the package of moss and mistletoe right from where I had left it. "Come. We need to get back to Baldua.

"But the m-mist is still strong," said Igraines.

"The way will not be barred," Moscastan declared, nodding toward the spear, the staff in my hand.

Igraines saw the nod. She looked at me with another look of confusion.

I walked out of the cavern, Igraines quickly following, Moscastan, with a knowing smile, trailing just behind her.

Indeed, the mist remained thick. But now I knew what to do. I breathed steadily, closed my eyes and went deep within. I held up the staff and saw in my mind's eye my deepest Self entering the spear and running through it, contacting the mist through the spear, contacting it at the smallest level of the mist itself; at the smallest and deepest level of being, where all things are made of the same substance, and are thus connected, and can therefore communicate. I knew to do this, at least in theory, through my Druidic training, but had never attempted to perform this type of feat with the depth of conviction I was feeling at that moment. Something in me had shifted back inside the cavern, on the slab. I now truly knew my *Source*, and I realized that by going within to my own deepest level of being, and aided by the spear, I could connect meaningfully with any and all things, for it is at this level, the level of Source, where all things are connected. I came to that level within the mist, merged with it (the mist) and asked it, urged it, to disperse, knowing that it would through the Law of Mind and Source. This Law, the workings of the One True Source, had been drilled into me on the Isle of Mystery since I'd been a lad, but I was only now understanding it! Moscastan knew. He had said as much earlier.

"It leaves!" exclaimed Igraines in perfect un-stuttered astonishment.

Her exclamation broke my concentration and brought me back to myself. No matter. The work had been done. Within a heartbeat, the mist began to vanish, rolling back as if it had a mind of its own, revealing a green glen just outside the cavern's entrance and a breaking dawn. I dropped my hand, holding the staff to my side, pleasantly astonished in spite of myself.

Moscastan smiled proudly at me.

Igraines nodded toward the object in my hand. "A w-wizard's staff that i-is, truly."

"Not really," I said.

"We shall now go find your friend," proclaimed Moscastan, more I think to divert attention from the topic of the spear, than to prompt us to get back to Baldua.

I headed down the path, the same one I'd approached the night before. Igraines and Moscastan followed.

It was early morning. The sun's disc could not have been up more than an hour's time. Had I really been in the crystal cavern all night long? It did not seem possible. Though a thin, dewy morning fog a mere foot off the damp ground was present, the choking, cloaking mist was completely gone. It did not take long for us to find the spot where Igraines and I had left Baldua. He was gone. I expected Moscastan to question us as to whether this was the right spot. He did not, especially after we found indications that perhaps our friend had been taken away from the place. The ground had clearly been chewed up quite recently by horses and men—many men.

"By the C-Christ. He was layin' there," muttered Igraines, pointing to a spot on the ground. There were marks in the dirt trailing off from the exact place Baldua had last laid before she left—marks that looked like someone had been dragged.

Yet, for some reason, at that moment, Igraines' words bothered me more than the drag marks and what they implied. "Why do you say that, Igraines? You are not a follower of the Christ, this Jesu. You suckle the Mother-Goddess, Dana," I said more harshly than I knew why.

"Wh-why do you care what I say? It's just words! You don't follow the Ch-Christ either," she replied, obviously insulted.

She was right. I understood very little of the Christ's teachings. I had learned more during my spirit's travel, my vision on the ocean-slab in the crystal cavern, than I'd known before. Besides, what I knew of this Christ's followers, I did not like. I doubted that even they truly understood the teachings, for they spoke utterly against all things natural. From all that I'd seen of them thus far in my life, hearing their beliefs through a few of the wandering priests and preachers that had been around, they seemed to care more about controlling others than advancing their own souls. Still, inexplicably, Igraines' words bothered me. Perhaps I was just misplacing anger at my friend's disappearance.

Igraines followed the marks as much as possible. They went back into the main grouping of prints in the small clearing in the center of the area, joining with hoofprints and footprints. All the prints then seemed to double back the way they had come, which was the same direction Igraines, Baldua and I had come from the day before. "They took him. We must f-follow the t-tracks," she declared.

"I agree that it appears the vile enemy you encountered yesterday has taken your friend, but we would do better to go to our village. That is where they have gone," said Moscastan, anger seeping into his voice.

Igraines considered him doubtfully.

"We can follow those tracks, but I tell you they will lead to our village and beyond. That is where Creconius was headed," Moscastan continued, with more venom than I've ever heard from him. "We may already be too late."

"You d-don't know th-that!" Igraines headed off at a near run, following the tracks.

"Igraines!" I yelled.

"Stubborn girl," observed Moscastan.

"Yes. Well, I suppose we should follow the tracks," I said.

In fact, the tracks led back to a place some quarter-of-a-mile from the battlefield of the day before. Here, the tracks converged with a mass of other prints—human and animal—and headed off in the direction of our village. It was now clear that what or who had found Baldua had been an expeditionary force sent out to track down those who had escaped Lord Creconius' army. It was the mist that had saved Igraines and myself. There was naught to do but head to our village, quickly. But when we finally arrived there, we nearly wished we had not been saved by the mist.

EIGHT

Fortunately, Moscastan had a water skin and dried meat with him to sustain us, for it took up nearly the whole day to reach our destination. We arrived at the village near dark. We had seen the smoke on the horizon and smelled the burned carnage from a mile out. There was nothing left. Everything had been razed to the ground and smoldered still. This must have happened the prior afternoon or evening. Those left alive—which numbered more than I expected—wandered in a daze, collecting what belongings remained or piling bodies in the cooking pits for disposal; the same cooking pits which Leoni used to make the meals. Now, beneath the corpses was wood for a different sort of fire. 'Twas the Celtic way: burning of the body in a funerary pyre instantly released the soul to travel to the Otherworld.

Yet, there was another faction in those dark days that was beginning to exert much influence on this subject. They even believed that it was evil to burn the body, for then their God—who was supposedly the Infinite and Only God—could not raise them in resurrection upon a Day of Judgment. How absurd! If their God was infinite, then He would be able to resurrect one no matter what! This faction was the Christians, and their view on death and cremation offended my sensibilities as a Celt and further convinced me that they did not understand their Christ's teachings. There was a group of them here now also collecting corpses, but not for cremation in the noble, Celtic way. They were placing them on a mule-drawn, flat-bed cart for a *Christian* burial. Quite a few of our clan members, though still practicing the Old Ways, which included consulting with

Druids on occasion, had, nonetheless, converted to Christianity, following the teachings of Jesu, or Jesus, as the present Christians called Him; the same man Centurion Longinus had pierced—that *I* had pierced—so long ago.

"Bring them," called a man in a drab brown robe tied at the waist with a simple rope. Looped over the rope was a twine of wood-beads which ended with a small dangling Crucifix. The man's head was shaved in the style of one the Christian Ascetics from the new Monastery at Glastonbury. A Tonsure, it was called— the crown of the head was completely shaved with a circle of hair rounding the skull front, back and sides. I didn't know its exact meaning, but it made these men stand out as priests of their Order. I thought that it also made them look ridiculous. This priest was fairly young, perhaps twenty-nine summers, comely and appealing. He had a firm yet gentle way about his countenance. And his eyes: a deep brown, yet there seemed to be something more—a depth perhaps of things not of this world. He spoke to the two villagers who had piled corpses, some already burned from the raid, onto the cart.

"Yes, Father Pretorius," said one of the villagers.

That was another thing I did not understand about these Christians; why they called these priests *Father*. Did they adopt these priests as fathers? Perhaps I would learn the answers someday. Right now, I wanted to find Baldua. Then I saw Leoni, bent over a small fire off to the edge of the village. She was cooking something, lifting the wood spoon from the pot and tasting its contents' worthiness.

"Leoni!" I called as I ran to her. I embraced the plump woman, who, to my surprise, did not return the gesture. "You are unscathed?" I said, as I pulled back and looked into her eyes.

"Yes, yes. Important work now, though. I must feed all these people. They're working hard at cleaning up, you see," she replied, vacantly, falsely. She was clearly trying to act as if nothing had happened.

I looked her up and down. She was not unscathed. She was filthy from head to toe. Her hair was disheveled and her face lacerated. Her dress was torn in places and on the spot under which her legs met at her crotch, there was blood; a lot of it. She had been raped, brutally. Anger welled within me, intense hatred for the ones who did this. I would cut their hearts from their bodies while they lived and shove it in their screaming mouths.

"Myrriddin!" Igraines called from behind me.

I looked around and saw her standing next to the Cart. Then I turned back to Leoni and touched her gently on the side of the head, caressing her hair. She jumped with a start, but did not pull away altogether. She was not entirely gone. "I'll come back in a bit, all right?" I said.

She stared into the air for a moment, then turned back to the pot without answering. I left it there for the time being, and headed over to the cart.

Moscastan was not with Igraines. Scanning the immediate area, I saw him near a woman and two children, no doubt tending to their needs. I stopped in my tracks briefly when I noticed that he had once again assumed his younger persona. Interesting trick, that! I would have to ask him exactly how he achieved that glam. I wasn't sure whom I liked better—the young Persian/Britton Moscastan, or the old man I'd met in the cavern of crystal, the *Crystal Sanctuary*, as I was beginning to think of it; at least the longer this hideous day wore on. And which one was the real, present-day Moscastan—the younger or the older? I had thought the latter upon first seeing him, but now I was not sure. Why would he choose to glam himself as an old man? Perhaps because of what the Old Ones represent, or perhaps because it suited him best to be as he was when I knew him during the life of Longinus: old Jacobi. That, too, was something I would have to find out.

I continued on toward the cart. My heart began to thump as I saw what Igraines was pointing to in the pile on the cart. I arrived there just as they started to move it away, one man pulling it, another pushing, following the priest Pretorius across a field, presumably to bury the cart's contents. Rather than stop the laboring men, I simply walked alongside the cart, as did Igraines, and I looked at the man she had been pointing to. Though the man's face was burned, I could tell that it was not Baldua. Besides, this man was wearing a cross, denoting him as a follower of the Christ. Baldua was Celt, through and through. "It's not him," I declared.

"Y-you sure?" she asked.

I looked again. The man's face did resemble Baldua's, but it was not him. "Yes. I know it looks like him, but it's not. Besides, Baldua would not be seen dead with that Christian symbol around his neck," I said with a forced smile.

My attempt at humor in this horrific setting was lost on her. I was just pleased that it was not my friend.

"What about that?" she said, pointing to a small shoulder bag lying in the man's grasp. It was Baldua's. Yet, I didn't remember him having it with him the previous day.

"It's his. I-I've seen it b-before," she said.

"But did you see him with it yesterday?"

She thought for a moment, then shrugged her shoulders, not remembering. "I don't think so," I said.

"That one was a raider," said the toothless, pudgy, middle-aged man pushing the cart; the same man who had addressed Pretorius a moment before. "Killed 'im myself, I did. Smacked 'im upside the head with a big torch and hit him a couple more times 'til he stopped floppin'. Stupid shit-holes. Who do ya think you are?!" he yelled at the corpse.

"He must have taken the bag from Baldua's hovel," I said.

We arrived at the burial site, a shallow pit had already been dug. Pretorius stood at the edge of the hole, eyes closed, apparently in meditation. I looked at Igraines who motioned with her head that we should get out of there. She obviously wanted nothing to do with this twisted practice.

"Stay, my children, please," said the priest. "No matter who these people were, what acts some of them may have committed in this life, they need to be sent to the Father properly. Your prayers and solemnity will aid in this."

I was loath to do so. Who was this person? Such presumption! I wanted to find my friend, to comfort Leoni and the others of our clan and destroy the demon that committed this atrocity. My anger, which to this point I did not even realize was there, suddenly burst forth. "Why? You are part of the cause of this, you and your kind," I exclaimed, pointing at the crucifix on his belt. "At least one of the dead men on that cart wears your symbol, and not one of our people!"

"Please," said the priest. "We are all of the One, regardless of what symbols we wear."

He didn't speak like most of the other priests of his religion that I had heard. He sounded more like Moscastan. There was something else, too: there was a familiarity about him; something about his countenance, his presence, that told me I knew this man. I sensed his spirit. I had known him previous to this life. I looked into his eyes and saw . . . a forest sanctuary in the mists from a long time ago.

"Paulonius?" I whispered.

"Pretorius," he replied, having heard my whispered recollection.

"No, I mean . . . never mind. You just remind me of someone from a long time ago," I said.

He looked at me quizzically for a moment before realization donned upon his face. "Ah, I see. You are a Celt and practice the Old Ways, then. Well, I understand your ways. Actually, my beliefs are not so far from yours. I am of a slightly different thought than most of my counterparts in the Church, more Gnostic, if you will. But I am Christian, and the need to tend to the Christian dead is great," he said, gesturing to the corpses in the cart.

"W-we need to find B-Baldua," Igraines said, grabbing my arm of the hand that held the spear.

The staff, the spear, had been silent; nothing from it. No vibration, glowing or anything since before we left the glen where Baldua had last been seen. With all that had happened to the village, I thought that the spear would have shaken in warning as we approached. It had not.

Father Pretorius was staring at the spear. "May I?" he asked, his voice nearly cracking, as he reached out tentatively to touch the object in my hand.

I could see in his eyes a recognition that he felt, but could not explain even to himself. I never let anyone touch this thing that I held. Yet, with this priest, it was different. I could tell that Pretorius *knew* what I possessed, but did not yet understand this knowledge. He did not yet fully understand his own soul's past enough to comprehend what it was that he was feeling. I held the staff, the spear, out to him. He touched it lightly and reverently, emotion welling up on his face in the process. Though still, I could see, he did not fully understand why he was feeling what he was feeling.

He touched the ancient wooden shaft lightly. Next, he caressed the crystal in its housing against the blade, touching the blade itself. Then it came: a tear of the soul long banished welled up in his left eye. "This is no Pagan Wizard's walking staff, is it, my friend? This is something from my Lord's realm. I feel it. It is old and not from here. Where did you come by it?"

"I . . . I cannot say," I replied.

"Cannot, or *will not*, Master . . . ?"

"Myrriddin, just Myrriddin," I answered.

He dropped his hand from the spear.

"Will you stay for a few moments to see these people properly given over to God?" asked Pretorius.

"Yes," I found myself saying.

"M-Myrriddin," Igraines said in frustration, not wanting to waste any more time in finding Baldua.

"'Tis but a short time to see the dead off, lass," said Moscastan from behind. He had approached quite stealthily, apparently having left the village remains for the time being. "Father Pretorius, good to see you again," he said, addressing the priest.

"And you, Druid Master Moscastan," replied Pretorius. "Will you help me perform this rite for the passing of the dead?"

I was shocked by the invitation—a Christian priest wishing to join with a Druid Master in performing a rite of passing for the dead? Truly, this priest was not of the Christian thought that I was used to seeing. He seemed to allow for, even embrace, the differences of our cultural, spiritual ways. Perhaps it was not so much our differences he focused on, but our similarities, all being of the One, as he put it. I was then even more surprised by Moscastan's response.

"Yes, Priest Pretorius. I would be honored," Moscastan said.

"Moscastan?" I said.

"Why do you look at me so, Myrriddin? 'We are all of the One'. Have I not said that a-thousand times? The One has a myriad of appearances and faces and aspects, but it all boils down to the One. Young Priest Pretorius sees this, even if most of his power-hungry counterparts do not."

"Ah, now Moscastan, do not be too harsh," said Pretorius.

"You are right. I just fear that those of your faith with less understanding than you, which, unfortunately is most of them, are bringing an end to our ways, violently and permanently," said Moscastan.

"Understood. This is not my wish nor should it be the way of things. We all need to recognize that our true Source is One Source. I will do what I can, Moscastan. I will do what I can," Pretorius responded.

Moscastan stepped forward and placed a hand on the younger man's shoulder. "I know that you will, my friend," he said.

Pretorius gave another look to the spear in my hand. I could see in his eyes that he wanted to inquire of it further, but this was not the time. He nodded to the men who had pushed the cart and then turned toward the grave's hole before us. The cart-men began to gently drop the bodies into their final resting place.

Pretorius then began to speak a prayer for the dead. "Requiem aeternam dona eis, Domine; et lux perpetua luceat eis. Requiescant in pace. Amen".

It was in Latin, of course. Where was Baldua when I needed him?

"By the Holy of Holies, by Dana and Luna, I release the spirits to the Otherworld, the crossing be blessed and whole . . . " intoned Moscastan.

Back and forth went the prayers for the dead, in Latin by Pretorius, in ancient Gaelic by Moscastan. I anticipated feeling nothing but loathing for the whole ordeal and resentment for being made to stay on account of Moscastan's desire for us, Igraines and me, to do so. Instead, what I began to feel was tenderness toward the souls of the deceased in the grave before me. Caught up in the moment, it took me a few heartbeats to realize that the spear was vibrating in my hand. It was not a vibration of warning; it was a subtle vibration of sympathy. It was an aide to the comfort being created for the departed souls to ease their crossing.

After a while, the vibration stopped; the rite was over. I knew not how much time had passed, for I had gone into a deep meditation, harmonizing in thought, in spirit, in mind, with the moment. I felt a tug on my arm. Igraines was trying to pull me away.

"C-come on. E-enough of this," she said.

I came back to my senses and agreed. "We are going to find Baldua," I said.

"Wait," said Pretorius. "I wish to go with you." He had looked at the spear as he said this.

"Why?" I asked. "Are you not needed here?"

The villagers who had brought the corpses began pushing dirt on the bodies, filling the grave.

"I have done what is needed," he said, indicating the grave and the bodies therein. "I am no longer needed here. It is time for me to leave. Perhaps I can help you."

Igraines stepped forward angrily, clearly about to say something abrasive to the priest.

I grabbed her arm to stop her, looked into her eyes and shook my head. Turning back to the priest, I said, "If you wish, but I don't see how you can help."

"We shall see," was all Pretorius said.

"Moscastan, will you come, too?" I asked.

"I will follow. Those left here need the comfort of the Old Ways, at least for a time."

"As you wish," I said, then turned to Pretorius. "Which way did those raiders go?"

"South, I think. Their Lord, their General, seeks something," he said, and again looked at the spear. Igraines saw the look, too.

"Then let's go south. I'm sure Baldua is with him," I said.

"How could you know that? Perhaps he tried to get back here? Perhaps something else has happened, God forbid it," Pretorius said.

I met his eyes and knew that he had more knowledge of Baldua and of what this so-called General was seeking than he was conveying. But what could that knowledge be? And why would Baldua be of any interest to this General? The spear vibrated in my hand again, giving me an answer for the moment; now was not the time to press Pretorius. Fine. The spear stopped vibrating. "I believe that he is with them. Regardless, I will find him," I said.

"So be it," said Moscastan.

"Indeed," said Pretorius.

"Would all of y-you stop fl-flapping your lips and m-move it!" said Igraines, angrily.

"So be it!" said Moscastan again. "Go."

I looked back toward the village, to where Leoni had been. She was nowhere to be seen.

"She will heal, Myrriddin. I will see that she begins the process," said Moscastan, reading my searching eyes. "I saw you speaking with her a while ago."

I nodded.

After a few minutes spent gathering some meager provisions, Pretorius, Igraines and I headed south.

It was not difficult to follow the trail of the "raiders," as the villager had called them. It is nearly impossible to hide the tracks of a passing army. Equally, it was not difficult to find them. By the end of that same day, we had them in sight. We were careful not to stay out in the open too much, as I was sure Lord Creconius would have scouts fore and aft of their position at all times. I was also sure that it was indeed Creconius and his followers. We had not been invaded since the Romans first came. Fighting between tribes and clans, certainly; that had been going on since the beginning of time. But no organized body led by an outsider had threatened us for some time. Until now.

We stood in a small grove of trees on a ridge near an outcropping of rocks, with an opening in the trees to see the enemy encampment in the valley below. The outcroppings made the perfect shelter to sleep under and the trees blocked us from the army below. Staying there for the night was the best option. We needed to make some sort of plan to get Baldua and would do that over a small evening meal. We had gathered up supplies enough for a few days—if we were disciplined with rationing them to ourselves—which Igraines had insisted on carrying in a makeshift satchel.

I was a little surprised that Pretorius was still with us. He did not strike me as the type to quest about the countryside searching to liberate someone that he did not even know, let alone liberate this person from a blood-lusting rabble. Yet here he was.

I was leaning on the staff, the spear, and looking through the trees, Igraines and Pretorius next to me, when I felt a subtle vibration from it. "Myrriddin," whispered the voice of the spear.

I must have given a startled look, for Pretorius gazed at me quizzically. "What is it, my friend?" he asked.

"It's that th-thing," said Igraines, pointing to the spear. "It s-speaks to him." Then, she walked back toward the outcropping.

If daggers could fly from my eyes, they would have killed her instantly. I knew that she was aware of my communications with the thing, but it disturbed me that she would be so cavalier in conveying that to a stranger. Besides, how could she have known I had just heard the voice?

"Is this true?" Pretorius asked.

Again, I sensed the man's depth of character and sincerity. "It is," I said. "You were right when you said that this was no mere '*Pagan* Wizard's walking staff,' as you put it."

An awkward silence ensued for a moment.

"Yes, well, that begs the question, doesn't it?" asked Pretorius.

I almost told him then that this was the spear of Longinus; the spear the Centurion had used to pierce the side of Christ while he hanged on the cross. But, I gave naught but silence.

"I see," he said.

"I don't mean to be rude," I countered, suddenly feeling guilty for being just that. "It's not easy . . . "

"You are afraid that I might not believe you," said Pretorius. It was a statement, not a question.

"Perhaps," I managed to say.

"L-lets eat," ordered Igraines, from under the outcropping. She had laid out a blanket and was divvying out food for the three of us. "They aren't going anywhere," she said, nodding in the general direction of the army encampment.

Pretorius and I looked at one another, suppressing laughter simmering beneath the surface. We joined Igraines for a humble meal of bread, dried meat, cheese and water.

After our meal, Pretorius went off to pray, leaving Igraines and me alone. It was dark and chilly. We lit no fire for obvious reasons, so we both huddled together for warmth. The spear was next to me, as always. We talked of things past and things perhaps to come, but mostly of the immediate threat posed by the invaders and what it might mean. Then, when the conversation seemed to lag, she touched the spear. To my surprise, I did nothing, somehow feeling that it was completely appropriate that she had done so; even that she had held it many a-time in another place, another time.

"Y-you know th-they seek this, too," she said in a whisper. "I don't kn-know how I kn-know. I just do."

I simply nodded, staring into her eyes. "Perhaps," was all I managed to say. I looked down at the spear, then gently placed it in a long nook in the rock next to me. I turned back to Igraines and stared into her eyes for a few a moments. We had known each other for a long time. In spite of her hard demeanor, she was becoming quite a woman through and through. And, yes. I admit that I was more than attracted to her; had been for a long time. I also believed that she felt the same toward me. The way she looked at me sometimes made me feel both excited and self-conscious.

She lay back, then, gently pulling me down with her and into an embrace. Slowly, tentatively at first, we kissed; a tender meeting of the lips. But soon the tentativeness abated, and our passion swelled. We became more excited and hungry by the moment, probing each other's mouths with eager lips and tongues. My heart was thudding. I could feel hers beneath her chest as well, as we pulled each other's body against one another. I do not remember exactly what happened next, save for the forceful caress of her hands, the heat of her body and the merging of our souls. If a paradise of *heaven*, as the Christians called it, existed, I entered it during that time with Igraines.

I felt her stir a little while later. I looked at her and a feeling of connectedness washed over me. Our passion for each other's body had been clear. But I realized that I felt more than mere lust for her, much more.

She insisted on taking a guard watch. Pretorius, back by that time and only half asleep nearby, did not see the need for any of us to stand guard. But then, he wouldn't. He was not a soldier. Not that I was, really, but I understood the need to keep a guard.

Still, she wanted to stand watch. "No," I had said to her. "Pretorius and I will stand watch through the night." That was a foolish thing for me to have said to her.

"Why? Am I n-not capable, that we three can't split the watch?" she asked, sitting up beside me, suddenly furious.

I always found it interesting that her stutter seemed much less pronounced when she was in a fit of anger. "Of course not," I said. "I just thought . . . " I began, looking at our bedding. To his credit, the priest said nothing about the coupling Igraines and I had obviously experienced earlier. Our clothes, though still on, were in quite the disarray, and our limbs, at least our legs, were still entwined. "Fine. Take the first watch, then," I said to her.

She got up and marched out to the small clearing not far away, near the tree where one could see the enemy's encampment.

We did not hear them come in the night. Nor, did we see them. I still, to this day, do not fully understand what happened. Thinking back, it seems clear that I should have taken the first watch. What I know for sure is that I awakened some time later with a broken body and another missing friend.

NINE

Floating. Flying, actually. I could see the green hills and mountains below, bathed in a pale sunset. It was as if I were a bird flying above them. I came in closer, spying more details. The green hills gave way to a rocky, forested area. I recognized this place. But parts of it were different than I remembered. Some of the trees were larger; some of the foliage more lushly sprawled, and some of the rocky areas more eroded. It was as if some time had passed since last I'd seen this place. Coming in even closer to one area in particular confirmed my thoughts as to where I was. There, before me, was an opening in the side of a rock formation, a granite formation. It was a cave's opening embedded in the side of one of the mountains. But not just any cave's opening; it was the entry point to Moscastan's Crystal Cavern.

Two people approached it. One I thought to be Moscastan. The other person was a lad, a young man of no more than fifteen summers. I looked again at Moscastan and realized quite suddenly that it was not Moscastan at all. It was me, a future-self? The vision-Myrriddin was adorned in the regalia of a Master Druid, the highest of Merlins: a purple robe with crimson trim flowed over his body. His hair, my hair, what was left of it, was nearly all white. He still had a clean-shaved face in the Roman way, showing the face to have the lines and crags of the years and the wise. But he also looked pale and drawn, having seen much of life's offerings and disappointments. I did not sense that this version of myself was all that far in the future, if indeed these images were prescient. Though somewhat pale and careworn, he also looked solid in his Unification with the One; his bearing and countenance conveyed a surety of purpose, a confidence of self. Which made me think, perhaps the coloring and apparent ragged features were reflective of an inner power that my present-self simply did not yet understand. I could see this in his eyes, *my* eyes, still bright and full of youth, depth and knowledge and inner power.

There was a walking staff—clearly a true Druid's staff—walking with him. A new and very large Crystal Druid's Egg with a glowing green hue, adorned the top, concealing the spear's blade. There was something almost trance-inducing about the Egg, the Crystal. It was unlike any stone I'd ever seen. A greenish light seemed to come from within it. It pulsated a power that was beyond comprehension. Yet, I quickly realized what I was seeing: the stone was taking the power that coursed through the staff—the power of the Merlin, the power of the One—and amplifying it. Amazing! Where had this Druid's Egg come from? However, I could not tell if this staff was the spear I presently possessed. *Why wouldn't it be?* I wondered.

The lad and Older Myrriddin were now very close to Moscastan's Crystal Sanctuary.

My vision-self, was in mid-sentence. He was speaking to the boy. "Arturius," Older Myrriddin said to the lad.

For amoment, I had the fleeting thought that I was simply dreaming, and that perhaps the boy was also a version of me some years earlier, speaking to his— my—future-self. But I had never been to the cave as a lad. No matter. Dreams are always strange that way, twisting our perceptions of time and memory and people. As I said, however, that was just a fleeting thought. This was no dream. I could *feel* its truth in the core of my being. This was a prophecy, a glimpse of some future event and time, a future in which I would tutor a boy named Arturius. The boy's name seemed familiar. But I knew no boy named Arturius in this life. At least not yet.

"Your father and Pretorius knew these things," Older Myrriddin continued, "but your father was wise in many other ways. He gathered many of the lands and clans together, did he not? You shall carry on that work, expand on it," continued my older persona. As they approached the cave's opening, the wonderful glow from within gently ebbed, flowed and spilled out of the entryway, onto the darkening ground. A look tantamount to pride played subtly across Oder Myrriddin's face. "I was a marvel at scrying and quite gifted with the *sight*, both past and future, you know. You may learn those things, too, during your stay here . . . if you wish it."

I felt my present-self grinning with heartfelt warmth at the older man's words.

"Yes. So you've said a-hundred times," the lad replied drolly.

They disappeared into the Sanctuary's opening.

"Merlin!" I heard from somewhere in the distance. "Myrriddin!"

The Crystal Sanctuary's entrance, the hills and mountains—the whole scene before me—evaporated.

My eyes snapped open. Slowly, they adjusted to the misty gloom. Cold. It was cold and damp. A hard surface was beneath me. Stone. A full moon was shrouded in misty clouds, peering out from its protective curtain on the mortals below. Light from torches flickered nearby. I should have been alarmed. Instead, I was disappointed. I was not quite sure why I felt that way. Perhaps it was because I half expected to wake up in the Sanctuary. Instead, I was outside on a cold, moonlit night, lying supine on a stone . . . altar?

Shapes took form nearby: upright, rectangular stone columns topped with stone lintels. I knew this place. Moscastan called it *The Grand Henge,* where the Ancients and ancestors plotted the course of the Universe; where the Otherworld met this one; where rituals of all sorts had been performed—from fertility rites to migrations of souls on All Hollows Eve; from sacrifices for various appeasements to the raising of the dead. This latter rite had only been a myth. But I got the feeling I wasn't lying on this Altar as some kind of living sacrifice.

It was then that I heard the chanting. Out of the corner of my eyes, I could see several white-robed, hooded figures, their faces obscured, but their voices clear. They stood six on each side of the stone altar, some ten feet away from me. They were chanting something in ancient Gaelic, only part of which I could understand. What I did understand, however, was unmistakable; it was a chant to bring the dead back to life, not the dead in the general sense, but one specifically: me. They were chanting to bring *me* back to life. Apparently, they had succeeded.

The chanting, the rhythmic voices, suddenly stopped. Sensing movement, I rolled my head to the right and looked at someone who approached the altar. Stepping forward, throwing off his dark hood and standing with his arms raised high to silence the twelve chanters, was Moscastan, somehow looking younger than I remembered him even as his younger self. Unlike the others, Moscastan was shrouded in a black robe adorned with gold stars and a prominent crescent moon on his chest. He stared at me. "You have returned. You have awakened," he said, stating the obvious, a hint of glee escaping from the upturned corners of his mouth.

But awakened from what? Ah, yes. We had been searching for Baldua and we had bedded down for the night; the priest Pretorius, Igraines and myself. "Igraines!" I opened my mouth to speak, but not a sound came out. Panic struck, I tried to grab my throat with my right hand, only to find that my hand would not move. Why? Trying my left hand proved slightly easier, but still challenging. I brought the heavily wrapped hand to my throat with difficulty and felt cloth around my entire neck—a wet, sticky substance seeping through the cloth.

I tried to sit up, but could not. The pain in my rib area and lower back sent searing bolts of agony coursing through my entire body. A slight, muffled animal noise emanated from my mouth in response to the pain. I remained lying down.

"Now, now Myrriddin," soothed Moscastan, "You've had quite an ordeal. We thought we had lost you. Your life's pulse faded and left not too long ago."

Forgetting the pain for the moment, I looked around as best I could, frantically looking for Igraines. Why I felt that she would be there at that moment, now seems ridiculous. I wasn't sure how or why I was there.

"It is here, Myrriddin. Fear naught," said Moscastan, pointing to a long, narrow object resting on a nearby portable wooden table, surrounded by ritual instruments. It was my staff, my spear. Not Igraines. That was something, anyway. Whatever had happened to us, my spear had escaped with me. But, how?

"It was . . . hidden, somehow, cloaked in a nook where the three of you had been sleeping. Did you place a glam on it when you retired that night?" ventured Moscastan excitedly. "So that no one else would see it?"

"I . . . " was all I managed to squeak out.

"My apologies a-thousand times, Master Myrriddin. I tax you needlessly. 'Tis good to have you back among us, truly, but you need to further heal," said Moscastan, turning to leave.

"Wh-where," I croaked, "is Igrai . . . "

"Igraines?" Moscastan stopped and turned back to me. "You must complete the healing. We will continue to aid you."

The tone in his voice sounded grim. "What is it?" Speaking caused searing pain to shoot through my throat. But I had to know what happened to Igraines; indeed, what happened to all three of us that night.

Moscastan hesitated before proceeding. I could see in his eyes that he knew I would not be put off. "No one knows exactly what happened," he began, "other than the fact that you were attacked by the same brigands that sacked your village—the ones camped near where you bedded for the night. They apparently overpowered Igraines easily. There were drag marks on the ground from where she had been 'on watch,' as you might say. The priest Pretorius was beaten and left near a tree. He's the one who came and got me, and a few others. They let him live because he had buried their dead comrades 'honorably.' He was able to hear most of what happened to you. They had been watching you all along, trailing you nearly since your visit to the Crystal Sanctuary. They want the spear and know you have it. But they couldn't find it. As I said, it's as if it cloaked itself, or you did, before you slipped into unconsciousness. I think 'twas the latter. I've seen you do something similar before, not even realizing you'd performed the feat of cloaking on the thing."

Yes, I remembered one occasion when I had willed the thing invisible during a bout with other boys. I was very young and the other lads wanted my "wizard's staff." They had pinned me down in an attempt to pry it out of my hands. At the very moment they were able to uncurl my fingers from around the shaft, the whole staff disappeared from sight. The boys jumped back at the display of apparent sorcery. I, however, could still feel the shaft in my hand even though I, too, could not see it for the moment. I remember laughing; laughing at my apparent power with the staff, or the staff's apparent power with me, and then laughing at the boys as they ran away. I almost laughed again now at the memory, but my face hurt too much.

Looking beyond Moscastan, I saw another figure lingering in the shadows just outside the sacred circle of stones. It was Pretorius. He, too, was in a white robe, but a large wooden crucifix dangled from around his neck. His hands were clasped in front of him and his head was bowed in prayer. I was surprised to see him in this Pagan place. I had a fleeting thought that his prayers were those of deliverance from this "evil place," as some of his contemporary Christians had called it. But I knew this man better than that. He had no fear of places like this. In fact, he would see it for what it had been: a place of focus for the One God to express in the only given way that our ancestors understood. In that sense, this place was sacred still. I had no doubt that his prayers were for me. I felt them; I felt their power. I felt the power of this priest and his understanding of the One's nature, which was the essence of everyone's nature. Pretorius stopped his mumbling of prayers and opened his eyes as if sensing my gaze. He smiled broadly and stepped forward into the Henge's inner circle. He halted short of those who had been chanting, however, and looked at them tentatively, as they looked at him and seemed to convey that the priest should venture no closer.

Moscastan, turning serious, leaned into my face. "You are still in a broken state, but your body heals itself as I speak. You had left us for a time—you'd no life pulse, no breath. We brought you here, you and your spear."

He paused then, and turned to the table next to us. Tenderly and reverently, he picked up the staff, the spear of Longinus, with both hands. Holding it horizontally, he lifted it briefly above his head, acknowledging it and the powers that flowed through it to the gods, to the heavens, to the One. Its tip began to glow.

Soft chanting began again. Moscastan brought the spear back down and held it in front of his body. The small branches and foliage I had tied to the blade were disheveled. Some of the thongs were loose and the crystal was gone. The rest of the thongs still held fast, though, which in turn still held the branches onto the spear overall. With the missing crystal, the spear's tip looked more like a claw than the crowning top of a wizard's staff. Yet, still among the twigged branches, the blade glowed.

Moscastan laid the spear gently on my body lengthwise, the blade on my upper chest, the shaft running down the center of my body, with the lower part of the shaft resting on the touching heels of my splayed feet. I rested my right hand on the part of the shaft just below the blade. My mentor then stepped back silently, joining the nearest chanters in proximity and voice. Pretorius, too, had stepped back and resumed his chanting of prayers.

I held the spear tightly against my chest and closed my eyes. I felt energy coming from it. At first, it was in the form of a pulsating, soothing heat. But then the feeling changed to something akin to a charged, static or as if I were suddenly near a bolt of lightning: a powerfully charged bolt of lightning that was in the spear itself. From there, it went into my body, coursing through to the injured region. A binding and pinching sensation came from within, as my muscle and sinew that had been torn and shredded were now being fused and mended back together in an instant. The chanting intensified, adding and aiding powerful energy to the healing that was taking place. I surrendered, giving in to the moment utterly. Leaving physical consciousness and physical body behind, my spirit—body and mind drifted above the scene. I did this so that the healing could complete itself without hindrance of my conscious thought.

Floating. I was floating over the Henge. My body lay on the center stone, the spear atop my body. I could also see all present, as well as an Otherwordly light that surrounded the whole area. This light, which I could only see with disembodied spirit eyes, radiated from the spear to those present and back again. All were connected in the beautiful light of power; for that is what it was: a light of divine, healing power. I felt it, knew it to be thus. Though I hovered above this scene in spirit, the cord of my soul, which connected my spirit-self to my body below, was present. The light of power coursed through this cord as well, and into my disembodied being. I knew, then, that not only would I be whole again in body, but more than powerful in spirit, too. The ritual, those chanting, the power of this Henge—this spot on earth—and the spear itself, all contributed to the immense surge of power happening to me right then and there.

Time seemed to stand still as I hovered and joined in mind with what was happening below. Then, I thought of being inside my body once again, and it happened in an instant. With a violent jolt, the scene before me went dark and I heard the chanting voices no more.

And so it began. It was on that night that I was born once more.

TEN

"He awakens, Master Moscastan." It was Leoni's sweet voice.

The lids of my eyes were as stone. With great effort, they struggled to free my sight from darkness and open them to my new world. Finally, they succeeded. I was no longer at the Henge, but in Moscastan's small earthen dwelling in our village, resting on his sleeping pallet. Leoni was there, as was Pretorius.

Moscastan's smiling face peered down at me. "How do you feel?" he asked.

I thought for a moment, assessing my entire being.

"He's groggy, can't you see?" said Leoni, answering for me. "'Tis no wonder," she said to me. "You've slept for near three days."

Moscastan gave her a reprimanding look, to which she simply turned up her nose. "Hmph, I say. Time you awoke. Ye must eat or ye'll have no strength at all. I have some leftover oat cakes and porridge from the morning's breaking of the fast. I'll get them." With that, she left, squeezing her ample girth into the narrow dirt tunnel leading to the outside. "Don't suppose ye could make this into a normal portal?" she said to Moscastan as her form receded up the passageway.

Ignoring her comment, Moscastan looked at me. "She has recovered quite nicely, don't you think?" he commented flatly in an obvious referral to Leoni's traumatized state after the village was razed.

"Three days?" I asked, my voice a bit scratchy from lack of use, but normal. "I've been lying here for three days? I remember the night at the Henge. I was outside of my body . . . "

"It was a night to behold," said Pretorius. "God was truly present, as He always is, but that night, His power was undeniably there."

"Indeed," agreed Moscastan. "Again, lad, how do you feel?"

I tentatively moved my hands, my arms. They moved a little stiffly at first, but were perfectly normal. I felt my throat and found it to be healed. Then I sat up. Aside from a quick and fleeting sense of dizziness, I felt completely healed and normal. It surprised me, for I sensed that my injuries had been devastating. "I feel . . . well," was all I could manage. I swung my legs off Moscastan's sleeping pallet and touched the ground with my feet. Standing slowly, I found my legs to be somewhat wobbly, but nothing that a few hours of walking wouldn't cure.

Moscastan beamed. "Yes, yes! You are indeed."

"Truly, you have been resurrected, Myrriddin. That night, all of us, acting as one, within the One . . . truly amazing," said Pretorius, clearly pleased to see me.

"Master Moscastan," Leoni called from outside. "If ye don't mind, I think it better for Master Myrriddin to eat up here, outside. Fresh air'll do 'im wonders."

"Yes, Leoni," I called.

"Myrriddin? Ah good, then," she said.

Moscastan leaned in close to me. "Aye, air will do you good, but me thinks she'd rather not squish through to get into my den again!" He patted my shoulder and pointed to the corner where my spear stood waiting for me. It still had the small branches tied to it, but was also still missing the Druid's Egg, thus exposing the blade. No matter. I picked it up and crawled into the passageway that led out.

The day was bright, clear and crisp. A more beautiful day there had never been. Everything seemed more vibrant, alive. Such were my thoughts as I re-entered the world through Moscastan's passageway. I stood near the opening to his hovel, staring at the trees, the sky, the foliage, three animals—squirrels, I believed—scurrying into the underbrush.

Everything had a slight glow around it, the energy which held it all together, and I could see it. Things that were living, plants, animals and people—had an extra tinge of color to their fields of energy which were in constant flux and change. I was transfixed.

"You see the aura of things now, yes?" asked Moscastan, having climbed out of his home. He was followed by Pretorius, both of whom stood next to me. "The colors and light of the life-flow, the energy that holds creation together, that is Creation Itself. The—"

"Yes, Moscastan," I said.

"I see it on your face and in your eyes. You have been transformed, elevated in the eyes of the One, and are now able to see the things of worlds merged," Moscastan said.

"What?" I said, playing dumb. Though I knew full well what he was saying, and he was correct, I wasn't sure that I wanted to admit it. That would mean letting go of my humanness to a certain degree. On the other hand, it meant that I was merging with and into my True Self, blending the baser with the divine.

"Here, now. Wonderful to see you up and about, Myrriddin. Truly," said Leoni, waddling toward me with a wooden tray full of fowl, oatcakes and mead. "Come," she continued, indicating a short table to the right with a stool in front of it. "Sit. Eat." She placed the tray on the table as I sat on the stool.

I began to eat. Ravenously. The more I ate, the more hungry I became. Soon, I was practically shoveling food into my mouth and washing it down with weak mead. The others, now sitting near me on stumps of stools of their own, simply smiled as I gorged myself. I suddenly stopped as a thought occurred to me. "Igraines!" All sensation of having been brought back from the brink of the Otherworld, being given the gift of the gods, The God, The One in the form of the amalgamation of my spirit and body fell away. The horror, and the beauty, of the night I lost her came flooding back. We had one night together wherein our bodies had found ecstasy in and through each other. It had been one night together wherein our souls had found bliss as one. Only one night. I had known her most of my life. Yet, on that one occasion . . . what a difference one night could make. And then there was Baldua. "And Baldua," I asked—afraid to hear the answer.

Moscastan looked to Pretorius.

"Baldua will be thrilled you're back among us," said the priest.

"He's here?" I said, excitement swelling my throat so that, at least to me, I sounded like a squealing little child.

"He is that."

"What happened to him?" I asked, gaining my normal voice once more.

"Perhaps you can get him to tell you," Moscastan said grimly. "He walked back into the village, or what was left of it, on the fourth day of your . . . incapacitation, the day before you . . . died."

So it was true, then! I really had crossed to the Otherworld. I had been dead and then truly brought back to life. Why could I not remember my journey to the Otherside, the—my experiences there? But this line of questioning I would save for another time. I wanted to know about Baldua and Igraines. "He just walked in you say?"

"Yes. And, wouldn't talk about his experience. He just kept looking around and saying 'Mea maxima culpa, It's all my fault,'" Moscastan explained. "He'd just shake his head when pressed for what he meant."

Baldua. My dear friend. I was silent for a few moments, contemplating what might have happened to him. "And Igraines?" I finally asked.

"No sign of the girl," said Pretorius. "You are . . . close with her, aren't you?" he asked gently, clearly referring to our coupling that night.

I stared at the man, debating how to phrase my reply, or whether to even give one. "More than I realized, Father. Much more than I realized."

"We'll find her, Myrriddin," assured Moscastan.

I simply nodded my head, hoping he was right, knowing in my heart that it may not be that simple.

ELEVEN

I walked. I walked with the spear in hand, using it, as always, in the manner of a walking staff. The blade pulsated with a glow quite frequently now; softly, subtly, almost imperceptibly. Except to me. Its glowing was the pulsating of my heart, my life-blood. I was linked to the spear more profoundly now than ever before. I had been healed *through* the spear, but not *by* the spear. I understood that well. I had been connected with this instrument for much longer than just this time's healing.

I walked on. Most of my walks had turned into meditations. I contemplated all that had occurred over the recent past; the meaning of all of it; the knowledge both spiritual and practical to be gained. It had been three moons since the night at the Henge—since my *resurrection*. I had searched for Igraines in the interim; searched in vain. Pretorius and Moscastan came with me on my expeditions into the wilderness in search of her—her and the bastards that had so disrupted our lives. We followed the trail of the raiders, of Lord Creconius and his men. It led to the sea. That discovery left me bitter and disappointed beyond belief. I was so vexed, that I nearly lost all control; nearly hurled the spear into the ocean at the non-existent receding ship carrying Creconius and the raiders that had long since made its escape. Instead, I shouted at the sea in anger. I yelled at the top of my lungs, cursing Lord Creconius for this present life's transgressions against me, as well as his offenses in my former-life. He had also been known to my spirit as Draco. I knew that now for certain. I was consciously aware of all the connections with people in my current life—connections that spanned centuries on the plane of the Earth; eons on the plane of the spirit; eternity on the plane of the Universal. I didn't pretend to *understand* these connections or why they were there. But, that never stopped me from musing and speculating on them. For example, I would ponder that perhaps different souls are together through the same aspects of existence because they came from the same batch of ethereal properties, so to speak, much the same way several oatcakes come from the same batch of oat mix. Though there are many batches or bowlfuls from a single vat of mix, only a certain number of oatcakes can be made from a single bowlful, and those from a given bowlful or batch are forever linked together because of coming from *that* particular batch of mix. Trite, perhaps, but not an altogether inaccurate analogy, though Pretorius thought me daft when I tried to explain it to him. "By your reasoning, our souls aren't then eternal because they were created. After all, I do not believe that an eternal soul has a beginning or end. It simply is," he'd said.

The more I got to know this man, the more I realized how unlike his fellow Christians he was. "Maybe," I replied, "but even before becoming the mix for oatcakes, the individual parts within existed in a different form. They are thus eternal." He wasn't really convinced.

Lord Creconius, Draco, had been a thorn in my side for more than one of my incarnations. He had been instrumental in my demise as Longinus. And, he had now stolen that most precious to me. *Well, near most precious*, I thought, as I felt the spear's solidity in my hand.

Moscastan had helped to calm me that windy, cloudy day on the beach—the day we arrived at the end of the trail at the waters' shore. My anger at the raiders' escape, at Lord Creconius' escape, was equal to the anger I felt over *wrongs* Creconius had perpetrated on my being over the centuries, and equal to my anger over his abducting Igraines. "*Be* angry. You should be," Moscastan had said. "But *see* beyond the moment and do not *become* the anger. Otherwise, it will consume you. Seek not revenge. Revenge is for the impatient, the simple. Creconius will have visited upon him that which he perpetrates on others. Trust in the Balance of the One for that."

I stood there, arm raised with spear in hand, ready to fling it at the escaping ship that was not there. The ocean's spray was dampening my face and blanketing my spirit. I did not fling the weapon into the water. Instead, I brought my arm down and stared at the spear. Its blade was normal, not aglow. Though the blade still had the small branches around it that once cradled the Druids' Egg, one could easily see the blade itself. What parts of it remained unstained gleamed in the partial sunlight. The clouds seemed to accentuate the stains on the thing, making them deeper and more pronounced. *His* stains, they were: Master Jesus' from so long ago. And yet, it was just yesterday. A blink of the eye of God; a breath in the journey of my soul.

"I know, Myrriddin," said Moscastan. "I know your frustration. But look into your own scrying bowl to reveal information on your own life. You will see that he is a trivial aspect of it."

Trivial? I thought. What was he saying? And, besides that, I had never been able to look at my own future through the scrying bowl.

"Perhaps you've just not tried hard enough," said Moscastan, apparently reading my thoughts.

"I *have* tried hard," I retorted.

"Or, you've hardly tried!" he insisted.

"You know that's not so, Moscastan. I have seriously attempted it on several occasions. I am too close to the source of the information to be foretold: Me. You have said as much yourself in the past, so don't pretend otherwise," I said, anger from the day spilling into my voice.

I stewed for a couple more minutes, then began to calm down. Moscastan stood in silence, as did Pretorius, both men allowing me to process the day's events and regain my composure. Finally, I turned to Moscastan and held the spear out to him. "You said Lord Creconius wanted this. Why has he left without it?" I asked.

"He will be back, I am sure," replied Moscastan. "He has taken the other items he wanted from the same location in which you found the spear."

"He is satisfied for now," Pretorius chimed in, "but Moscastan is right. Lord Creconius will return to gain the rest of what he seeks," he said, glancing at the spear.

But it was what Moscastan had just said that stunned me. "What're you talking about, 'other items,' Moscastan?" I asked, looking from one man to the other.

"You found the spear in the Temple ruins on the Isle of Mystery when you were a wee lad," Moscastan began. "You found it along with a few other items which you considered at the time to be of . . . lesser value: a piece of wood—"

"A piece of the Rood—the Cross on which our Lord Jesus was hanged," Pretorius said for clarification.

"A bowl—"

"The bowl or cup is believed to be the one that *He* used during his final meal," Pretorius said, excitement creeping into his voice.

"And a book—"

"The *original* Testimonies of Thomas, Disciple of Jesus', and Mary of Magdalena, who was also a Disciple of Jesus. There have been ancient *copies* circulating for decades. These testimonies and others like them, which were also written by eye-witnesses to our Lord's life, are presently being condemned by my Church as heretical," Pretorius spat, with obvious disdain and contempt for those doing the condemning.

A silence fell between us all. Except through legend, I knew nothing of the other items they spoke of. And, Moscastan was right. To my child's mind at the time, the spear was the only real treasure there. Then again, perhaps there was more to it than that. The spear was not just a treasure—it *spoke* to me, even as a youth. I was particularly surprised just then, however, by something else that Pretorius had said about Mary. Had she really been one of the Disciples? Can anyone know for certain how many Disciples there had actually been? Truth be told, I knew little to nothing of the woman Mary. This Church of Pretorius', as far as I understood, shunned women, considered them to be inferior beings. But then again, the more I learned of Pretorius the man and his personal beliefs, the more I realized he was disenfranchised from *his* Church, even at odds with it. "Why?" I finally asked, turning to Pretorius. "As you say, the accounts are from eyewitnesses. Why would the church condemn firsthand accounts?"

The priest regained his usual stoically reverent demeanor and stepped toward me. He placed a hand on my shoulder and said, "The Church has turned secular, my son."

It always made me laugh inside when he spoke to me as if he were my elder.

"The Church or many of those who run it," Pretorius continued, "are not as much interested in Truth and Enlightenment, as they are in power and control. Some in the hierarchy of the Church have twisted the teachings of our Master Jesus so as to reflect an agenda of earthly ilk. A handful of us know this and will never adhere."

"At the risk of sounding naive, why do you stay a part of it, the Church, I mean?" I asked.

"Because I love it so. *God* imparted His teachings through Jesus. *Men* made the Church, or at least, made it what it is. It has simply lost its way. Perhaps I and others like me can bring it back to fold," answered Pretorius.

"*Now* who's being naïve?" Moscastan said sardonically.

"I believe that in their hearts, the Church fathers, from the Pontiff to the Cardinals, know the Church won't survive unless they hear and live the teachings of the Anointed One. They cannot twist and turn the teachings to suit their will. They will perish and the Church with them," insisted Pretorius.

"Please, Pretorius. They continue to destroy our way of life and subjugate our people in the name of your Jesus, and show no sign of letting up," Moscastan countered.

"Rome has done that."

"The Church *is* Rome now!" Moscastan said, displaying a rare moment of pure agitation.

"Now, now, Moscastan," I said, mocking his earlier tone with me. "Do not *become* the anger!"

My mentor smiled. "No, no. No anger. A bit of frustration is all. Come, Myrriddin. You, too, Pretorius, my friend. Let's go back and eat. We will consider more options in the finding of Creconius and Igraines. Perhaps Baldua will be receptive this night and he can aid us in this endeavor." Though Moscastan attempted to sound positive in his postulation, his eyes belied his true feelings. There was sadness there, a sadness that spoke to the truth of our mutual friend's condition.

Few words had passed between Baldua and me since my own recovery. He was tormented in the head. I was sure he'd break through whatever demons had hold of him; whatever demons Creconius had poisoned him with. But with each passing day, he seemed to sink deeper and deeper into the grasp of his demons. He had stopped saying that it was all his fault, which was something, I supposed. The problem now was that he was barely saying anything at all. He had withdrawn with his demons almost completely. I feared more for the loss of my friend's mind than ever.

It was near dark by the time we got back to the village. Our community had been rebuilt with astonishing speed and alacrity. A feasting hall had been built. We had a smaller one before the raiders came, but this one was grand; grand not because we needed a large hall—we didn't. It was grand as a symbol of defiance to those who thought they had destroyed us in flesh, as well as spirit.

Moscastan, Pretorius and I entered the hall. It was dimly lit, but lively. Many of the villagers were at several tables in the large room's center, feasting on the evening's meal. Leoni was in the middle of it all, serving food and drink, and scolding those who were grabbing at the fare for being impatient. Just near her was Baldua, sitting in the middle of a table, surrounded by many villagers clamoring for a meal, yet utterly alone. A vacant look filled his eyes. I turned to Moscastan. "I'll join you soon," I said.

Moscastan turned his gaze to where I had been looking. "Yes. See if you cannot bring him round. Be gentle and at ease, though."

I nodded and headed to my friend.

"Salve, Baldua! (Greetings, Baldua!)" I said in Latin, lightly, happily, as if nothing was wrong with the world.

Baldua had been absently pushing food around on the platter before him. He stopped, apparently recognizing my voice, and looked up at me. Though his gaze was upon me, my friend was not there. His eyes were empty. I sat next to him, facing out with my back to the table and hung my head for a brief instant, sadness nearly overwhelming me. I quickly shed the emotional weight and placed my hand on Baldua's shoulder. He didn't draw back from the touch, but he did turn back to the plate of food before him, and resumed playing with the food there. "What is it, Baldua?" I asked him. "Where've you gone, huh? You need to come back. *I* need you to come back. We've work to do, you and I. We need to find Igraines. We . . . we need to find the treasures that were stolen from the Temple ruins—you know about those, right? We need to find and destroy this Lord Creconius."

Baldua's head snapped up and his gaze bore into my eyes at the mention of Creconius' name. Hatred and fire spewed from those light colored orbs. He was present once again.

"Yes, Creconius," I said the name again, not sure how far to push my friend, but pleased that it was eliciting a response from him, any response.

He turned back to the table, fists balled up on either side of his plate. His body began rocking back and forth, anger spreading across the features of his face. He was fighting; fighting to get back. That is what I wanted to believe.

Moscastan appeared next to me. We exchanged a look. "I was wrong before. Press him. None too gently, I should think."

"My fault, my fault. It hurt, hurt badly . . . " Baldua said between clenched teeth. He was now rocking back and forth; a gesture both of comfort and of liberation, as if he were trying to shake off the demons.

"Why? Or, what? What is your fault? The village's destruction? *Creconius* knew where the village was without your help, so what could be your fault? And what hurt? What did that piece of shite, *Creconius,* do to you?" I pressed, emphasizing Creconius' name more and more with each saying of it. Baldua could be swallowed by the demons entirely, I knew that. But it was a risk I was willing to take to bring my friend back.

He suddenly stopped his rocking and began pounding his clenched fists on the table. His right hand landed on the side of his plate, catapulting the contents into the air and across the table. It landed on the arm or a large villager. Jostin was his name. He was of forty summers with many a swirled tattoo on either arm. He had the longest mustache I had ever seen, but kept the rest of his face and his head completely shaved for reasons none of us were ever able to figure out. We had not seen him for many a summer, for he'd relocated to his wife's clan four miles into the valley, and only came back when our village, his home village, had been razed. He stood now, ready to pounce on whoever had thrown the food at him. "Who dares?" he bellowed.

"Peace, Jostin," said Moscastan. "'Twas Baldua here, and he meant it not. You know that."

Jostin checked his anger and stared at poor Baldua, as many others in the hall were now doing. My friend continued to pound his fists on the table, bloodying his right, and breaking the other, as evidenced by the odd angle at which his pinky and ring finger were now bent.

"Baldua! What did Creconius do to you?" I yelled. Then, it hit me. Gently, I lifted the spear and placed the blade near my friend's head. The blade, indeed the whole spear, was glowing. I heard gasps from those nearby, as they pointed and wondered at the spear. "Breathe, Baldua." I reached up and broke one of the small branches of the wicker cage that still hugged the spear's top, so that I could touch its blade to Baldua's head.

At first contact, my friend ceased all activity. As if frozen in time, he sat there, stiff. Then, his breathing eased and he blinked three times and closed his eyes. Tears squeezed from his closed lids, dampening his cheeks. "Yes," he finally said to no one in particular

"What?" I asked.

"It is not you to whom he speaks, Myrriddin," said Moscastan.

Well, then who was he speaking to? And then it dawned on me. "Could it be?" I wondered aloud.

"Yes," answered Moscastan.

I looked at him with a mixture of confusion and I knew not what. *I* was the only one who had ever heard *His* voice through the spear.

"Oh come now, Myrriddin. Jealously does not suit you," said Moscastan.

"I'm *not* jealous," I said protesting a little too vigorously. *Stop it, Myrriddin*, I thought to myself. I realized that my friend was in need of the healing right then and there, and if part of that was to hear His voice through the spear as I had in the past, then so be it.

"Yes, I understand and know this to be so. So it is," said Baldua to the air. He fell silent then and breathed deeply, easily for some five minutes. The entire hall had fallen silent as well, as if in silent support, even prayer. I looked around and saw that many had their heads bowed, there lips moving in silent supplication. Pretorius, too, now standing near Moscastan, was uttering prayers under his breath much the way he had for me that night at the Henge. I, too, joined the silence, going within my being and seeing my friend as I knew him to Truly be: a whole and perfect being. Whatever was happening to him on the outside was of the human condition and not of his own True nature. With such a realization, anything could be overcome.

"You know this to be so," said the Voice of the spear in my mind, but not to me.

"Yes, I understand and know this to be so. So it is," Baldua said in reply.

Somehow, someway, I was hearing the communication between the Voice of the spear and Baldua. After a moment, I opened my eyes. The spear had ceased to glow and I withdrew it from my friend's head, realizing its work was done.

Slowly, Baldua's eyes opened. Silence still filled the halls. Baldua turned his head and stared straight into my eyes. I thought I saw my friend there, and not the vacant, demon-filled shell of a man he had been a moment ago. But, until he spoke . . .

"Well, how ye be, my boy?" came Leoni's voice from behind me.

Despite the situation, I smiled at hearing the matter-of-fact way in which she always expressed herself.

Baldua, still staring at me, then smiled, too. "She's always been rather gruff, Nonne consentis, Myrriddine, mihi frate? (Do you not agree, Myrriddin, my brother?)" he said, the first part in our native Celt, the second in his pretentious Latin.

"Indeed!" I agreed. I then flung my arms around his neck, embracing him as if he were in fact a long-lost brother.

"That . . . spear. It spoke to me, the way it speaks to you, Myrriddin," Baldua exclaimed.

"I know," I said.

"Ye still have not answered me question!" insisted Leoni.

Baldua took a moment, seemingly assessing his person. Finally, he nodded. "Fine. I am fine. But . . . I must admit to being the cause of horrible things." He said this last thing with a heavy heart and much remorse, but in a detached and accepting manner.

"You don't have to say it if you don't wish to," I said.

"A moment ago, you were prodding me for the information," replied Baldua.

"A moment ago, I would've done anything to bring you out of your . . . state of mind, to take off the weight of your burden."

"Still, I must say it to cleanse it from myself. "I . . . " my friend began tentatively. " . . . unspeakable things were done to me, to my body, to parts of me that only a lover should touch. I . . . the pain was unbearable. The fungus he forced down my throat, its poison drugged me, made the pain feel even worse and made me say things. He wanted to know where the ruined Temple was, and where the artifacts were that had been brought there three centuries past by a man called Joseph Of Arimathea. I broke down. I told him where they were, at least where I thought they were. All but the spear. I didn't break with that. Something stopped me," Baldua said, looking at the spear which was now at my side. "He still is unsure of where that is." More weight seemed to lift off Baldua in the telling of his torturous tale.

"'He' being Creconius?" I asked, even though it was the obvious.

Baldua cringed slightly at the name, but otherwise remained unaffected.

"But . . . how did *you* know where those things were?" I continued.

"Ach, Myrriddin," scolded Leoni. "Ye thinks ye be the only boy who's ever explored those ruins? Baldua was on the Island longer than you, lad."

A part of my childhood had just been shattered. I found that I was actually a bit hurt that my secret place on the Island had not even remotely been *my* secret place.

"What's more," continued Baldua, bursting my momentary bubble of self-pity, "I was the one that led a small group, including the pig Creconius, onto the Island and into the Temple ruins in the dark of a new moon."

A soft murmur arose in the hall. No doubt, most of our fellow villagers had no idea that there were *treasures* in the ruins of an ancient Temple on the Island of Mystery. How could they, unless they had been chosen to serve or be educated there? So Baldua's revelation was just that to them: a revelation. The murmurs quickly started to become more ominous, though. "How could he have led *them* to that sacred place?" whispered someone behind me.

"Let alone robbed it," said another.

Moscastan whirled around and addressed those in the general direction from which the accusing words had come. "Enough of that talk!" his voice boomed, with an Otherworldly quality.

Everyone in the hall was silenced with awe, bordering on outright fear. "How dare you—you who would condemn without knowing the toll this lad has paid. Shame be upon ye! Show yourselves, those who speak so."

No one came forth.

"I thought as much. Those items which were in the Temple did not belong to us and most of you here knew naught of their presence to begin with. So, do not pretend to be sorely offended at their disappearance. Now, that being said, they were brought here for safe-keeping all those years past. They have been usurped by a force of evil and will be retrieved and kept safe once again, mark my words," Moscastan assured everyone. "In the meantime, help your fellow clansman back into your arms," he continued, extending a hand toward Baldua. "Keep him and understand what he's been through."

Those present looked to one another almost ashamedly. "Come," said Leoni as she picked up another full tray of food. "I did not slave over an open fire most of the day to see this venison and fowl wasted. These grilled roots are scrumptious, too, and you all *will* enjoy them!"

A festive rumble rose in the hall once again as those near Leoni began clamoring for food and drink once more. A tray that was precariously filled with mugs of mead rested on the table near Baldua. It, too, was descended upon by men nearby, as wolves to a kill. The evening's feasting continued.

TWELVE

The day dawned bright, but damp. Our voices rose in chant when the sun's brilliant disk appeared as a sliver of reddish-orange light over the distant peaks. In a semi-circle, we stood in the middle of the Wood Henge: a smaller-scaled, wood version of the Grand Stone Henge where I had been healed and brought back from the Otherside. I had made it my morning ritual to join others here at the dawn of each day to give praise and thanks to Dana, the Goddess, for the light and *Light* of my blessings, and to welcome the rebirth of Creation in the form of a new day.

We were all in earthen-colored, hooded robes, faces obscured. We were spirits only, in harmony and synchronization in welcoming the new dawn. Spirits, perhaps, yet I knew full well that it was Moscastan leading the rite on this morning, and my friend Baldua, standing next to me. And, if I was not mistaken, it was Pretorius next to Moscastan.

Our voices soared at the rising of the sun's disk and the rapid spreading of its light. As the solar body quickly crested the peaks and became whole in its morning ascension, so, too, did my soul soar, ascending with the sun and the rise of our voices, declaring the new day, and with it, the rebirth of life; the rebirth of our souls.

All of us greeted the renewal of Creation as the renewal of our beings. And, we expressed this greeting with elation and a sense of oneness. It could be heard in our voices. We could feel it in our spirits through our connection with each other and the One. There was no separation.

As the sun continued its ascent, our voices became a crescendo, then faded. We ended the rite, filing out of the Henge in a single line, leaving the sun to continue its journey as we continued ours. None of us removed our hoods until we had all gone our separate ways.

Moscastan, Pretorius, Baldua and I met in the hall to break our fast. There were many others there, as well; no doubt some of whom had been our companions-in-ritual only a short time ago.

"Brother Pretorius," Baldua began in a jesting tone, as we all sat at the center table, food tray and mead cup in hand. "Was that you with us this morn, at the rite of dawn? Not *too* Falsorum deirum cultor (Pagan-worshiping of false gods), was it?"

"Don't be rude," I said to my friend.

"Back to old Baldua, as I understand, my lad?" smiled Pretorius. "Good to see. *I* don't consider the rite of dawn to be pagan. Are we not all of the One? Especially, when two or more are gathered, so is *He*. There ceases to be individuality for the moment. The robes accentuate that by hooding our features. So, you can't be sure it was me, can you? And if you *are* sure, why were you placing your attention on me and not giving your *all* to the moment, to the rite, to God?

"Indeed," Moscastan said, laughing.

"Pagan, so called, or not, Baldua, I know that we all adhere to the same Source, the same Laws, the same One, no matter what earthly form a given rite might seem to take," said Pretorius.

"All right, all right. Sorry I said anything!" Baldua conceded.

Yes, it appeared that my friend Baldua was back to his old self. A wave of sadness overtook me then. In that instant, I was reminded of the way things had been between me, Baldua and Igraines; between myself and Igraines, in particular.

"What is it, Myrriddin?" asked Baldua.

"She's around, lad," Moscastan assured me.

Baldua suddenly became sheepish, as if he realized that he should have understood what was the matter with me just then. "I'd not known your feelings for her, Myrriddin, truly. I'd have kept better watch on her, you know."

"None of us could do that. She's her own person. Besides, you weren't even there. 'Twas you we were searching for," I replied.

"Then perhaps *I* should've been more vigilant," Pretorius interjected.

"Thank you, but we've been through that. You know better," I said.

Moscastan looked thoughtful. "Try scrying again tonight, Myrriddin. Per-haps—"

"No," I said a bit too harshly. "No. It hasn't worked. Someone or something is guarding her closely with a glam I can tell. She is veiled."

"Or perhaps she's too far from here to see," Baldua offered lamely.

"Distance is irrelevant when using the *Sight*, Baldua. Have you learned noth-ing?" I snapped at him, instantly regretting it. "Sorry." We fell into an uneasy silence as we finished our meal.

"All right, then, my brethren," said Pretorius at last, breaking the gloomy mood that had descended upon our little group. "I've something to tell you." He said this last part with a heavy heart mixed with the subtle, adventurous glee of a child. "I must be off."

Baldua and I looked at one another somewhat confused. Moscastan smiled slyly. I could tell that he already knew what the priest was talking about. "Uh . . . all right. We will see you later, at the evening meal perhaps," said Baldua as a response, clearly fishing for more information.

Pretorius smiled indulgently. "No, lad. I must be away. I must leave. I've been recalled by the great Constantine himself. I go to Rome then to Constanti-nople."

"Ahh. Your heretical views have caught up with you," quipped Baldua.

Moscastan's sharp look to my friend showed that the latter's verbal arrow was closer to the mark than any of us knew.

"Is that true, Pretorius?" I asked.

"It will not be the first time, but I am not sure. The missive was vague," the priest replied.

"When do you leave?" asked Baldua.

"As soon as possible. I've delayed too long already."

"What? Why have you just now said this?" I asked, somewhat incredulously.

"You have had more important matters to occupy your time, Myrriddin," Pretorius said gently. "I will say this: it would please me greatly if you three would accompany me on my journey. You would be wonderful ambassadors. You could explain better than anyone what has befallen your people and all the people in this region. I'm talking of the Church's influence, for better or worse, yes, but also the lawlessness that has come here. Rome has abandoned you. Your testimony would be valuable," Pretorius finished.

"No," I blurted out.

Moscastan and Baldua looked at me surprised.

"My apologies, Father Pretorius. I thank you for your offer, but I intend to find Igraines," I said, softening my tone.

Pretorius and Moscastan exchanged a cryptic glance. Did they know something of her?

My heart began to race. "What? What is it?" I asked.

"Nothing, nothing, lad," soothed Moscastan. "As I said a moment ago, she is around. I feel it."

"Aye," I said, somewhat disappointed. "I know it, too, which is why I'll not leave now."

"But the question is where? Where is she? We all believe that she was taken by *him*, Lord Creconius, across the sea," Moscastan said. "What good then, to stay here?"

"What good then to leave?! What if she returns in my absence? What if I find out where they've gone, where they've taken her? I could then mount my own trip to retrieve her *and* the items that were stolen," I said, unintentionally directing this last part at my friend Baldua. The color of shame splashed across his face for a brief moment.

"But we believe that he has headed back to the Holy land, to the origin of these things. 'Tis where they'd be most powerful and valuable," offered Pretorius, looking to Moscastan, apparently seeking the other man's agreement.

"Is this true, Moscastan?" I asked.

"You have been scrying for the incorrect query, Myrriddin. You need to be scrying for Creconius, himself. He's not very good at hiding himself in a glam of concealment. Never has been," Moscastan stated, absently. "You seek Igraines when you should be seeking Creconius. There you'll find your love."

I felt my own face blush at the mention of Igraines as my love. All at once, I questioned my motives for finding her. *My love?* Was she that? True; I had feelings for her that I'd not realized until *that* night. But perhaps I was making too much of them, making them something that they were not because of her absence and the guilt I felt over her disappearance.

"Nonsense, and you know it, Myrriddin," Moscastan said, apparently reading my thoughts. "You and Igraines have known one-another for many lifetimes, and have things to accomplish on the level of the soul together in this one. Do not dismiss that."

The intensity of his gaze gave me pause. The spear vibrated slightly in my hand; not in warning, but in a sympathetic echo of what Moscastan was saying. The spear knew Igraines' soul as it knew mine. I shook my head at the thought. *How could it?* But it was true. I felt it. The spear *knew* all of us at that table. Or at least, the power that coursed through it did.

"Scry for Creconius tonight," Moscastan continued. "Ask the spear to help you, too. You will see."

"Where we will end up will not be all that far from the Holy Land," added Pretorius.

I thought about what they were saying for a moment, not altogether convinced by it.

"I believe you'll come to join us. We're not leaving for three days' time," Moscastan said, interrupting my thoughts.

"*You're* going then? Just like that?" I said, surprised by the declaration. It didn't take much time for the entirety of what he was saying to sink in. It wasn't just that he was leaving for a day-expedition. He would be gone indefinitely. I suddenly felt like a child whose parent was leaving him in the care of another for the first time. It was true that we Celts reared each others' offspring, fostering them out to our neighbors and fellow clansmen. It usually didn't take place until one was six or seven years of age. Many times, that first moment of separation from one's actual parents was traumatic. But even so, that child would still see his parents from time to time around the village. Yet, actually, this was different; Moscastan was leaving and I did not know when, or if, I would ever see him again. There had simply never been a time that he was not there in my life. "That's not fair of you," was all I managed to say.

Moscastan leaned forward, placing a gentle hand on my shoulder and smiling. "'Fair' is nothing in this case. I need not a bye-your-leave, Myrriddin. We've been together for a good long time, now and in previous lifetimes, and our journey on that level will continue. But I must be off for my own growth. I trust that you understand. I also trust that you will come, too, so the point is moot."

"Heus! (Here, now). What about me?" Baldua said with mock offense.

"What about you?" retorted Moscastan, smiling broadly.

"As I said, Baldua, I would like all three of you to come," answered Pretorius.

Baldua's demeanor suddenly changed. I saw on his face high adventure and sights unseen in his life thus far. His excitement grew by the moment. "Yes!" he finally exclaimed. "Oh, but . . . I should stay, abide by you, Myrriddin, help you

. . . " he trailed off as he looked at me.

"It's fine if you want to go," I assured him.

My friend thought for moment, clearly weighing the importance of staying versus going and clearly making a show of the decision-making process.

"Ahg, for Dana's sake! Just go, you know you want to," I said.

"I'll wait to see what you scry and what you decide," Baldua said, his tone turning serious. "'Tis the least I can do."

"So be it," Moscastan said.

THIRTEEN

The night was filled with darkness and foreboding. The mist swirled within the forest on the hillside and chilled my bones. A wolf howled in the distance, calling its mate or its maker, I knew not which. The moon was bright, made more so by the light's reflective quality from the mists. I looked up the hillside, to an opening in the side of the large earthen mound, a cave. The opening was manmade, its frame shored up by wooden beams. It was then that I saw her.

Igraines stood framed in the opening's threshold, silhouetted by light from within the cave itself, a fire for warmth, perhaps. Her face was lit by the moon's light. The light showed something else, too. Her form was different than I remembered: rounder. It took me a moment to realize what the roundness was. She was pregnant. Panic suddenly filled my being. Igraines was pregnant! It had been six months since last I had seen her. Could it be . . . mine? The other thought, what her captors might have done to her, was unthinkable. But where was she? I was scrying. Or was I?

I had entered my dwelling and begun scrying as Moscastan had suggested, looking for Creconius. Nothing had been revealed. I had stopped after an hour or so and decided to wander outside in the misty damp night for a while. I had only wandered a short distance when the spear began to vibrate violently in my hand. Its tip glowed, pulsating a blood-red. The energy I felt coming from it nearly knocked me to the ground.

"Heed the call," the spear's voice—Jesus' voice—said in my head. "Heed, Myrriddin, and learn."

I sat on the ground, my back against a mighty oak. Heat from the sacred tree emanated from within its core and engulfed my being. Perhaps the heat was from the day's sun, absorbed by the tree. Or perhaps the ancient sentinel was more alive than any of us really knew, generating its own source of heat from within. In that moment, it mattered not, for the tree's very being became a part of mine, as did the spear.

I looked out through my human eyes, but saw a land far away imposed upon the landscape before me. It was not all that different from the land I was now in, but it was more arid. It took me a moment to realize that most of the trees I saw on the hillside were from my own realm, but the hillside itself was from the . . . vision, for want of a better word. It was difficult to tell where the vision's world began and mine ended; the images were blending more and more. But it was clear that Igraines was in the vision's world. I tried to speak, to call out to her. "Igraines!" I yelled. She paused, tilting her head to one side as if hearing something well in the distance and attempting to identify it. In the end she gave up, turned back and went into the cave.

The scene changed. Soldiers I knew to be of a far away land, the land that now ruled the world—Roman, but not *Old Roman,* Old Roman being those who had occupied my land in centuries past—lined a road leading to palaces near a port. Creconius was there! He was speaking to three well-dressed men. Possibly, leaders of the community, by their dress and bearing. One was dressed in the black and collar of high Christian clergy. Next to Creconius was a wagon laden with wears under a canvas. He was gesturing to the wagon's contents for the men's perusal. All at once, Creconius stopped what he was doing and looked seemingly in my general direction, as if sensing my presence, my probing *Sight.* I immediately drew my attention away from him, and onto the palaces and nearby area. If my focus was taken off him he might no longer feel my presence. Near the palaces was a hillside. I could see a light coming from a small opening in the hillside. Though the opening was far away from this perspective, I had no doubt what it was. Igraines was there; I knew it! This place was either Rome or the other place which Pretorius had spoken of, Constantinople. Either way, my decision as whether to accompany Pretorius or not had been made.

I was late. I knew it as I ran for the hillside, stumbling on my robe as I went. I heard their chants and saw the sun's light splash over the valley as the disc crested the peaks in the distance. The crescendo of voices told me at what point the rite was located, and there was no need for me to attempt to join in the circle. I would only disrupt the proceedings, which many would take as a bad omen for the day and the rest of the week's solar cycle. So, I halted. Catching my breath, I was moved to do something: to join in from right where I stood. I was perhaps fifty paces away from the circle of chanters. No matter. The robe's hood covered my face and my spear was hidden in the folds of the robe. I was simply a lone figure adding voice to the final phase of the morning's ritual. Perfectly acceptable. I was merely letting go of my haste, feeling the oneness with the moment, the sun—

"Ah! Greetings, Myrriddin! I thought *I* was the only one too late to join in. Saw you coming up the hill back there. Well, you have it! Grand idea to stop here and give voice, since we can't make it to the circle!" declared Baldua, much too loudly for my ears.

The moment broken, I snapped at my friend. "What demon's in you, man? Have you no respect?"

"I'm just observing that you are brilliant to stop and join in. None'll be the wiser, eh, that we weren't here most of the rite, since we couldn't make it earlier?! Can't disturb it once it's begun."

Sometimes I just wanted to throttle my *friend.* "I stopped because I was compelled to, not for false praise while I hide under my robe?" I countered, between nearly clenched teeth.

"Who's hiding?" said Baldua, as he gave voice to the final chorus of the rite, hood off, face exposed.

I shook my head and attempted to refocus on the remaining moments of the rite, as the vocalizations nearby were fading.

"By and by," Baldua's voice said. Though, his voice was more of a whisper this time, it still crashed into my thoughts, disintegrating the moment for good. "Have you decided if you will go with Pretorius and Moscastan?"

I suddenly had the devilish thought of butting him with the end of the spear beneath my robe. The spear gave a short vibration as if laughing at me. "You'll find out soon enough," was all I trusted myself to say.

"Oh, come now," Baldua whined.

"No," I said, somewhat satisfied. Petty for me to hold out on him, but being an annoyance was something that my friend was adept at, and I felt that he must learn the consequences of that. Or so I kept telling myself. I knew he probably never would.

The circle of chanters broke and everyone began exiting the area single-file, hoods still on. Baldua apparently had a sudden change of heart. He hastily and clumsily reached over his shoulders and pulled on the hood of his robe, thus concealing his face. We both stood there, heads bowed, as the silent line of hooded participants began to pass by us on the nearby trail. Two of the hooded adherents stepped out of the line as they came close to us. They came to a stop and stood next to us, each flanking either side of Baldua and me as the others continued on. Though I still couldn't see their faces, I could guess who they were.

"Pleasant morn to you both and kind of you to make it," said the voice of Master Moscastan beneath the cloth cowl next to me.

"Aye, better to be late and seen than absent and not, right boys?" spoke the voice of Pretorius on the other side of Baldua.

"Thought we weren't supposed to know who each other is here!" Baldua said, whipping his head back to forcibly throw off his hood.

The other chanters had passed and were receding from us down the trail back toward the village. Moscastan and Pretorius pulled off their hoods, as did I.

"We'll speak with you now, lads, rather than at the morning meal," replied Pretorius somewhat gravely.

"'Tis something amiss?" I asked light-heartedly.

"We want to know if ye've decided to come with us," said Moscastan.

Baldua remained silent and looked at me, a smirk of victory tugging at one corner of his mouth. It seemed he would find out my decision sooner rather than later, after all. "I . . . was going to tell you at the evening meal and—"

"We'll be gone by then, Myrriddin," said Moscastan, now sounding as grave as Pretorius.

"What is it?" I asked.

"A vision," Moscastan replied cryptically.

"Well, what sort of vision?" said Baldua, sardonically.

"Hold your tongue, lad," Pretorius said gently. "You know Master Moscastan is quite the channel of the Otherworld, just as your friend, Myrriddin, here."

"I had a vision, too, Moscastan," I said. "I saw Igraines. She was, is, with child . . . I think."

"That would confirm what was shown to me," said Moscastan.

"I think it . . . well, I think it might be mine," I confessed, sheepishly.

Moscastan placed a tender hand on my shoulder. "There are larger things at stake here, my friend. She was betrothed by Creconius, Myrriddin, to a man named Lot of Orkney."

"What? What are you saying? That it's his child Igraines carries?" I asked, more harshly than I meant, feeling more hurt than I realized I would.

"I don't know, Myrriddin, but I don't think so. At least not yet. What I believe *you* saw was a future Igraines, not our girl of the present," mused Moscastan.

"But, she looked as she does now, or at least as she did when last I saw her. Besides, she looked right at me when I was scrying. Well, it seemed like it anyway. Just like that Roman officer did—as if she knew she was being watched," I insisted.

Pretorius looked at me. "I don't completely understand how these things work. Officially, the church's position on this is that scrying and any kind of *magic* are of the devil. Simpleton reasoning, me thinks. There's a lot more to God's Universe than the narrow view of one religion. But, why wouldn't the future Igraines feel she's being watched? She exists there as here in the *Now*. All are present-tense in the One."

I mulled over what the priest said.

"What the hell does that mean?" asked Baldua. "Never mind. Myrriddin also said she looks the same as she does now. Is that part of your *present-tense-ness*?"

"She's an eternal look of youth about her, I would presume," offered Pretorius.

"Enough," Moscastan interjected. "Myrriddin, do you come?"

The spear in my hand vibrated. I held it up for all to see. The blade was glowing a soft green.

"Myrriddin, what's it saying?!" asked a wide-eyed Baldua.

I stared at the blade, the glow, and was pulled in. *It is your destiny, Myrriddin*, came the voice in my head, the voice of the spear, *His* voice. *It is the continuation of your work here, the work you started during your time as Longinus.*

I looked at Moscastan, a vast smile suddenly spread across his face. "Ah. I see *He* speaks to you still. Just as before. Will you heed?"

I nodded. "To Rome first?" I asked, more to Pretorius than to Moscastan.

But it was Moscastan who answered. "Nay. We go to find Uther."

"What, pray you, is an Uther?" asked Baldua.

"Not what, but who," replied Moscastan. He then turned to me. "A distant cousin, for starters. All will be revealed. Come. Enough daylight has burned." With that, he walked briskly toward the village. There was naught to do but follow.

FOURTEEN

We were on the road within the hour. I hadn't the vaguest idea why it was so important to find this alleged cousin named Uther. Oh, Moscastan explained again to me the importance of what he, this Uther, was doing: driving out the likes of Creconius, uniting the various parts of the land under one banner—his banner; the Pendragon—but I could not get my mind off Igraines. Had she been given to this King Lot by Creconius as a slave? But why would a noble—a King, no less—marry a village girl? Unless, she really was much more. She *had* been on the Isle of Mystery for a time. When she was still very, very young, no more than eight summers, the priests there decreed that she was destined for the life of a Royal, which was something that many scoffed at in private. She was sent back to the village elders for leadership training. She never quite took to it, which only served to prove the scoffers' point, at least to those who'd done the scoffing. Perhaps becoming the wife of this Lot was what the priests had seen. No matter. All I could think of was that she was now truly gone from me. Someone I felt as though I had known forever was now more out of reach than ever.

Moscastan gave her marriage even more weight than I did. He also clearly saw her pregnancy as even more significant, even momentous. I only saw it as annoying and hurtful, especially the fact that Moscastan insisted that the child she carried was not only not mine, but not Lot's either. Uther was the key to this mystery in more ways than one. Such was my dark mood as we plodded along the trail leading south.

"You'd understand a lot more if you'd get out of your own way," he said, seemingly able to read my thoughts yet again.

I snapped out of my melancholy state of mind to see that he was walking next to me. "I hate it when you read me so," I said.

"I'm not 'reading' you in the way you think. It's obvious, lad. I'd ask that you step outside your little self to see the bigger picture. Consult with the spear, that staff you walk with. You've barely used it 'til now. Allow it to help you see the truth of things to come. You'll be playing a pivotal role in the events of the near future."

"Well, I'm glad you think so." We walked on in silence for nearly a league.

"She will always be with you. She always has," he finally said, cryptically. "Your spear will tell you that as well."

"Moscastan," said Pretorius from a few yards ahead.

Moscastan hurried along to catch up to the priest, who had stopped at the mouth of the trail where it emptied onto a main road. He was not alone, but was speaking to a man dressed in very worn traveling togs. As Baldua, who had been trudging behind up to this point, caught up, the other man turned back to the main road, which I now saw held a large party of wagons and other travelers.

"We will go with these people for a time. They are from the Tremoriddin clan and are going to the Hallows Eve feast in the next Clan-dom," said Pretorius as I halted next to him.

I was surprised at the priest's carefree attitude regarding the matter. "All Hallows Eve festivities? That's about as *pagan* as it gets. Not too much for you?"

"Quite the contrary. I find the concept of allowing dead ancestors to inhabit the body for a night fascinating. Besides, I know the fellow to whom I spoke — stayed with his family last winter season. He's a Christian at heart," answered Pretorius.

"Ah, there's the rub of it," Baldua interjected. "A chance to convert him, aye?"

"Now, lad, you know me better than that by now," countered the priest. "Come."

We joined the Tremoriddin clan on the main road.

Darkness descended quickly. We had walked only another five miles or so when the whole company, the Tremoriddin clan and our little party, came off the main road and into a sparse grove of oaks to make camp. Cooking fires were started in the camp's center, and many of the women, and men, were preparing the evening meal. Venison was brought forth from some of the clansmen and we were invited to join them. Baldua, being Baldua, had already begun chatting to a comely lass with red-blonde hair. The odd thing was that she kept looking in my general direction even while engaged in conversation with Baldua. I turned more than once to look behind me in an attempt to assess if it was actually me she was looking at or someone, or something else. I could not figure it out, so I simply let the matter rest.

The meal was more than satisfying, and afterward, I sat near one of the fires for a time. Moscastan and some of the clansmen talked about the festivities to come the next evening. One clansman, in particular, was especially excited to allow his father to live again through his body for the night. Apparently, the debauchery of his dead father was insatiable—not unlike his son's it seemed, judging by the way he was speaking—and the son was more than willing to give up his physical form for the events this one night. I had never participated in the holiday in the purest sense of it. Our village and clan had ceased the practice of the tradition many generations before, though we certainly still honored our ancestors on the night.

"Will you join the rite?" asked a lilting female voice.

I didn't turn at the sound of her voice, not right away. I could smell her: light honey-suckle and lily. It was enchanting. Her voice only added to the odd sensation I suddenly felt wash over me. She sat down on the ground next to me, at which time I turned my head and looked at her. I hadn't even heard her approach, this young woman whom Baldua had been speaking with earlier. Her features were smooth and gentle in the firelight, and more beautiful than I saw earlier. Her hair seemed more red then blonde in the light of the flames, as well. And her eyes were amber in color.

"Your friend—Baldua, is it?—said that you've never been a part of a true All Hallows Eve night," she said.

I looked around. Baldua was nowhere in sight.

"Oh, he's talking with my sister," she added.

"Who?" I asked lamely.

"Your friend," she replied, laughing. "He also said that your walking staff speaks to you from the Otherworld," she said, pointing to the spear at my side. "Is that true?"

"My friend says too much," was my curt reply.

"Please, don't be angry. I know his talk is just that. That is why I pointed him toward my sister. She likes to play those kind of games. But you—something tells me you've much too much of a deep spirit for such things," she said, smiling warmly, genuinely, her straight white teeth glowing in the light of the fire.

I was glad of the darkness and firelight just then, as I could feel my face flushing from her comment.

"Nimue," she said by way of introduction. "I am called Nimue, in case you were wondering."

"Ah. I am Myrriddin."

"I see. And are you one?"

"Am I one what?" I asked, confused.

"A Myrriddin?"

"Are you serious?" I asked, not sure if *she* was playing a game with me.

She nodded. "I ask sincerely. My grandfather was a great Merlin, and people used to call him Myrriddin as from the old tongue," she said. "You come from the land of the Mystery Isle, where you spent some time, or so I understand, so . . ."

"No doubt you understand that from my friend as well," I said, laughing.

"'Tis true."

A round of laughter burst forth from nearby as Moscastan, being a grand bard in addition to his other many talents, began a tale of love and woe and triumph over demons. The story began with a woman, the story's eventual heroine, singing a sardonic, stinging lament of love lost and revenge sought. Moscastan's falsetto and comedic rendition of a scorned woman singing was apparently what was garnering the laughter from those present, whose numbers seemed to have swelled in the past few minutes to include most of the clan. I had heard him perform this story before and always cringed when he began it, hoping that none of the women present would take offense and hurl hot coals at him. Offending anyone was always furthest from Moscastan's mind. Yet, he maintained that he must remain true to the story.

Nimue and I sat in silence for a long span of time, listening as Moscastan weaved magic with his story telling. It was the magic of transporting an audience to a different place, a different time, a different life. And, judging by the expressions on the faces of those present, all were entranced by the magic.

"Ye have not answered my question," Nimue finally said in a quiet voice.

"Oh?" I whispered back.

"All Hallow's Eve, the rite. Will you join in?"

"Well," I began, "Yes. Why not?" I found myself saying.

We sat in silence again, listening to my mentor, watching him animate the characters of the plot.

"But," said Nimue a while later, shortly after Moscastan passed the arc of his story. "You've not participated before, true?"

"Participated in the ritual?"

She nodded.

"I've honored my ancestors every Hollow's Eve since I was a lad," I said, a little too defensively. "But not in the way that you mean," I added, my tone softening.

"Then I shall be your guide, your partner," Nimue declared.

I felt my brow crinkle in confusion. "What do you mean? Will we contact our ancestors together?"

She laughed, giggled really. It was a sweet sound, but elicited a hushing scowl from two older women close by. "That's not exactly how it works," Nimue whispered to me. "Some drink the potion to help them go into a trance and . . . how would you say . . . to help them step aside so that an ancestor may come forth from the Otherworld. Something tells me, though, that you won't need any potion. Either way, 'tis best to have someone stay in their right spirit or right mind to serve as an aid to the one in trance. You understand?"

"I think so," I said, suddenly regretting having professed participation. I knew from personal experience that interesting things sometimes happened while in a trance state—things that a person might do without conscious recollection when finished. Though I had only just met the woman next to me, the thought of doing something potentially embarrassing before her while in a trance state, however unlikely that might be, was enough to make my face feel flushed once again. I could not back out now that I had declared my participation, though. That would mark me as dishonorable—to myself, at least. *A man's honor is only as good as his actions are to his words*, Moscastan once said. It had stuck with me. "I agree," I continued. "I don't think I'll need to take a potion."

Cheers and the slapping of hands on thighs suddenly burst forth from all those listening to Moscastan's tale as it reached its climax.

Suddenly and unexpectedly, Nimue quickly rose to her feet.

"Where are you going?" I asked, hearing too much disappointment in my own voice.

"Tremel said he'd take vespers with your companion, the priest," she answered.

"Tremel?"

"Yes, Tremel. My father," she said.

"Ah," I replied. I looked around at those present, but saw no sign of Pretorius.

"I don't see Tremel, either," Nimue said, apparently reading my look. "I'm sure they've begun the prayers and I know Tremel wanted me present."

I was unsure which I found more amusing: the fact that she called her father by his given name, or the fact that she and her father held with vespers *and* still practiced traditional so-called *paganisms,* such as the rite of All Hallow's Eve. "You would pray in the Christian way?" I asked.

She laughed liltingly. "Of course, the Christian God is simply an expression of the Mother Goddess."

"Aye, well, the good priest's church would see it much differently," I pointed out.

"Why?" she asked, genuinely perplexed. "There is only One Mother/Father Source for everything by *any* name," she said, sounding a bit like Moscastan. Before I could respond, she looked at my side. Her eyebrows suddenly lifted in surprise. "Your friend tells the truth, for the walking staff speaks to you now, me thinks."

I followed her gaze and saw that indeed, the spear's upper half glowed dimly, pulsating gently. After a moment, the pulsating glow ceased. The spear, my staff, looked normal again.

"What does it mean?" she asked sincerely, more with curiosity than awe.

"I'm not sure. I don't always understand it."

"Hm," she said. "Something tells me you will eventually."

Those around us who had been listening to Moscastan's story were beginning to leave the fires.

"Until the morrow, Myrriddin," Nimue said as she turned to go.

I hurried to get to my feet, but she had already walked away. "Indeed," I said, more to myself than to her receding back.

We heard the revelry from the main road, faint though it was. After a time, we left this roadway and traveled down a narrow path which wound through a dense forest. I could no longer hear the revelers very well and questioned Moscastan as to whether Tremel was leading us all in the right direction. Foolish, that, for I knew the answer before he spoke it. "come now," was his smiling response. "You know how a forest deadens sound."

"Yes, yes," I said curtly. Indeed, the forest we now found ourselves traveling through was thick with rowan, adler and oak.

The deeper we went, the deader the sound became – until a ringing silence filled the ear. Darker, too, it became. The forest's thick canopy thrust us into near blackness, though it was only late afternoon. Even though the actual path beneath our feet was packed – presumably from the trodding soles of many other travelers these past days who were also heading to the festivities – it was far from dry. There was a perpetual dampness to the forest floor which was due, like the darkness, to its thick canopy preventing Belenus' drying warmth from touching the earth's skin. This was also the reason for the pungent smells that bombarded our nostrils: sickly sweet mint, stale moist bark, foul rotting flesh and leaf, and everything in-between.

Nearly two hours we walked through the woods until finally, the path suddenly spilled out onto a large, beautifully flowered, thinly-grassed meadow, with mountains on one side and the forest on the other. Bright sunlight splashed on my face as we came out of the forest, warming my spirit though the day was chilly, and the cacophony of hundreds of voices hit my ears as if a door to a festival had been thrown open. Many, many people were already in full regalia and celebration of the sacred day – All Hallow's Eve. Traditionally, the actual rite did not fully get underway until late into the night: midnight to three by the Roman way of keeping time. That particular window of time was considered optimal for crossing between the world of the dead and the world of the living. "Worlds swirl near worlds and sometimes they are closer to each other than at others," a Druid priest on the Isle of Mystery had once said. Yet, in spite of the time of day, the festivities here – if not the rite itself – had already begun in earnest.

Some of the celebrants were painted with blue or gold woad, a preliminary preparation for the main experiences of the evening. Others seemed to be slightly out of their heads, perhaps having already taken the potion Nimue had spoken of, or something entirely more potent. One man, for instance, stumbled toward us as we came into the meadow. "Welcommme to the realmmmm of the Inbetweennn, where all who live shall die, and all who've died shall liiive!" he said, speech slurring eerily in a high-pitched tone. The man was shirtless, and his skin unusually sweaty, which was odd because of the chilliness in the air – 'twas cold enough to see one's breath plume in misty vapor before the face. And his eyes had a far off, almost crazed look, pupils severely enlarged, as if he were possessed by demons or several creatures from a nether world. My guess was that he had ingested some of the small, leafy foscal plant that grew on the lower trunk of the sacred oak or the toxic mushroom that grew at its base. For some reason, both of these growths became a somewhat poisonous item when grown in direct contact with the oak. Mushroom and foscal that grow in contact with other trees do not develop this tinge to them. The poison is not enough to do any lasting harm – unless the mushroom or foscal is eaten in large quantities, of course; yet even then, the one ingesting the large amount would probably vomit most of it out before enough of the poison was assimilated in the body to kill. But, it is enough to alter the mind and *"open the soul"* as some claim. The fact that the mighty oak is where the *"magical"* foscal plant and mushroom were found exclusively only added to the mystique of sacredness to these wonderful trees.

Baldua had tried the foscal plant once in the hopes of crossing to the Other-side for a visit. "I'm simply curious," he had said. Truth is, I suspected that it was more because he had recently been informed that his birth mother had just passed to the Otherside during childbirth – the little one, the new life within her, hav-ing succumbed to death as well. We were isolated on the Mystery Isle at the time, having had no contact with our parents for some nine moons, having already been adept on the Isle for many solar cycles, many years. Baldua had been unusually close to his mother. Some even said – without judgment, mind you – that they were much more than naturally close; the child she had carried and died trying to give birth to was their proof. She had been seen with no man for many, many seasons. *"Who else could be its father?"* they had said. I'd made sure Baldua never heard these musings. If he had heard them, he paid no heed; gave no indication that he gave two shites what anyone else thought, what anyone else said. Such was his love for his mother. Whether the musings of others had been true or not, only Baldua knew. I cared not one way or another. He was my friend, had been for many lifetimes. His mother's death had been a hammer's blow to his soul. I had no doubt that his desire to visit the Otherside was perpetuated by his desire to see his mother.

In the throes of the plant's toxic effects, Baldua had appeared much as this man in the meadow – sweaty and crazed. Baldua must have had some kind of wonder-filled experience during his supposed sojourn in the Otherworld, for upon his return to his normal self, his normal state of being, he was more happy, more euphoric, more convinced of the reality of the Otherworld—the Other-side—than I had ever seen anyone be. He claimed that he had indeed seen his mother and spoken to her during the experience. What's more is that she had become the Goddess Dana during his time with her. Having left his body for travel to the Otherside, his mother, Dana, the mother of all, then took his spirit to yet another world altogether: a place in the future or distant past—he could not tell—but he knew by what the Goddess said that it was not of our time. All Baldua remembered of it was that this place was filled with tall glass or crystal buildings, and flying machines and carriages that moved rapidly on the ground without the aid of horses. Both the flying machines and the carriages transported people! He was utterly convinced that what he'd seen was real.

I, on the other hand, felt that the substance he'd ingested to aid him on to the Otherworld, the foscal plant, had simply twisted his mind. But then again, I had never swallowed the plant myself; never felt its effects, and thus was in no position to judge another's perception of the experience.

The man in the meadow before us began to spin, twirling on the balls of his feet with his arms flung out. "All manner of spirit awaits theee!" he sang. Like a dancer, he continued to spin, suddenly oblivious to all but the song in his head.

We moved past him, further into the meadow and across it toward the base of the mountains. There, people were not at a celebration point, but rather, were setting up tents of animal skins or make-shift shelters from bound, leafy branches. Trees of birch and small rowan were scattered about near the base of the mountains. Some of the people had draped canvases over the branches of a few of these trees, thus creating temporary shelters for themselves. This area had become a small village, complete with central cooking fires, set to one side, thereby leaving the center of the meadow for the celebrations to come.

Father Pretorius led us to a larger rowan whose low, over-hanging branches created a natural covering some eight feet off the ground, sheltering about twenty or so square feet of ground beneath it. The priest walked quickly to it, apparently surprised, as I was, that no one had claimed the spot yet, and stopped in the center of it. He turned to us as we caught up and raised his palms and face skyward – or toward the overhanging branches, now only a couple of feet above his head; I couldn't tell which. "Thank you," he muttered. He then looked at us and said, "'Twas meant for us, you know, this spot. We'll camp here."

"Indeed," agreed Moscastan, moving close to Pretorius. He turned toward Baldua and me. "You wish to partake in the festivities, lads, yes?"

"I don't . . . not especially," said my friend, his voice somewhat tinged with apprehension. He had been on edge since we had entered the forest from the main road.

I wasn't the only one who noticed. "What is wrong, my son?" Pretorius asked Baldua, gently.

"Nothing," replied Baldua a bit too quickly. He became thoughtful for a moment before continuing. "The forest, I suppose. Brought up . . . things."

"The past cannot harm you, lad, unless you allow it to," said Moscastan.

"Easy to say," remarked Baldua, with a bitter edge.

"Easy to do," countered Moscastan. "Just let it go. Let it flitter away. You are far more than any earthly experience you may have. Your spirit is eternal and therefore larger than anything that may befall you on this earth."

"Aye, 'tis true," put in Pretorius. "You are 'in this world' of experiences, but not 'of this world' of experiences. So it has been said. You understand?"

"I understand," said Baldua doubtfully, dismissively. "Why did we come here anyway? I thought this journey carried urgency. Why dally here in this place?"

"Do you tire of your new lady already?" Moscastan asked teasingly.

Baldua turned three shades of red, but held his head up high, defying embarrassment.

Moscastan smiled broadly and laughed. "Very well, lad. We do not dally here. These people are intrinsic to our goal. We began the inquiry for what we seek with Tremel, their leader, last night."

"At vespers," added Pretorius.

"But these things must be sought delicately, lest an affront to Tremel's hospitality be seen," continued Moscastan. "We should find out what we need to know this night." As Moscastan said this last part, his gaze drifted past Baldua and me to something beyond our shoulders. I heard soft footfalls approaching from behind, dead leaves on the ground crunching gently beneath them. They came to a stop.

"Forgive the intrusion," came the female voice from behind me. I recognized it at once. I turned and there she stood—lovely Nimue. I opened my mouth to speak, but then realized by her look that she was not here for me alone. She addressed us all. "Tremel asks that you join us for refreshments and libation presently, before the night's activities." She said this last bit to me, smiling as she ended the sentence, her secretive thoughts for me and the night to come left floating in the air for all to detect. With that, she turned and left.

I turned back to Moscastan and Pretorius to find both of them staring at me, each in turn with a gentle smirk on his face.

I felt my face flush and my brows crinkle.

"Me thinks that Master Baldua be not the only one smitten of late," Pretorius said to Moscastan.

"Indeed!" my mentor replied.

As Baldua defied embarrassment before our travel mates, so did I. Mustering my courage, I planted the butt of my staff onto the ground with authority. "Enough, gentlemen! You heard the lass," I said with more bravado than I felt. I spun on my heels and followed in Nimue's wake, leaving the others to secure our camping spot.

The fire was hot on my face, its flames intense, dispelling the chill in the night air around me. There were more than thirty of us huddled around the large fire. There were many such fires scattered about the meadow, lighting the area, each with as many or more people huddled around them as the one I was at. Around my fire some sat, some stood, but all – whether directly participating in the night's rites or simply being a guardian to another—felt the effects of this unique time. Those participating directly, each one, whether having taken a potion or not, had on his or her face an expression of . . . what? How can I describe another's journey to the Otherside, or his stepping aside to allow someone from the Otherworld to come through them? Judging by the expression on the faces of those participating, though, that is what they were experiencing. Some had another person near them – their partner, their guardian for the night's activities, as Nimue had described. These folks appeared watchful – not at all in the throws of the ecstatic passion of traveling to and from the Otherworld. They were watchful, but also solemn, some chanting as an aid to their charge.

Nimue and I had come to this particular fire two hours after dark-fall. It was now three hours past midnight. I had been in and out of trance since sitting down in front of the fire. But now . . . now I felt the inner pull on my spirit stronger than ever. There was something in the air, the energy and alignment of this particular time – this particular moment of the year, when worlds meet – and the alignment in mind and spirit of those present, made my head spin. Though I had been in and out of trance since we sat down, I had not as yet crossed to the Otherside, nor had I been contacted by any spirit from that world. In between my trance states, I simply observed those around the fire.

"You're very sensitive to this night, are you not?" Nimue asked. "Your eyes . . ." she trailed off.

I said nothing, but pulled my gaze from observing those around the fire to the fire itself. I had laid the staff down on my right side. It rested between myself and Nimue, who was also on my right and sitting very close. She was so close, in fact, that I could smell her scent and feel her body heat in spite of the heat coming from the fire. Her left knee rested against my right thigh and over the shaft of the staff between us, on which my right hand rested. It was tempting to let my mind wander to Nimue, to her smell and closeness. Yet, there was another more powerful force drawing on me. A threshold of crossing was at hand.

I stared into the fire, concentrating on the primeval essence within. Gazing into the flame was much like staring into water – the water of a scrying bowl, for example. Yet, it could be even more powerful, for fire is more of a living thing – evolving, changing and expressing in every instant of its existence.

I continued to stare into the flames and felt the rest of the world recede. Forms began to take shape in the flames. Some were indiscernible spirits; some were clearly human. Some of the human forms looked at me as I looked at them – strangers from different worlds gazing upon one another through a seemingly impenetrable window. I heard things then: strange and ghostly whispers from the Otherside; from the forms within the flames. I heard something else, too—a sweet, lilting feminine voice singing a melody in an ancient tongue; a language so old, I had thought it lost to time. Though I did not understand the words, I recognized the tune. I knew it from somewhere in my past. Then I realized from whence I knew it. The image of my Na-na—my maternal grandmother—came to my mind as she looked down upon me in my cradle of rushes and fresh leaves. She had been beautiful with auburn hair and green eyes, and dots from the sun all over her face. I was no more than three summers as she sang the ancient song of protection in the archaic tongue to me. 'Twas a beautiful melody whose every note surrounded both singer and listener with an ever strengthening glam of protection. I suddenly felt that blanket of protection in the form of Love enfold me, both my toddler self and my adult self.

My mind came back to the present and once again concentrated on the flames. There within, among the forms from the Otherworld, was Na-na, just as I remembered her! I could still hear the melody of protection being sung, but I had the sudden realization that it was not coming from her. Her spirit's lips did not move, 'twas true, yet the song could have been coming from her mind to my mind, but it was not. It was coming from my world, from someone close to me – from Nimue. I knew that Nimue's people were of an ancient clan. Not surprising then, that she might know this tune. But to be singing it – something so obscure and from my childhood . . . Nimue was singing it for my protection, as my guardian and partner. The song also served another purpose. It helped propel me further into my trance. Deeper and deeper I went, until all the rest of my world vanished from my awareness, from my mind.

"Come, young Myrriddin," said the deep female voice from within the flames. My heart leapt at the hearing of her voice. "Come. I must show you something. Time on your side of the veil grows short. The portal will close sooner than anyone realizes," she finished, extending a hand to me.

Within an eye's blink, I was standing next to Na-na in the flames. Rather, my spirit was. In my hand, I held the spear, or a spirit form of it, an essential representation of it. The spear now looked as it must have soon after it was originally made. It did not have the additions I had put onto it. Its shaft was smooth and new. Its blade was polished and bright, except where crimson stains from *Him* remained. Though we stood in the flames of the fire, I could feel no heat. Indeed, though we were surrounded by an expanse of orange-yellow, I sensed that beyond it lay the infinite realm of the Otherworld. I could still hear Nimue's lovely voice singing the ancient song. When I looked in the direction of her sound, I saw her through the warbling effect of fire. More than that, it was also through the mysterious veil of looking from the Otherworld back into my own, where I saw Nimue sitting next to my in-tranced physical form that caused the warbling appearance. I, my spirit or soul, truly was now on the Otherside. I looked back into the expanse of flames, trying to see beyond.

"There are many levels to this side, this World, Myrriddin," my Na-na said.

I simply stared at her, realizing for certain that it was her, her spirit, and not some phantom from a dream.

"'Tis good to see you, my child. You've become quite the strapping lad. Although, I've watched you grow from this side, it's still pleasing to see you thus," Na-na said.

Even in my disembodied spirit form, I felt a slight self-consciousness at her words. "'Tis good to see you too, Na-na," I said, embracing her.

"I be surprised ye remember me. I passed through the veil when you were but five summers," she replied.

It was true. My Na-na had died when I was very young. Though it was tradition generally that we Celts fostered our children for the community to raise, such was generally not the case with our village and clan – except, of course, when a child was chosen by the Druids and Mystics for study on the Island of

Mystery. In my very early years, I stayed on the Isle, yes, but Na-na was there. I remembered her all my life and what came from her even more than what came from her own daughter, my mother. What came from my Na-na was always love, unconditional.

"Be not hard on her, lad," Na-na said, reading my thoughts again. "She always had one foot in the physical world and one foot in the Otherworld when she was alive, your mother did. She could never control it and it made her not well in the head, don't you know."

I looked past Na-na just then, half expecting to see my mum somewhere in the expanse.

"She's on one of those other levels I mentioned a moment ago," Na-na said.

"I see," I replied, somewhat at a loss for words. I suddenly had another thought. "Would you like to come into my world for a time, Na-na?" I asked, already expecting the answer. "'Tis what this night's truly for."

"It's easiest to journey between the two worlds this night, but I've no desire to inhabit another's body. Besides, I visit your world often in various forms and ways. I've been at your side many-a-time to nudge you to a decision and such. When you took that, for example," she said, gesturing to the spear. "Oh, 'twas yours many life-times ago, 'tis true—I was there, too—but you needed a nudging to truly recognize it, to reclaim it in *this* life, you see," she finished.

The spear began to glow softly, whether in warning, or why I could not tell.

Na-na saw it, too. "There's no time to explain. You must see something, something to come if you choose wisely," she said. With the wave of her hand, the flames around us faded, revealing another place, another time. Rolling green hills surrounded us and a sky as blue as the brightest day I could have imagined crowned our heads. Na-na stood next to me. She was looking off to her left, smiling. A sound came to me then; not Nimue's singing, but a sound equally as pleasant – children at play. I looked in the direction of Na-na's gaze—in the direction from which the sound of the children came. A group of children gleefully frolicked nearby. They were all dressed in rich and ornate gowns, not the offspring of peasant villagers were these. A short distance past the children, in the shade of a mighty oak, sat what looked to be a king and queen, judging by their attire and the craftsmanship of the chairs on which they sat. They were not exactly thrones, but nor were they field stools, either. Other people were around the king and queen – their court, I presumed. Standing off to one side of all of them was a very old man clad in the robes of a High Druid. It was me, a much older version of me – the same persona that had been at the cave with the boy, Arturius, in another vision. The old sage, my older self, next to the king and queen held onto a Druid's staff in one hand. But it was not the spear in guise that I now possessed.

The king was in a heated discussion with several men in front of him. He suddenly turned toward my older persona. "What say you, Merlin?" he asked.

"They possess the items, the Moors do, it is true. But, be sure that it's what you truly seek, Arturius," the older Myrriddin, or Merlin, said. Obviously, I would not be rid of the *name* Merlin in this life, if this future held true. But who was this Arturius, the boy who had now become king? And this land in which he was king, and I, his High Druid—was it still my homeland or was it elsewhere? And how was it that I could see future things or possible future things in the Otherworld?

I turned to ask Na-na the meaning of these things. She was gone! Panic briefly ran through my mind. The spear now glowed an intense red-blue, as if it were searing hot, even angry. Now, I had no doubt; it was a warning. All became silent. The sounds of the children ceased; the chatter of the king, queen, and the court went mute. I looked back at them. King, queen, court and children were still, frozen in time. And my older, Myrriddin self, Merlin, was no longer there.

Then came the rumbling. Steadily, it grew louder; so loud, in fact, that I should have been able to feel it as well as hear it. But this was the Otherworld, after all. Perhaps I wouldn't feel it since this was not my actual body in this world; not my physical body which I would need to *feel* such things. It then dawned on me what the rumbling might be. Next came the screams. They became louder and closer and left no doubt in my mind that they were coming from the Otherside, or rather, my side—the world of the physical. The veil was closed again.

"By the God," I whispered. The spear shook violently in my hand and I closed my eyes, commanding a return to myself. I felt a shuddering jolt, opened my eyes and found myself back in the world of men next to Nimue, and in the middle of utter, violent chaos.

FIFTEEN

It took a moment to come full to myself upon arriving back in my body from the Otherworld. In fact, for a moment or two, I was paralyzed; my body would not respond to my will, nor could I hear anything. I felt my hand still resting on the staff, but that was all. I could see, however. I could see Nimue out of the corner of my eye. She was now standing next to my still seated form. Breathing. Breathing was difficult, not because I momentarily felt paralyzed, but because something was in the air, something I was breathing in. *Was it smoke, smoke from the fires?* I wondered. No. It was dust. It was then that my hearing came back and I heard the screams of terror, and felt the jostling of those nearby as they attempted to flee in panic. Some, still in their trance—induced stupor, stumbled and fell directly into the fire, adding to the terrible screams in the night. My body finally responded and I jumped to my feet, staff in hand, and spun to face the mêlée.

The attack had come at the height of the night's activities, when most of those who had gathered for the All Hallows Eve celebration were in the throws of ritual, including myself. I was fortunate in that I made it back from the Otherworld before anything befell Nimue or me. Na-na. For a brief instant, I let my mind wander to her. I felt the warmth of her love and presence.

"Pagans! All of you! Destroy them!" yelled a man wielding a battle-axe. He brought the weapon down on a defenseless naked man, cleaving off the man's right shoulder and arm. I recognized the victim. He was the one who had been boasting of allowing his debaucherous, deceased father to live again through him for this night. The man was obviously still in his trance, for his eyes were glazed and his face had on it a mindless smile. Perhaps his father's soul within was experiencing death again. The man crumpled to the ground in a fountain of blood. More and more of the attackers were appearing at the edge of the firelight, some on horseback—clearly the rumbling I heard from the Otherside—all brandishing weapons with crazed bloodlust in their eyes.

"We must fight or flee!" yelled Nimue over the din. There was no fear in her voice. She was simply stating fact.

I stayed rooted where I stood. I grabbed for the Roman short sword I kept at my side. It was not there. I had left it at our campsite. No need for weapons here, or so we had thought. I was sure, too, that no sentries had been placed at the meadow's perimeter. Why would there be? This had apparently been a gathering place for many, many generations. Someone crashed into me from my left, knocking me sideways into Nimue. We toppled to the ground in a tangle of limbs. I slammed to the ground partially on top of Nimue and heard a loud, horrible cracking sound as we landed. "Nimue?" I said, immediately believing that I had landed awkwardly on her and somehow broken a bone, or bones, within her petite body.

"It's all right. I'm not hurt," she assured me.

I quickly untangled myself from her and pulled us both to our feet. I then saw, to my dismay, what had caused the frightening sound: the housing of small branches I had attached to the blade of the spear to hold the Druid's Egg had broken and splintered into dozens of pieces when we hit the ground. Part of my body weight had landed on Nimue, but the other part had landed on the staff, crushing the branched housing. All that remained of the spear's disguise was the leather thong which now dangled loose on the shaft where it met the blade. It was no longer my walking staff, but a Roman spear again.

Nimue stared at it for a moment. "Interesting Druid's staff, Myrriddin," she said. "You know how to use it now?"

I was confused by what she said and must have looked it.

"As a spear, is what I mean!" she added. "Do you know how to use it as a weapon?"

Two more of the gatherers crashed into us, flailing in their panic to run away. We were not knocked over this time, though, but held our ground. The two who ran into us moved by us, and the assailant who was chasing them saw us and stopped short of Nimue and me, his quarry all but forgotten. He was a hairy brute with bare, muscular shoulders. He gripped a bloodied long sword in his right hand and was panting from his gruesome exertions. I brought the spear to bear its sharp tip pointing at the man's belly. I was not exactly sure how to use the spear as a weapon, but my anger at the turn of events of the night would guide me. Any advance toward us and I would skewer the brigand. But he made no move. He simply stared at us, then at the spear. Like its counterpart on the Otherside, its blade began to glow an angry red. The brigand's eyes grew huge at the sight, fear and awe shining forth from them. He took a step back and opened his mouth to speak, but nothing came out—at first.

"Here! It's here!" he said, facing me, guarding me, but yelling over his shoulder to the fellow raiders who had not caught up to him. "Holy Mother of Christ," he whispered to himself. "It's here!" he yelled again, this time turning his head to see if anyone had heard him.

In that instant, Nimue was shoved into me by others who were desperately trying to escape. Inadvertently, I lunged into the brigand, stabbing the spear into his abdomen. He howled with rage and pain. I froze for a moment, not believing what had just happened. I quickly recovered myself, though, and yanked the spear free. Though the blade had gone deeply into the man's belly, there was no blood on it, save for *His* blood from centuries past. Yet, even more odd was the smoke that trailed from both the blade's tip and the man's wound. He stood there for a moment staring at the wound which was now not just a slice into the skin, but strangely becoming an ever-widening, bloodless gaping hole. The brigand looked at the sky, with a faraway expression. He then looked at me with a genuine smile of peace and happiness before he crumpled to the ground dead.

My astonishment at what had just taken place—the stabbing of another human being with the spear and the bloodless, gaping, smoking hole it left in the victim—was the only thing that was preventing me from vomiting over having just killed the man. Before I had any more time to think about it, Nimue was trying to pull me away.

"Come! There're too many of them. We must vanish into the night," she said, as she started to back away.

I turned to follow her. Corpses lay strewn about, making our escape slow and difficult. The more I saw of them and the violent hacking of these defenseless revelers, the more disgusted I became. My anger grew with each passing second. I had the only weapon on behalf of our side: the spear. I could not just run. I stopped in my tracks.

"What're you doing?" asked Nimue, stopping a few feet ahead of me.

"Defending these people," I replied, turning back to face the enemy.

"Just you and that spear against killers and Romans?" she asked sardonically.

Romans? I thought. I looked closer back in the direction from which we had come, toward the fires. There was a pocket of fighting, or rather massacre, taking place near the fire we had just left. Among those committing the atrocity, but with more practiced, disciplined efficiency, were Roman legionnaires, approximately two platoons worth. Nearby this pocket, just on the firelight's edge, were three men on horseback. They were still, observing the slaughter from their mounts. One of them was dressed as a Roman officer, a General. Another appeared to be wearing the cloak of a high-ranking official in the Christian church. A large, gold crucifix on his chest gleamed in the firelight—a Papal Legate, perhaps. But the third man . . . the third man on horseback was the one who had led the initial attack on my people, kidnapped Igraines and Baldua, and left me for dead: Lord Creconius.

He pointed directly at me and bellowed, "Seize him! Seize that spear! It is the spear of Longinus, the spear of Christ in Pagan hands!"

By the gods. My blood boiled at the words. The only *Pagan* on these grounds was the lower-than-shite thing from which the accusation came. And, how dare he attempt to usurp that which had been mine for centuries. *I am Longinus!* I screamed in my head. As if to reflect my own outrage, the spear's tip pulsated a rage-filled red. I silently swore an oath to kill them all before allowing them to take it.

"That is not to be the way of it, Myrriddin. Have you learned nothing?" said the voice of the spear, *His* voice.

The voice conveyed power. I froze with indecision. I wondered where Moscastan was. He would know what to do. I attempted to calm myself; to call forth the power of the spear, my own power.

Guttural yells of bloodlust broke into the noise of the night from twenty yards away, as brigands and legionnaires converged against me, breaking my concentration.

"Myrriddin!" yelled Nimue, in a warning born of desperation.

That was it then; I would destroy them, regardless of what the voice had said. I ran toward them, planting myself some ten yards from my previous spot—more to give Nimue more room to escape than hasten the combat to come. In spite of my bravado, I did not know how to use the spear as the weapon for which it had been originally created. Impulsively, I began to swing the spear back and forth in wild arcs in front of me, daring anyone to cross the blade's threshold.

"Myrriddin!" It was Moscastan. I saw him off to my right. He looked dirty and bloody, as if he, too, had been in the fray. "Myrriddin, no!"

Too late. I was committed. "Leave here!" I called to him. "Take Nimue."

He moved toward Nimue, leaving my field of vision.

The first of the attackers arrived, followed quickly by the others, some ten in all. They stopped before the arcing spear, but none of them tried to come any closer to me. What they waited for, I had no idea. My feeble attempt at keeping them at bay could easily be thwarted with numbers. I never could have kept the spear arcing fast enough to keep them all away. Then I realized what had stopped them: fear. I could see it in their eyes. They believed that I held the spear of Christ and thus all the power it could yield. For whatever reason, that realization made me even more angry. I wanted nothing more than to make these men drop where they were; to have the power of the gods shoot forth from the spear and annihilate them. I brought the spear to a halt, bringing the blade's point to bear at the men before me. And then it happened: two of them attacked me at once. The lightning charge happened so fast that all froze in disbelief. A bolt of lightening shot from the blade of the spear and into one of the attackers, searing right through him and into the other in less time than it takes to blink. They contorted and screamed in utter agony. They were incinerated from the inside out and dropped dead as only the shells of men. Briefly, a silence filled the meadow. Only the crackling of the fires and the moans of those wounded or dying from the initial attack could be heard.

"Cowards!" Creconius yelled at his men, trotting his horse forward.

"Hold, Creconius," said the General, he and the Papal man keeping pace with Creconius. The three men halted their horses next to their men on the ground.

My arms felt weak, fatigued from arcing the spear and the slight electrical charge I had received when the bolt spewed forth from its blade. I held the blade toward the remaining brigands and Romans before me. It no longer glowed. I'm sure I appeared a pitiful threat. The General then raised a hand in the air and brought it down in a sharp chopping motion.

I never saw them coming, especially in the night. They hit me with such force that I was slammed to the ground on my back, dropping the spear in the process. The pain in both my shoulders began a few seconds later. In my fall, I had broken the front of both arrows, which had gone through my body and protruded out of my back. I now lay on my back staring at the night sky and seeing two feathered arrow shafts, one sticking out of the front of each of my shoulders. The pain was intense, like a poker in each shoulder. And, I could move neither arm.

"Myrriddin!" It was Nimue. Her voice came from far behind in the distance. I could not tell whether that was because she was escaping, hopefully with the aid of Moscastan, or whether it was because I was beginning to lose consciousness. I hoped the former.

My vision began to waver, but I could see two faces above me, looking at me with a mixture of fear, awe and curiosity. It was easier to focus on them than the pain. One was the young face of a legionnaire who couldn't be more than sixteen summers. Though his face was dirt-smudged, I could see that he was not from this land. My guess was that he was a conscript from the land where Moscastan hailed. The other face belonged to a toothless, filth—encrusted man, who prodded me none too gently with the butt of his weapon; a spear of some kind—a large stone, honed to resemble a sharp spear-head, tied in the fork of a split, hand-made shaft created from what appeared to be an oak branch. The spear was short, maybe four-feet long, but looked effective. The man, himself, was dressed in little more than rags and brandished a makeshift wooden crucifix on his chest. The thing dangled from a leather thong and looked to be little more than two twigs tied together cross-ways. He also stank of stale mead and human waste. I doubted whether the man had bathed in a fistful of seasons, and I guessed that he probably wiped his arse with his own cloak, if at all. His stench did more to prevent me from losing consciousness than any rough prodding with his weapon.

"He's alive!" declared the legionnaire in an accent that told me my guess about his origins was correct.

Other faces appeared over me.

Where is my spear? I suddenly wondered, panic gripping me. I could feel the dirt beneath my hands. My arms could move again. I moved one hand to feel the ground around me for the spear. "Agh!" I screamed. The movement sent a bolt of pain through my upper body. One of the men laughed.

"Looking for this, lad?" Creconius asked. I turned my head and the legs of those around me stepped aside. Standing some fifteen-feet away, holding the spear, was Creconius. The men around him were standing off by a few feet, giving him, or the spear, a wide berth. Fear drenched their features. It was as if they expected it to burst into flames. In spite of the situation, I almost laughed. These fools knew nothing of what they now possessed. Then again, for that matter, nor did I. All the time I had it, I never truly understood it or my relationship to it. Yes, I had the visions in the Crystal Sanctuary, and elsewhere, of my life as Longinus. But I no longer felt connected to that life, that person. If we have lived in human form previous to a given life, then why do the majority of us need to relearn the lessons there-from? Only a few Master Druids I have known were able to have that kind of recall.

I forcefully brought my attention back to the moment, my pain, the loss of the spear, all of it. I felt weak for having allowed the spear to leave my grasp. Then again, the arrows had clearly been targeted so that I would drop the weapon. I was alive. A part of me thought it better to have died if I was going to lose this sacred thing which had somehow been put in my trust . . . again.

"Kill him!" ordered Creconius.

"No," said a squeaky voice. This came from the mousy figure mounted next to the General. Compared to Creconius and The General, who, like Lord Creconius, was very tall even in the saddle and had the largest chest and arms I'd ever seen on a man, the Papal Legate was the size of a small girl with a voice to match. He was short and thin. His face was mostly obscured by the hood of his garment, but what I could see of it looked pale, even sickly. For an instant, I thought that perhaps this was a woman. *Impossible*, I thought. There was no doubt in my mind that he wore the Robes of the Church of Rome, complete, as I said, with the large gold crucifix. He trotted his mount forward to get a better look at me. When he stared down at me, something coursed through my body. I tried to discern what it was; fear? Awe? No. 'Twas power, but uncontrolled and unharnessed. There was no way of telling, therefore, if his power was used for good or evil. Power knows no person or intent. Only law; its own law of action. The intent, and thus the ultimate use, to which power is put, is up to the individual wielding it. In that sense, it is more frightening to face one who has the kind of power I was sensing now, but knows not how to use it, than it is to face one of evil and does know how.

The Papal Legate looked into my eyes. "Bring the Relic," he said to Creconius while staring into my face. The Legate held out his hand in apparent expectation of the spear being placed there.

"*I* am leading this party. You will not order me to do anything, Bishop," spouted Creconius calmly.

The Legate now whipped his head to face Creconius. Though I could not see the man's face, I heard the shift in power to his voice. It still squeaked, but there was now an undeniable force to it. "You dare defy the Church?"

I *could* see Creconius' face. It flinched, briefly. He, too, felt this power coming through the Bishop. He recovered quickly, though. "I care naught for your Church and . . . "

"You are here at the Church's pleasure, Lord Creconius. Do not forget your place. These soldiers are mine. Those," the Bishop continued, motioning to some of the rag-tag fighters nearby, "things are yours. If you insist, I can have the General demonstrate my point." With the nod of his head, the Legate signaled the General, who, in turn, inclined his head.

A yelp, and a sickening slicing sound came from nearby. Suddenly, the upper half of a body fell on top of my legs. His falling had moved the air around me such that I knew exactly who it was. I almost vomited from the fetid stench of the man who had only a moment ago been staring toothlessly into my face. The legionnaire who had been next to him came back into my view, wiping the blood from his Roman sword. "I was tired of your shit-smell anyway ya scum," he said to the dead man, in his Persian accent.

The Legate moved a cloth to his nose beneath the hood, obviously having just received a pungent whiff of the man, now made worse by the loosing of his bowels upon death. "Och! Remove that putrid form," said the Legate, indicating the corpse on my legs. Two other legionnaires moved in and dragged the dead man away. The Legate again turned to Creconius. "I'll not ask again," he said.

Silently, arrogantly, Creconius walked over to the Legate and handed him the Spear of Longinus, the Spear Of Christ, my wizard's staff, defiance dripping from his face.

The Legate looked over the weapon with curious and loving eyes. He stroked it tenderly as he examined the shaft and made his way up to the blade. Upon arriving at the blade, he made a sharp gasp, seeing something there that delighted and astonished him. "*His*? Truly?" It took me a moment to realize that the question was directed at me.

I strained my neck to see to what he referred. But I need not have bothered. I knew what he had found on the blade: the dried Blood of Christ. I would give nothing away, however. "I know nothing of what you say," I replied.

"Come now!" said the Legate. Something in his voice caught me off guard. He said it like an excited little boy, not as the killer he had displayed himself to be a moment ago when he had ordered the General to make an example-kill. He slid off the horse and rushed to my side, kneeling next to me. He held the spear for me to see. "Here, the blood. It is My Lord Christ's, is it not? I have heard that it remained, that even the Centurion who possessed it, Longinus—the one who had pierced the Lord's side—could not remove it."

"It's just an old spear, man," I said. Stupid, that. Had I forgotten that bolts of lightening had just flown from the thing and killed two men?

"Yes. And the display you just created with it, what was that, dumb luck? Your . . . Druid's training?" asked the Legate. He said this last part also with boyish excitement, as if he were genuinely interested in the Druid's craft, not contemptuous of it. He was beginning to seem more like Pretorius than a true Papal Legate. "Besides," he continued, "I had seen it before you broke its disguise. Why disguise it if it weren't important?"

In spite of myself and the situation, or maybe because of it, I found myself warming to this man. "Perhaps you're right. But it is simply my . . . staff by any other name," I said.

He stood then, and pointed the spear at three of the men standing nearby: two more of the raiders and the legionnaire who had just carried out the murder of the foul-smelling man. All three of the men started. But the Legate made no threatening move toward them. Instead, he kept the spear's blade pointed at the men and threw off his hood. His face was indeed boyish. But in the light of the night's fire, he could have been fifteen summers or thirty-five; such were his features. His eyes seemed to be of a light color and sparkled in the sparse light with gleeful anticipation. He then closed his eyes and contorted his face with what appeared to be concentration. I knew exactly what he was trying to do. A part of me wanted to burst into laughter: he looked like a child trying to make an adult's toy work without knowing how. The other part of me, though, knew that even *I* didn't know how it worked. It just seemed to be a part of me, responding to my deepest, most intense intentions and emotions at any give moment. But then there was the voice: *His* voice that came unbidden from time to time through the spear. Could this boy-Legate hear it now? Would he make the spear do his bidding? If so, then I would surely die this night, for I now realized that this was why he had stopped Creconius from killing me.

The Legate shook with the effort of making the spear do his will. Nothing happened; no bolt of lightening shot forth, no glow emanated from its tip, and no vibration shook its shaft. He halted the effort, much to the relief of the three men at whom the Legate had pointed the spear. "Hmm," he voiced. "Yet we all saw the light that shot forth, killing the two unfortunates."

He approached me once again and resumed his kneeling position. "You are Merlin, are you not?" he asked sincerely.

"My name is Myrriddin," I replied.

"Ah, forgive me, Myrriddin," said the Legate. "But your name is simply the ancient form of Merlin, no? And, a Merlin is a high-ranking bard or magician within the ranks of Druids, no?"

I made no reply.

"And, you have studied for many years on the great Isle of Mystery, no?" he continued.

I was astonished that he knew so much about me, but tried to hide it. "Why would you care? And even if that's all true, why would someone like me have this sacred relic—if it's what you say it is, is what I mean?"

He laughed, giggled, really. "Oh, Merlin—Myrriddin—you know precisely why. Hundreds of years ago, several sacred relics of the Church, of the then fledgling new religion, were deposited on your Isle of Mystery for safe-keeping. They're all gone from there now." He leaned in closer to me, so that only I could hear his next words. "I've a good idea who has taken two of them," he whispered, inclining his head backwards slightly to indicate the now impatient Creconius. "In fact, I'm sure of it. My sources say so. Can't confront him on it, you see. Then we'd never get them back." He leaned back to his previous position. "They're probably long gone," he said loudly, so that Creconius could hear. "But the spear . . . my sources have kept me informed of you for some time. I feel as though I know you, Mer—Myrriddin," he said correcting himself again.

Why was he telling me all this? He wanted me to wield the spear's alleged power for him, no doubt, perhaps to train him in the use of it. But there was more, I sensed. Perhaps he wanted me, with the spear's help, to also help locate the other sacred items.

"I understand that you can view remotely even without the spear's help. That's a gift, you know. Oh, the Church frowns upon such things, but I think the Universe is a vast place and God is infinite in the way He uses it . . . and us," said the Legate.

I laughed out loud then, for he indeed sounded just like Father Pretorius. But, the mere act of laughing caused intense pain to shoot through my shoulders, and I grimaced at the agonizing sensation.

"I don't know what's so funny, my son, but we need to attend to you. General," he called, rising to his feet.

The General trotted his mount close to us.

"Let us be gone from here. See to my friend Myrriddin. Take him to my tent and summon my surgeon," ordered the Legate.

Creconius was incredulous. "You cannot be serious!"

"I can and I am," The Legate said to Creconius. Turning his attention back to the Roman, he said, "Carry on, General!"

The General saluted fist to chest, turned and barked orders into the night. Within a heartbeat, six men approached, one carrying a make shift field-stretcher. He laid it open on the ground next to me. None too gently, they jostled me onto the stretcher and lifted me up. I felt as though I would pass out from the pain. I looked over at the spear, still in the hand of the Legate. I then looked at Creconius, who was also eyeing the relic.

"I think not, Lord Creconius," said the Legate, reading Creconius' desire. "It'll be safer with me." He then approached my stretcher before the men started to walk away with me. He placed a hand gently on my left arm. "We'll have you fit in no time, my friend. And, trust me, Myrriddin. I will take great care of this," he said, holding the spear so that I could see it.

For whatever reason, I believed him. With his words, my world went black as I lost consciousness.

I did not know where I was when I awoke. The pillow beneath my skin was the softest thing I had ever felt, lulling me into a sense of Otherworldly comfort and safety. I thought I could lie there forever on this cloud of softness. Had I crossed to the Otherside permanently? No. I could still feel the pain in my shoulders, but it seemed lessened by ten-fold. I opened my eyes and stared at the ceiling. Directly above me was a cloth, a very rich-looking cloth for it shined and shimmered as it moved slightly. I had never seen any cloth so shimmery as this. I thought at first that it was the ceiling itself, but quickly realized that it was a billowing drapery hung from its edges just beneath the real ceiling. I could see through the seam of the cloth to the actual ceiling: a canvas, the top of a field tent. I was disappointed. I definitely was not in the Otherworld, but some kind of lush commander's tent. Then it all came back to me.

I noticed that the arrow shafts were gone. I then began to look cautiously around at my surroundings. The interior of this *tent* was huge. Ornate and expensive accoutrements for living were everywhere: four wooden chairs, apparently handmade—each appeared slightly different, but were clearly from the same craftsman—polished and stained to perfection, complete with golden inlays and gold lion's paws for feet stood a short distance away. A very large matching table was nearby the chairs. Thick and large carpets and rugs, rich in appointment and artistry, covered every inch of the floor, and many hung on the interior of the tent's walls as tapestries. Each of those on the floor, at least the ones I could see, depicted a battle being fought by Romans of old. But the tapestries on the walls were different. Each of these had a scene wherein a specific man was being hanged on a Roman cross, or brought down from one, or showed a moment where it was at some point in the middle of this event. My eyes landed on one depicting the latter; one in which a particular bearded soldier of Rome held his spear point to the ribs of the man on the cross. My heart suddenly leapt. It was clear who this Roman soldier was supposed to be. I studied the soldier closer. *The look is all wrong!* I found myself thinking. *I, he, didn't look like that. To begin with, there was never any beard!*

A sound came from nearby, from behind and to my left. It was a quiet, breathy, wheezing type of sound. It broke my concentration; my analysis of the tapestry.

"You recognize it, do you not?" said the squeaky voice of the Legate.

I strained my neck and head to see him. The pain shot through my shoulders again and my chest with the effort, too much so this time. I brought my attention back to my body. I raised one arm, then the other. The pain was there, but not as bad as when I tried to move my whole body.

"Three days," said the Legate.

I heard the creak of a wooden chair from behind as the Legate rose and stepped to the side of my . . . bed. I was on no mere pallet with rushes for a mattress, but a bed approximately four feet off the ground and covered with fluffed and sumptuous pillows; feather-stuffed by the feel of them. The Legate stood over me and I looked into his boyish face. He was no boy, however. The beginnings of wrinkles tickled the corners of his eyes. And, though he certainly looked youthful in features, he was sickly in color. He coughed then, spitting something into a sage-colored cloth, which he quickly brought to his mouth.

He quickly regained his composure. "Forgive me," he said. "A chill in the chest I cannot seem to be rid of. I no sooner think that it has run its course when it comes back again. I'm sure the activities of the other night helped it not," he said, pausing for a time. "Three days since that night—that you've been here, in case you were wondering," the Legate offered.

I simply nodded. Three days. Better than the last time I was in a similar circumstance, I supposed. My gaze then drifted back to the tapestry.

The Legate turned his attention to it, as well. "You recognize it," he repeated while looking at the wall hanging. He said it as a matter of fact, not as a question.

I was not sure whether he referred to the whole scene in the tapestry, the soldier and the spear, or just the spear. Given the events of the night two or three nights past, it had to be the spear. I wasn't about to tell him that I was the reincarnation of the soldier in the scene. Still . . . "The beard looks strange," I heard myself saying.

"Eh?" replied the Legate, obviously caught off guard by my comment.

"The beard on the soldier stabbing the prisoner on the cross," I clarified. "I thought soldiers of Rome were clean shaven."

"Ah, well you see, this tapestry is a product of its time. The artisan who created it lived during the time of Emperor Hadrian who lived not all that long ago. He always wore the facial hair. It became quite acceptable for a legionnaire to fashion one, as well, at least for a time," the Legate explained.

"So, this is a crucifixion at the time of Hadrian, then, not at the time of the Christ?" I asked almost dismissively, trying to deflect the direction of the conversation.

"Nay, Myrriddin. You know it's of Jesu. The artisan simply used the look of his time." The Legate paused again and studied me. "You'll notice, too, that the rank of the soldier is wrong as well. Is it not?"

It was true. The soldier depicted was a common foot soldier, a common legionnaire. Of course, he should have been depicted as a Centurion. But to the Legate, I feigned ignorance. "Is it?" I asked lamely.

The Legate simply smiled. He turned and walked across the tent's floor to a tall flap, an opening on the far wall of the tent. "I wish not to tax you too heavily. We'll talk again soon," he said over his shoulder. He stopped then, racked by another fit of coughing. He recovered quickly enough and looked at me from near the tent's entrance. "I'll see that a proper meal is brought to you," he said, and turned to leave.

"Wait," I called.

He stopped and looked at me, an indeterminable smile tugging at his lips.

"What of my staff, the spear?" I asked, a whiff of desperation filling my voice.

"As I said," he replied calmly, "we'll talk more later."

"And . . . my . . . did you take anyone else . . . prisoner?" My friends. Had Moscastan and Nimue escaped? What of Baldua and Pretorius?

"I would not call you a prisoner, Myrriddin," he answered.

"Oh?" I asked, incredulous. "Let me take stock," I began sarcastically. "You chased and killed many of the people I was with, you shot me and took my possession and brought me here against my will. Does that not make a prisoner?"

"As I said, I'd not say you were a prisoner."

"So I'm free to leave, then?" I said, becoming more angry by the moment.

The Legate stepped up to the tent's opening and pulled back the flap, silently inviting me to freedom. Daylight streamed in, as well as the sounds of activity in an encampment, surprisingly muted until just then.

I sat up and swung my legs off the bed all in one motion. And, I instantly regretted it. The pain shot through not only my whole body, but my whole being. I nearly passed out. I lay back down quickly. I panted heavily and was sweating from what ordinarily would have been a small exertion. One doesn't truly appreciate the body's abilities, no matter how minute or seemingly insignificant, until it is taken away. I then felt liquid on my shoulders. My wounds were seeping blood again.

"I'll have food brought to you, Myrriddin. And, my surgeon again," he said from the tent's flap.

"Thank you, Legate," I said, defeated.

"Rozinus," said the Legate. "My name is Bishop Rozinus," he said as he left me alone in the plush quarters.

SIXTEEN

"Fear not, Myrriddin," said Moscastan. He leaned over the pallet I lay on and looked into my face. I could move not a muscle. I tried to speak, but could not. I could not even move my lips. What had happened? I could not turn my head to see if I was in the same place, in the tent wherein Rozinus had left me. "You needn't have the spear. You have the Merlin within to do your bidding. You always have and always will," he continued.

"M-Myrrid-d-din, my l-love," stuttered Igraines. Her face appeared next to Moscastan, both stared at me with concern, yet joy in their eyes. *What was happening?* I screamed in my mind. *I am here! Help me! I cannot move.*

"You tried to safeguard the spear, but it matters not, lad. You did what you could," said Moscastan.

"Salve, mihi care amice (Hello, my dear friend). Are you coming back to us?" It was Baldua, speaking as his face joined the others above me. He turned to Moscastan and Igraines, "I think he's gone. His stare, it's blank," he said in perfect Gaelic.

'Twas true. I could not even move my eyes to focus on any one of them.

"No," said Igraines. "Th-they're still m-moist." Her face disappeared from my view for a moment as she turned away. I then heard an amazing sound: the wail of an infant. Igraines appeared back in my view, now holding a beautiful baby. "Look, Myrriddin, l-look. My son. I have named h-him Arturius. Y-You must teach h-him the w-w-wonders of the gods," she said, tears brimming her eyes.

Arturius! Yes! Yes! I know the lad. I've seen him, foretold of his coming, I yelled in my mind. *But . . . I no longer have the spear to guide me, to guide us to . . .*

"Look! His eyes water!" said Baldua. "He *is* with us still!"

Cold liquid dripped down my face, a small amount at first, then more, and more until I felt as though I would drown. I coughed, struggled for breath and sat up.

"I sorry," said the terrified girl sitting on my bed of fluffed, feathered pillows. "I bathe you, say Bishop. Too much water in cloth. I sorry," she rambled in broken Gaelic. She could not have been more than twelve summers. I knew little of the northern countries, but what I did know of them, this lass fit. She was yellow of hair and blue of eye. She spoke with the guttural accent of a Germanic tribe. She had, no doubt, been picked up as a slave during the Bishop's travels.

But what kind of slave she was, I did not want to think. I understood that most of these Christian priests now took vows of celibacy. I wondered if Bishop Rozinus did. I'd be not surprised by him either way. I did not understand their reasoning for such a vow. According to Pretorius, they thought by taking a vow of celibacy, it brought them closer to God and away from the so-called evil and baser aspects of being human. Yet, physical urges were not just natural to my people and the old ways, but brought us closer to creation by engaging in the act of creation itself; whether for the creation of new life, or the creation of something else, an outstanding harvest of a blessed crop, for example, by bringing together the opposite energies and spirits. There were those among the Druids who had reached a level of being beyond the physical; they were truly spirits living from their spirit only while housed in body. I saw that with them, the desire for the act of physical coupling was something that had simply fallen away; something that they had moved beyond, like a child that has outgrown a toy. To move beyond it for any other reason was to miss the whole point. One does not lead the ox with the wagon, as it is said.

"I sorry," the girl repeated. She looked as though I were about to strike her; not fearful, but simply resigned to it. Obviously, it was part of her master's routine.

"Do not worry," I said, realizing I could not only speak, not only move, but that I was also sitting naked on the bed. And, I realized, too, that my friends had been a dream. I remained a . . . guest of the Bishop's in his tent. "I was dreaming and you startled me, that is all," I said to the girl. "I can bathe myself."

"Nin," she insisted, shaking her head. "I water the hurts wid my mix," she said, pointing to a nearby bowl containing a dark, gelatinous liquid.

Though I was dubious, I looked at the wound in my left shoulder. It was nearly healed. If her *mix* had aided in that, then so be it. I then wiped off the remaining water from my face.

"I try to give you drink with cloth, but too much, me thinks," she said sheepishly.

I laughed, perhaps for the first time in days. "Me thinks too," I agreed. I then turned to her and motioned for her to apply her mix. As she worked, my mind drifted to the tent, to the fact that I'd lost track of my time here, to my friends and the dream I just had. To the spear! I resolved then and there to get it back. I needed it to fulfill the destiny that kept coming to me. Arturius, the boy who grew to be a king, at least if my visions were correct. Son of Igraines? But who was the father? I wanted to believe that I was, from that night Igraines and I lay together, which now seemed a lifetime ago. No matter. My destiny, or at least part of it, was apparently intricately interwoven with this child and with the land he would rule. And the spear; I must have the spear to guide me, to give me the power and ability to guide us all. I saw that now more than ever. It was truly *my* Druid's staff. "Quickly, now lass. I have things to do, you know," I said to the girl as she continued to slather her concoction on my wounds. The mix, or salve felt cool and soothing, and something else: it tingled. It felt as though tiny little creatures crawled over the skin. Not in a frightening or disturbing way, however. It was a special type of tingling and tickling sensation, like skin being rapidly mended back together. I had never felt anything like it.

"Yes, Master," she said shyly, but with a look that said, "*You've been lying here for days and now you suddenly 'have things to do'?*"

"Well, I do," I said defensively.

She continued about her work, saying no more.

The sun was bright and harsh as I stepped out of the tent. Or, perhaps it was more the fact that I'd been inside and bedridden that made it seem so. Two guards, helmeted, armed Roman legionnaires, flanked the sides of the tent opening as I stepped out. Neither moved, but stood stiffly, looking ahead and away from me. They made no move to stop me or question me. The girl who had been applying the salve to my wounds squeezed her way between me and one of the guards as she left. "Thank you," I called after her. She simply held up a hand in acknowledgement and walked on, never turning back to look at me. One of the guards snickered at this. I could guess what was going through his mind.

The activity outside the tent was sparse. I expected to see more people and soldiers. There were only a handful of legionnaires scattered about and a few of the raiders that had been with Creconius. It was then that I heard the voice of Creconius, heated, as though he would spew forth venom at any moment. "You said so," he claimed in a loud growl.

I took another step out from the tent and looked to my right, in the direction of his voice. There, near a corner of the tent, was Creconius, face-to-face with Legate Bishop Rozinus, who was flanked by two other Churchmen, judging by their brown robes and tonsured heads. "My good Creconius, I said no such thing," replied the Bishop calmly, even sweetly. "It is plain to see that you misunderstood."

I knew not of what they spoke. But something told me it was about me, and or the spear; more likely the spear. I took a step toward them. A strong hand grasped my arm and stopped me. "No, Myrriddin."

I almost spat at the man. How dare this rat of Rome be so presumptuous as to call me by my name. I looked into the man's face and nearly passed out from the shock of what I saw. Beneath the brim of the helmet were the eyes of Baldua. "Salve, mihi amice (Hello, my friend)," he said in his pretentious Latin. 'Twas Baldua for certain.

"Enough with that talk!" said the other legionnaire guard; a female—Nimue.

I was stunned. With dirt smudged on her face and her hair obviously pulled back and up under her helmet, she looked more like an older boy than a woman to be sure. "What the . . . " I began.

"'Tis come in quite useful getting us this far, lass, don't ya think?" Baldua replied haughtily to Nimue's slight.

"What are you two doing here, and dressed like . . . like that?" I said too loudly, pointing to the Roman garb.

"Stop it, Myrriddin. You'll give us away now," said Nimue.

"Obviously, we came for you, ya ingrate," Baldua said to me. "You've been too ill 'til now. Thought we'd lost you."

"Yes," said Nimue, sternly but tenderly. "That we did."

"But . . . how did you . . . "

"Ah, by the gods, Myrriddin. Enough. We're here, are we not?" said Baldua, clearly thinking we were talking too much.

"Moscastan had us lead two soldiers into the woods," explained Nimue. "He glammed them—spelled them, I think. We took their uniforms and their place."

"And their compatriots didn't notice?" I asked.

"They were breaking camp when we arrived in the uniforms. Most of 'em were leaving with that general. Someone barked for us to stay. Didn't give us a second look," said Baldua.

"Lucky for you! Could you imagine if he had barked for you to go with those leaving?" I laughed at the thought of Nimue and Baldua serving in the Legions of Rome for the remainder of their days. Well, at least the thought of it happening to Baldua made me laugh for a moment.

Creconius yelled what sounded like a threat to the Bishop. He sounded as though he was losing control. His voice had shifted to a very high tone, almost to that of a woman's shriek. "I'll cut you through, I will!" he yelled again. Suddenly, a ringing sound was heard: the sound of a high-grade metal blade being un-sheathed. In a whirl of his body, Creconius had brandished a hidden sword. The thing was nearly as long as a man and shined with the brightness of a full moon. Where he had pulled it from, I could not tell. He brought it down with the fury of a god, straight at Bishop Rozinus' head. But the bishop was fast, faster than anyone I had ever seen. In one move, he stepped slightly to one side and pulled one of the tonsured Churchmen toward him, effectively using the unwitting man as a shield against the sword blow. It worked. Creconius' blade missed the Bishop, but cleaved the other Churchman in one shoulder close to the neck, nearly cut-ting the man in two lengthwise. Everyone froze for an instant.

The man who was just hacked in two was fully awake and comprehending, at least for a moment. He looked at his mortal injury with stunned disbelief. "Oh, oh, oh," he said. He then turned his gaze to the sky, to the heavens. "I was not done here, my Lord. But if thine will is . . . is . . . " He dropped silently to the ground in a pool of blood. No one was watching the man die, though, for some-thing more astonishing had happened.

Those who were within viewing of what had just taken place were watching Creconius; his face had changed, as if a glam had suddenly been lifted with the exertion of this shining sword. He had always had decidedly feminine features. But, now his face appeared even more soft. It was feminine, yes, but more that of a crone, a hag, a female Sorceress from the Old Ways—one who uses the knowledge and power and law of the Infinite, the One, to do Dark biddings.

"What treachery is this?" Bishop Rozinus asked, menace dripping from his words. "What demon are you, for you are not Creconius?"

"I am Creconius, you fool," Creconius said, regaining some of his normal voice. But his appearance remained that of the old crone. "I am Creconius Mab, seeker and keeper of the Old Ways, and I'll have the spear or your head, Rozinus. Your church ways are an abomination and will be destroyed. I already have your other precious relics and the power they hold."

I felt Baldua tense up next to me. It was now I who reached out and placed a hand on my friend's arm to steady him.

"I knew it!" bellowed the Bishop. "Where've you taken them?"

"Far from here." Creconius Mab laughed thunderously then. When he stopped laughing, his face became deadly serious. He brandished the point of the mighty sword at the throat of Rozinus. There was a crackling in the air, as if an electrical charge had pierced the area. The tip of the sword glowed a fierce red. Bishop Rozinus stared at it, transfixed. Not only did the blade shine immensely bright, but there was a glow to the hilt of the thing. It was not like the glow of the blade's tip, however. This one was soft and bluish-white and conveyed a feeling that was . . . what? I could not understand it for a moment. And then it hit me. Creconius Mab was having difficulty maintaining his glamour because of this sword—because of the power coursing through this sword. It was not meant for such a Sorceress as Creconius Mab. The blue light glowing from the hilt—it was the power of goodness; the positive attributes of the gods, The God. I could feel it; it was the same feeling I always felt from the spear. It took all of Creconius Mab's power to stay in control over the magnificent sword.

"Impressive, is it not?" Creconius Mab asked Rozinus as the Legate's stare remained transfixed on the sword. "Forged from a metal no man has seen before, honed to perfection and wielded by a so-called holy man of your ilk," continued Creconius Mab. I looked at it closer. Indeed, the blade looked different than any I had ever seen; shining polish, yes, but it also appeared to be more solid, stronger than any blade I'd ever seen. It had sliced through the tonsured Churchman as if he were naught but air. There were symbols adorning each side of the blade, from hilt to tip. I recognized some of them as ancient Gaelic. The others looked even older, and more obscure. I believe Moscastan had drawn some like these once— said they were glamours of divine providence; invocations of ancient and sacred trusts. He had called them runes. The hilt and grip were plain enough; a sturdy iron cross bar to protect the hand, both of its ends fanned out, and a smooth-handled grip with leather strips wrapped tightly around it. I could see part of the grip beneath his hand. It ended with a round crystal-like pummel. Nothing too special about the hilt, grip and pummel. It was the blade that set this weapon apart, and the power which coursed through it.

"You see the caliber of the blade, the weapon. You sense its power," he continued, taunting the Bishop.

"I . . . " Rozinus began, regaining his composure, no longer transfixed by the sword. He looked straight into the eyes of Creconius Mab then, menace and contempt spewing forth. "I see one who is unworthy of such a weapon and sense that he is terribly weakened by the controlling of it. If you were worthy of such as this," he continued, as he casually brought a hand to the blade, "your wielding of it would be effortless." Rozinus then touched the flat of the blade with a finger and gently pushed it away from his throat.

Creconius Mab began panting, his breathing labored as if from extreme exertion. For an instant, his glamour dropped completely. Before us stood a stooped, short, ugly hag leaning on the large sword whose point was now in the ground.

"Take him . . . her! Take the sword!" yelled Rozinus to no one in particular.

Before anyone could respond, or even know to respond—there were very few people left in the camp, very few soldiers—Creconius Mab, the hag, gave a blood-spilling scream, threw her head back violently, and suddenly became Creconius Mab, the murderous scum once more, fully glammed with the large man's presence and being. Creconius Mab then howled with rage and took three steps backward. Still howling his demented anger, he thrust the sword into the air and suddenly disappeared, vanishing completely from sight on a bright and clear day.

"By the gods!" exclaimed Baldua. The remaining tonsured Churchman standing next to Bishop Rozinus dropped to his knees and began to fervently pray through unbridled terror and tears. His words were in Latin, but his meaning was clear.

"He prays for deliverance from evil and . . . "

"Yes, Baldua. I can guess what he's praying for!" I snapped at my friend as he began to play the role of interpreter.

He fell silent, as we all did for a moment, not quite believing what had just happened. The only sounds were a bird cawing in the distance, and the frantic mumblings of a terrified priest.

"Myrriddin," Nimue whispered from behind me.

I turned and looked into her eyes, beautiful even though her face was a dirty mess.

"You want your precious spear, follow me," she said. She seemed not at all affected by the Sorceress' disappearance. Slowly, she started to back into the tent I had just exited.

"You can't be serious," I said. "I'd know if it were in there."

"Obviously, you know not as much as you think," she countered as she went in.

"Go, Myrriddin. I'll watch here," said Baldua.

I said nothing, but followed Nimue into the tent.

It was stale. Though it was still the same large and luxurious space, the smell was sickly. My head hurt and my stomach lurched. I also felt weak. Perhaps I had *made* my exit from the tent too soon, I thought. The girl had been sent in to bathe me and continue treatment of my wounds. Maybe I was still injured and weak.

"Here," said Nimue from a large, freestanding wardrobe cabinet. It stood at least seven-feet tall. I recalled taking notice of it before at some point, but paid it no heed. Perhaps because of its location in the tent—several yards behind the head of the bed I had been in for . . . two weeks maybe? Had I been here that long? Nimue stood holding the wardrobe's intricately-carved door open. A soft glow came from within. I approached slowly, cautiously, and peered inside.

It stood leaning against the back, right-hand corner inside the cabinet, the blade glowing softly with the same bluish hue as the sword hilt for a few moments. Was it in sympathetic connection with the sword? And how could I not sense the spear's presence in the very place I was convalescing, not think to look in the cabinet?

"You're scowling. I thought you'd be happy to see it," said Nimue.

"How'd I not feel its presence? And why did the Bishop not hide it away?" I asked, feeling a mixture of confusion and unworthiness.

"He probably kept it here to aid in your healing, don't you think?" she stated flatly as if it were the most obvious thing in the world.

"But I didn't *feel* it . . . " I started.

"I don't know," she said, exasperated. "Ah, Myrriddin, we haven't time for this. Take it." Nimue looked back to the tent's entrance flap and made a soft, bird-like cawing sound. A moment later, Baldua entered.

"We must leave. It's clear for now, but the shock of that Sorceress vanishing is wearing thin," he said as he stopped before us.

I took the spear in my hand. Its warmth was comforting. I took a deep breath and instantly felt my connection to it reassert itself. I was at home with this instrument, no matter where I was. Holding the spear, I suddenly realized that I also felt invigorated, healed, the sickly feeling I had upon re-entering the tent all but gone. I looked at Nimue. "How'd you know it was here?" I asked.

Baldua answered. "The little lass that tended you a while ago – she's quite the chattering goose," he said, a smile pulling the corners of his mouth.

"What does that mean?" I asked incredulously.

"What do you mean, 'what does that mean,' Myrriddin?"

"Well, did you frighten her or did you . . . "

"No! Of course not," he replied, genuinely hurt.

Nimue stepped in and said, "It means, Myrriddin, that your friend is a charmer of little girls as well as older ones. Well, some older ones," she said, clearly implying that she was above such things from him. "Enough. Let's leave."

I stepped toward the entrance when Baldua grabbed my arm, stopping me. "Not that way. There's a short flap at the back. The tree line is ten feet from it on the outside," he said.

Nimue led the way as we went to the very back of the tent. She pulled aside a lovely, expensive looking two-seat couch. There, near the base of the tent's wall, was a tied flap approximately three-feet-by-three-feet. "It's for ventilation, but makes a good escape hole," she said.

"You certainly reconnoitered the place," I observed.

She said no more, but dropped to her knees, untied the flap which hinged at its top, and crawled out. Dropping to my knees, I followed her out, Baldua behind me. Outside the back of the tent, the way was clear and we quickly made it to the tree-line. We entered the protective covering of the forest, escaping the Bishop and the remainder of his soldiers and Creconius Mab's rabble. As I crossed the threshold of the tree-line, I looked back toward the tent. Not too far from the dwelling, in the midst of what had now become a bustle of activity—the group was apparently breaking camp—stood Bishop Rozinus. Standing before the Bishop and speaking to him, much to my surprise, was Pretorius. I looked at Baldua, who was looking in the same general direction as I was, but only briefly.

"Go, Myrriddin," Baldua said, as he pushed me into the forest.

SEVENTEEN

We crept through the forest, quickly but quietly. We traveled for over a mile, weaving in between rowans and oaks and saplings as they became thicker in trunk, denser in population. At first I kept turning, expecting to see pursuers on foot. I stopped on two occasions simply to listen and nearly fell behind. No one was trailing us. The spear still glowed a soft blue; it had neither intensified nor diminished since leaving the tent. That was odd. Of course, it had glowed occasionally since the day I'd discovered it – in warning, in conveyance of some thought or message from the Otherworld; in empathic harmony with my own soul. Yet, it had never glowed this shade of color, nor with this consistency. I was still deeply connected to the spear; I felt it. But this glowing was in harmony with the sword Creconius Mab had wielded, or had tried to wield. I did not understand it, but I felt it. Little did I know that the sword Creconius Mab possessed then would one day aid in the making of a king. My immediate concern, however, was to proceed to safety.

We had traveled deep into the forest when we burst forth into a bright meadow near a large rock formation in the side of a green hill. Nimue, who had been leading us, stopped, Baldua and I alongside of her. The three of us stood in silence for a moment, the twill of birds and the soughing of tree branches in the late afternoon breeze the only sounds coming to our ears. Then Nimue added her own bird twill to the mix, calling forth a moment later a figure from between the craggy rocks. Moscastan. My heart leapt at the sight of him.

"Moscastan!" I yelled, nearly dropping the spear in my rush to embrace him.

"Ah, Master Myrriddin," he said. "We were a bit concerned there for a while." He turned to my two companions. "Well done." It was then that I noticed Moscastan appeared . . . different. He did not look as old as he had in the Crystal Sanctuary, but he certainly did not appear as young as the mentor I knew. The person before me was someone in between. There was something else, too: he was pale, as if something was draining his energy, his very blood. I was about to question him on this when Baldua interrupted my thoughts.

"Father Pratorius—he was there. We saw him when we made our escape!" my friend said, as he began to strip his body of the Roman uniform.

"Yes," added Nimue.

I had completely forgotten about seeing the priest. But in that moment, I knew not which caught me more off my guard; the fact that the priest had indeed been in the Bishop's camp, or the fact that my friends were surprised by it. I supposed that in the back of my mind, I had simply assumed the priest to be there as part of the ruse to free me.

"And the sword! Creconius Mab was there and he had a sword the likes of which you've never seen, Moscastan!" Baldua was near babbling in his excitement.

"Calm yourself, lad. Come," Moscastan said as he turned and walked back the way he had come. The three of us followed, weaving our way into and through a craggy rock maze. We then ascended a steep, long set of natural rock steps and emerged onto a large plateau atop the hill, which was actually, as it turned out, not a hill but one gigantic rock formation the size of a small mountain that was covered with mossy grass, giving it the appearance of a smooth, green hill. The plateau was some seventy yards off the floor of the meadow and boasted naturally formed rock walls some four to six feet high around its circumference or perimeter. Thus, it was a perfect hiding place; a naturally formed and hidden refuge from prying eyes. The only way a potential intruder could spy on us here was if he climbed to the top of one of the tallest trees on the edge of the forest, which was not more than thirty yards away. But even so, the tallest of those trees could not reach the height of the plateau. I looked out over the nearby segment of four-foot wall toward the forest from which we'd emerged, and could only see the top of the forest's canopy. The sight of the canopy, the height and seclusion of the plateau— it was breath-taking.

"Wonderous," I said to no one in particular.

"Come, Myrriddin," Moscastan beckoned. I turned. He was standing near a cold fire-pit in the center of the plateau. Around the pit were many folks, celebrants from the evening of the All Hallow's Eve rite turned massacre. Some sat with arms and other appendages in wrappings still bloodied from wounds received that horrific night. Others stood nearby but with the vacant look of the undead in their eyes; that night's carnage leaving them so disturbed in mind that they had one foot in this world, one foot in the Other. The remainder looked fine in body and mind and were clearly giving comfort – or attempting to – to those in need. Anger rose within me. Rage again filled my being as it had the night of the raid, the murderous rampage. The spear in my hand finally ceased to glow blue. It vibrated in my hand and began to pulsate a vibrant red, reflecting the anger seething within me.

"Calm yourself, Myrriddin," said my mentor. "They need your help, not your anger," he said, noting the spear.

"My anger is for those that committed this," I said, waving my hand at the victims before me. *And* for Rozinus, I thought, feeling another surge of anger rise. I had allowed myself to feel complacency toward the Bishop for allowing me to heal. *He'd* have done better to finish what he started rather than allow me to live, I thought maliciously.

"Myrriddin," Moscastan said.

I walked toward him when he turned and entered a small nearby animal skin shelter approximately four-square-feet in size. It obviously had been hastily erected, using broken branches from the forest below. He pulled back a flap and disappeared inside the small shelter. He clearly wanted me to follow, but a part of me wanted to stop and immediately help the people here; I could feel it in my bones. I could feel it from the spear. It's what we were supposed to do—the spear and I.

"Go, Myrriddin," prodded Nimue. She had already shed her legionnaire's costume and stood before me as the daughter of Tremel. She was dressed now, however, in a green cloth tunic and animal skin riding breaches. She hastily wiped the dirt smudges from her face and revealed the beauty of it which I had nearly forgotten. Something stirred within me at a deeper level than what I thought I held for Igraines: a connection that was at least as old as the one I felt I shared with Igraines. I could not quite put my finger on it just then.

"Go," she said again, as she bent down to a man with an arm wound. She began to unwrap the bloody cloth. The unwrappings released a putrid odor of gangrenous flesh. I nearly gagged. Nimue paid no heed to the smell, or to my reaction. "He has something for you," she said, indicating the nearby shelter with a gesture of her head. "And in case you haven't taken note, he's not well, either." She stated this with a bitter edge. Why, I was not sure.

But at her words, my anger abated and genuine concern for Master Druid Moscastan took its place. I looked at the pitiful group around me. Yes, they needed my help and the spear's. But they could wait a few more moments, I supposed. I abruptly turned and entered Moscastan's shelter.

The space was tiny and dank and smelled faintly of Moscastan's underground hovel in our home village. A sense of comfort and security suddenly washed over me; a sense of freedom and learning and fondness of memory and peace. But it was false and fleeting.

A muffled scream came from outside. Clearly, it was from someone enduring pain; the kind of pain that comes from the tending of a wound that simply won't heal.

Moscastan already sat cross-legged on the hard ground and indicated that I should do the same. I did so, sitting opposite him, facing him, laying the spear next to me on the ground. It had ceased its red, angry glow and emanated the blue light once more. Moscastan stared at it for a moment. But I could see in his eyes that he wasn't just staring at the spear. His pained look also told me he was waiting for the muffled sound of the one in pain to subside. It almost seemed as if he himself was feeling the pain of this person, taking it on himself to lessen it for another. The sound finally stopped and my mentor brought his eyes to my eyes. What I saw there frightened me.

"I've done what I can for them, Myrriddin. You must heal them, break the glamour that binds them to the pain and suffering placed on them by Creconius Mab that night as they fled," he said heavily. "I have fought it, but cannot break it. The wounds these people have do not heal. The spell must be broken for them to become whole. It is a travesty of the use of the One, the Law." He fell silent and became older in appearance before my eyes. I tried not to show surprise, but felt my eyes widen. "I have taken on their glamour as much as I can," he continued. "Attempted to show them that they have the power within them to deny the essence of pain thrust on them by another. But they're a simple lot. Some of them have even turned to the Christian's influence they've apparently experienced these seasons past, and now see their present condition as some form of twisted retribution for the *sin* of participating in the ritual that night. Absurd. 'Tis their own thinking that perpetuates the condition." He paused and drew a labored breath. "But I tell you nothing you don't know."

I stared at Moscastan, my heart suddenly feeling as though it were breaking. I had never seen him so. "Moscastan," I began, my voice cracking. "By the gods, what glamour could destroy you thus? You wield more understanding, more power of the Law than anyone I know."

"'Tis not the glamour, but the one who invokes it—uses the same laws of the Universe available to us all, but for the most sinister of purposes, the most reviled of reason, the most ... "

"Moscastan." He had started to babble. "Save your strength, please," I said as I reached out and placed my hand on his shoulder. He was shaking ever so slightly. "What is happening? I've been in that Bishop's camp for over a fortnight. Meanwhile, the world I knew went from bad to worse still. Who could throw a glam of this power? One strong enough to keep those people out there in a bondage of evil and nearly destroy you? Is it Creconius Mab? He is not what he seems. A Sorceress! He changed before our eyes. Vanished too! He ... "

Moscastan shot a hand in the air to silence me. I was now the one who babbled.

"Yes, it is Creconius Mab. But it is worse than that," my mentor said cryptically.

"I don't understand. Does he have a legion of demons at his bidding?" I asked sardonically, half joking.

Moscastan said nothing for a moment. I suddenly had the thought that perhaps my comment was closer to the mark than not.

"Baldua and Nimue said Father Pretorius was at the Churchman's camp. Was it so? Did you see him?" asked Moscastan.

"Yes. He was there at the Bishop's encampment," I replied.

"And Creconius Mab, as well?"

"Yes," I replied, confused by the line of questioning. He seemed to be linking the Priest and the Sorceress together. Then my thoughts shifted to the amazing weapon that Creconius Mab had brandished. "The sword! He or she; Creconius Mab had a sword. It was nearly as long as he was and intricately designed. It was of a metal I'd never seen and infused with a power, too! Creconius Mab had trouble with it, he did. Wasn't meant for him, I don't think. His glam dropped when he tried to use it and ... "

Moscastan's hand shot up again in the gesture to silence me. "So, it does exist," he said, his voice heavy with awe.

"Yes," I said confused. "How could you know about the sword?" I asked.

"Tell me this," he said, ignoring my question for the moment. "Were there . . . symbols on the blade near the edges?" he asked.

"Runes. Yes," I replied, surprised. "They ran the length of the blade."

Silence filled the space. Soft moaning could be heard from outside, but that was all.

"This sword," I finally said. "'Twas clearly endowed with great power. Creconius Mab said that it had been used by a Holy man of the Church. He implied that its power was from this man.

"One named Constantinius, yes. But it was forged here, on one of the lesser islands in the lake, near the Isle of Mystery," Moscastan said. "It was indeed forged from a metal never seen before. But before Constantinius had it, the legend goes that it was used to kill one of the Church's truly Holy men. He was said to be much like the Christ, and as with your spear there, his Holiness, his power, was somehow transferred to the sword. After a time, the sword made its way back here, to the Lady on the island of its origins. A good woman and a high priestess of the Old Ways." Moscastan stopped his story. The look in his eyes became far and away as if he were reliving a memory. A smile of pleasure touched his lips. Obviously, the memory was a fond one.

It dawned on me what the memory might be of. "You knew this lady, this High Priestess?" I asked tentatively.

"Aye. She was my friend, my lover, my wife – for a time, at least."

"I never knew."

"No. You didn't. 'Twas before your time. She etched the runes to hold in the power of the divine that apparently coursed through the sword. It's much like your spear," said Moscastan.

"But the spear doesn't need runes to hold its power," I replied.

"Your spear actually pierced the Christ's side, did it not?" countered Moscastan. "The Christ's blood is the sealing stone for whatever power courses through it. But like your spear, the sword's supposed divine power can only be wielded by a righteous and just man."

His eyes bore into me then. I saw in those eyes the depths of his soul; many lifetimes of existence and trust in me, my soul. Am I worthy of such a title –*righteous and just?*

"Yes, Myrriddin," said my mentor, reading my face, my thoughts. "You're indeed such a man. You will help to found a kingdom based on truth and justice, and in the process, become the most famous of all Merlins."

Moscastan's eyes had glazed over. He was on the edge of trance, prophesizing. But something he said struck me. "I can't see that now. I always thought I would be father to a great Merlin to carry on what I've started," I said.

"No. The line of Merlins will end with you. You are already birthing yourself a-new. *You* are the son and the father," Moscastan said. "This supposed power in the sword will aid you in birthing the kingdom."

"And the spear?" I asked.

"A powerful Druid Staff indeed. But you will outgrow it," he replied.

"I don't understand," I said, confused and concerned.

"The power of the spear, the power of the sword, though clearly detectable, is naught but the power of the One focused. Nothing can harness this power more than the mind, the spirit. Nothing. You know this, but will soon fully embody it, thus outgrowing your need for the spear," he answered. He paused for a moment before continuing. "Yet, the spear and the sword are important symbols and instruments for now. The sword is in part what we sought."

"We?"

"Pretorius and I," Moscastan said nearly spitting the priest's name. He was also out of the semi-trance.

I wanted to know why he spoke Pretorius' name so, but a different question came to my lips. "How is it that Creconius Mab has the sword?" I asked.

"She stole it from her sister."

"His . . . her sister?" I asked, completely confused. He said nothing for a moment. "You mean the Lady, the runes lady is the sister of Creconius Mab?"

"Aye."

I was stunned. My face must have shown it.

"There's more," said Moscastan heavily. "I ask you this; When you saw Pretorius at the Bishop's encampment, was Creconius Mab there?"

"No," I replied, struggling once again to discern this line of question.

"And when Creconius Mab *was* present, was Pretorius?"

"Moscastan," I exclaimed, shocked, "what are you saying?!"

Moscastan sat staring at me for a long moment, thinking. "I'm not sure, Myrriddin. I'm not yet completely sure. So, I will hold my tongue. For now." He said this last bit with finality. Though a hundred questions leapt into my mind, the matter was obviously closed. He reached behind him to a bundle wrapped in dung-colored cloth. Gently, reverently, he lifted the bundle – which was nearly the size of a young man's head – and placed it in front of me. "As I said," Moscastan began, "the spear is presently an important symbol and instrument. "This," he said, indicating the bundle, "will go a long way to disguising the spear, and the Egg is exceptional. It will truly help to accentuate the spear's supposed – forgive me – the spear's power."

I unwrapped the bundle and found a beautifully woven oval-shaped wicker cage containing a flawless green crystal, a Druid's Egg, the size of a man's fist. I'd never seen anything like it. "Moscastan," I said, awed. "It's exquisite."

"Indeed. The cage is much sturdier than the last one you had. Place it on the spear's blade. It should fit well," he said.

I did as he bade, slipping the housing, the cage, over the blade's tip and onto the blade. The Druid Egg made a tap-sound as it came to rest against the metal. Instantly, a green hue lit the space around it. I could no longer see the blue glow that had been emanating from the spear.

"Secure it tightly," said Moscastan, pointing to the leather thongs on the top and bottom of the cage.

I did. When I was satisfied that the oval cage and crystal would not be going anywhere, I held it at arm's length, admiring it. "'Tis beautiful, Moscastan. Better than anything I have ever done. Thank you."

"Indeed. You're welcome, lad. Now, it's time—time to go out and help these people. Time to heal the land and found a kingdom, Master Merlin," he said smiling.

EIGHTEEN

As I emerged from Moscastan's shelter, the spear turned into a powerful Druid's staff once more in my hand. All those present around the cold fire pit stared at me, or rather, at my Druid's staff and its glowing green Druid egg, with awe and respect. All but Baldua and Nimue, that is. Baldua smiled, apparently glad to see the thing back to a familiar appearance. Nimue scowled. "If it and you are to aid these people," she said as she continued wrapping the wounded chest of a man, "then come."

I hesitated, but only briefly. I approached the man whose chest was being tended to by Nimue. "Remove the wrap," I said to her.

She looked at me with an expression of annoyance, having just wrapped the wound by running the bandage all the way around the man's torso. She quickly complied, however, and undid her work. When the last of the wrapping and the poultice pack was removed, the wound stood gaping before me. It was in-between his lower ribs on the right side of his chest and had the appearance of a stab wound. The wound was too large to have been caused by a knife or a sword, though. *A spear must have caused this*, I thought; a spear not unlike the one now disguised as my Druid staff – a soldier's spear. My heart raced as I stared at the wound. It was oddly familiar. The wound itself was festered, and the ridges of curled back skin around the opening were inflamed and pussey. I looked into the man's eyes. It was then that I realized who he was: Tremel, Nimue's father. I looked at Nimue kneeling next to him. "Help him, Myrriddin. Help them all," she said.

I simply nodded. There was nothing else to say. Looking at Tremel, I saw fatigue in his face and fear in his eyes. He stared at the staff, the glowing crystal. "Fear not," I said gently. "Lie back."

"Do as he says, Tremel, please," Nimue begged, the girl within the woman peeking out.

Tremel did as he was bade, relaxing on his back as best he could on the hard ground.

"Breathe deep and steady," I instructed.

He winced at first with the painful effort of simply breathing, but quickly settled into a steady, slow rhythm. Breath; life's essence. I too breathed deep and steady, but focused on the Druid Egg and the spear blade behind it, fusing with it in my mind. It started as a tingling in the hand that held the staff, but quickly became a constant charged vibration, as if a bolt of lightening were coming from the Universe, entering my body and the staff and collecting, converging in the blade, and especially the Druid Egg. It pulsated with a bright green-blue light. Several people nearby gasped at the sight. Slowly, reverently, I placed the cage of the staff directly on the wound. Then something amazing took place. The light that had been pulsating around the crystal and blade became more intense; then bent and streamed into the wound. I closed my eyes then and saw in my mind the wound being cleaned by the light, bathed in its healing power, and closing in an instant as if the wound had never happened. This final image had no sooner solidified itself in my mind when I felt the vibrating of the spear cease; the lightning charge disseminate. I opened my eyes and the light of the Druid Egg and blade were gone. But most importantly, the wound on Tremel's chest was completely sealed and healed. Only a pink line remained.

"By the God!" whispered someone nearby.

"How do you feel, Tremel?" I asked.

He thought for a moment, a look of astonishment and peace intermingling on the features of his face. "Hale and fit," he finally said. "As if something evil has been sucked from me."

A man hobbled toward me from behind Tremel. He hobbled because he was aiding a woman to walk. Blood seeped from a gash on her head and her eyes had the look of the walking dead. He stopped before me, holding his charge on her feet with great effort. He did not appear to be injured. But he did seem both fatigued beyond human limits and desperately sad. He looked at the woman he held, a comely lady of perhaps thirty odd summers – the same in years as he appeared to be – and then to me. Tears brimmed his eyes. "Some say ye be a Master

Druid, a Sorcerer of the Old Ways. Some say ye be a wizard that practices the arts of magic. Some even say ye be a priest of the new religion of the Christ," he said as he looked at my Druid staff, his eyes narrowing to see the spear blade within, I was sure. "But use the truth of Druids to wield great power. I care not what ye be. Do for my wife what ye did for Tremel. Please, my lord." His hold on his emotions broke. The man began sobbing as an infant. Two other men and Nimue jumped to their feet to steady the man, Nimue holding the woman, as the sobbing man nearly crumpled to his knees.

My heart and spirit went out to the couple and I motioned for Nimue to gently lay the woman down.

Darkness had long since descended by the time I finished treating those on the plateau. With each ailing survivor that I treated, the next healed even faster. It was a testament to the fact that their belief in the success of the treatment—whether they called it magic or not—was helping to dispel the glamour and heal them properly; as much, if not more than anything I was doing. Spirits had been raised; some even ventured forth to find kindling and wood to create a fire in the cold pit. Two of the men even brought back fresh water and venison – a feast compared to the paltry diet of roots and nuts they had been subsisting on for over half-a-moon's cycle. I was leery of starting a fire in the pit; didn't want to give away our position. But Baldua pointed out that there were only two ways to get to the top of this plateau: the way we had come and an even narrower passageway on the opposite end of the plateau.

"Two men could defend this place if need be," Baldua said. "Come, Myrriddin. We've all been through much and we've all been healed, including yourself. A decent meal and a warm fire is not too much for tonight."

I found myself reaching beneath my tunic to feel my own wounds. Each area where the arrows had penetrated was naught but a puckered scar; otherwise completely healed. They had not been so upon leaving the Bishop's camp. The only explanation that came to me was that the aid I had performed on the others had been instantly returned to me many fold.

"Praeterea, mihi amice(Besides, my friend), it's clear we've not been pursued," Baldua continued.

"Yes, but why not? is the question. And we still don't know why Father Pretorius was at the Bishop's camp," I said.

"You did not find out from Moscastan?"

"He alluded to something, but wouldn't complete the thought," I replied.

"Odd that. That Pretorius was there is what I mean."

"Odd too, that Bishop Rozinus did not pursue us once he saw I'd gone. He wants the spear, you know," I pointed out, needlessly.

Baldua smiled. "What spear? I see naught but a Druid's staff!"

"Yes, well, the Bishop will see through that," I said.

We stood in relative silence for a moment. Laughter came from nearby, near the fire pit which was joyously being prepared for night's fire.

"Your point is taken, Myrriddin. I'll post a man at both access points and a lookout on the walls," he stated matter-of-factly, authoritatively.

I looked at my friend quizzically. I had never seen him so serious, so commanding, so . . . grown up.

"Agh, now, Myrriddin! Why do you look at me so? These good folks have looked to me and Moscastan since that night. Moscastan began to take on their ailments of the glamour and they looked to me for leadership. I can do it. I'm not just yer jester, don't ya know!" he finished, passionately.

"I know," I said after a moment. "I'd not be your friend if I saw naught more to you then a Latin-speaking jester," I replied sincerely.

I smelled smoke then and heard laughter from near the fire.

"Bring the meat!" said one of the men.

"Ney, let the fire burn hot first," replied another.

Both Baldua and I watched those near the fire pit ready for a meal. They appeared happy, celebratory. "I've not the heart to make three of them take watch. I'll take one," said Baldua.

"Show me the other path to this place and I'll take watch there," I said.

"No, Myrriddin. You've done enough for one day. Besides, they'll want you near. You're their . . . guide now—their spirit leader and healer – their shaman and, dare I say, their Merlin," my friend said.

"And what of Moscastan?" I asked. "And Pretorius?"

"Moscastan is *your* Mentor. He helped keep the glamour from destroying them. You took it away and healed them. Pretorius? He's become a mystery, has he not?"

Moscastan. I suddenly realized I'd not seen him since being in his shelter many hours earlier in the afternoon. "Excuse me, my friend," I said and headed for my mentor's shelter.

I crossed the short distance to the other side of the plateau, passing the fire pit on the way, which now contained a brilliant blaze.

"Hail to thee, Master Merlin! We be in yer debt forever!" called the man from earlier, whose comely wife now beamed with life and health by his side.

"Indeed!" she said in a sweet voice, tears of joy brimming her eyes. She let go of her husband as I neared and dropped to her knees before me, stopping me in my tracks. She grabbed my free hand and kissed it. "Thank you, Lord Merlin, thank you," she said through her tears.

Of all the things I could say to her, I was about to correct her on my name; *Myrridin, not Merlin*, I wanted to say. But I did not. How trivial, it seemed. Myrriddin or Merlin. It, they, meant the same. "Rise," I said to her, pulling her to her feet. "You are welcome. But do not forget that you are whole again because you allowed yourself to believe you could be so," I said.

She looked confused. "I was aware of what you were doing," she said, "but . . . I . . . " she trailed off.

"Just trust that it is so," I replied.

She stood on her toes, kissed my cheek and ran back to her husband.

I smiled to myself and walked the rest of the way to see Moscastan. Three feet before his shelter, the staff in my hand began to vibrate softly, the spear's blade and Druid's Egg within, to glow softly in warning. I sensed that it was not a warning of impending hostility, though, but of something much more solemn. I didn't understand it just then. I approached the shelter's entrance and stopped before it. "Master Moscastan?" I said softly.

There was no reply.

Slowly, I poked my head in. He was lying down on a mat of straw, sleeping.

"I'll come back," I whispered, suddenly feeling foolish for saying something out loud to someone asleep. I was about to duck my head back out when the staff's subtle vibrations became more pronounced, more insistent. The Druid Egg and blade began to glow a soft, soothing white. It was then that I saw it: a misty, ethereal form floating just above Moscastan. I entered the dwelling and stood before my mentor, and the smoky substance began to take shape. Within a moment, it was in the form of a man, one that I knew—Moscastan. He, the ethereal Moscastan, floating above the physical one, appeared as aged as his counterpart on the mat. But the floating form began to change, becoming younger in appearance by the moment. Next, his face changed entirely. It changed to that of a stranger to me in this life, but one to whom I'd been close in another. This new/old face smiled at me and I recognized the toothless grin deep in my soul. "Jacobi," I said.

The form before me smiled even broader. The face then changed back to Moscastan – a young Moscastan. He looked at the aged form lying on the mat, then back to me and I understood; his mind speaking to my mind, not in words but in thought, understanding. It is simple to do, this conversing mind-to-mind, I now realized. "There is only the One Mind in which ours reside and are thus not separate, but connect points within the One Mind," Moscastan had once said. I now completely understood what he had meant. I also understood what was happening here in the dwelling. I looked down at his aged body on the mat, to his now craggy face. He had been much older than I'd ever known. Moscastan did not rest on the mat in sleep. He rested on the mat in death. And, his spirit was making the transition to the Otherworld. I suddenly found myself dropping to my knees, sad but honored to be witnessing this . . . event. I felt a tear roll down my cheek as I looked up at his still floating spirit. He smiled a sweet and loving smile and inclined his head toward me.

The white light from the staff suddenly brightened the entire inside of the dwelling. It became so bright that it was blinding and I had to cover my eyes. Immediately, I sensed that a doorway, a portal to the Otherworld was opening. My mind and spirit took over, aiding in thought and spirit to shoring up the portal. Connecting to the spear, my staff, I also asked for aid in this from those I sensed nearby on the Otherside. They abided and after a moment, I heard Moscastan's thoughts – in words this time—in my mind. "It is done, Myrriddin. Farewell," he said.

In an instant, I sensed the portal close and the white light dissipate. I opened my eyes. The ethereal spirit of Moscastan was gone. All was still in the dwelling, especially the now empty vassal of my mentor lying on the mat.

I sat in the shelter for quite some time, partly out of respect for my mentor; partly because of the sacredness of what I had witnessed. I felt no heaviness at Moscastan's transition to the Otherworld. A small bit of sadness, perhaps. I loved the presence of my mentor. More than his presence. The truth of it was that I loved him. Yet, he was not *gone* in the sense of a cessation of existence. I knew that for certain. Thus, I would be able to converse with him, feel his presence, his essence at any time. It would start in my imagination. Some may say it ends there, too. I pity those that do not know themselves and the nature of the Universe. Imagination is simply the mental imaging of Truth. I *see* Moscastan in my mind's eye and he is with me in truth, becomes himself to me again because it is him, his essence peeking back into this realm.

"Myrriddin? Moscastan? Is all well?" whispered Nimue from just out side the shelter.

"Aye. 'Tis well now," I replied. I leaned forward and kissed Moscastan's brow, stood and exited the shelter.

Nimue stood a few feet from the shelter silhouetted against the fire in the pit a few yards away and the light of a nearly full moon overhead. "We were beginning to wonder if something was amiss. You've been in there near four hours and . . . " She stopped speaking and stepped forward toward me. Though her face was still partly in shadow, I could see enough of its loveliness to tell that she was surprised by something; something she was seeing in me, for she stared directly into my eyes. She scanned my face and body. "Myrriddin," she said almost breathlessly. "There is a light that emanates from you."

I held up my free hand and saw a faint white glow surrounding it. In fact, the light was around my entire arm. It also surrounded my lower body and all parts I could see, including my staff. The blade and Druid Egg within also glowed with the white light. "So it seems," I finally said.

"What does it mean?" asked Nimue, with a touch of reverence, even awe.

"It means that Moscastan has begun his next life. It means that I aided in the opening of the portal and the perpetuation of his journey to the Otherworld. And, it means that I was truly blessed and honored to have witnessed his stepping through the veil," I said, as I felt a tear of joy mixed with sorrow slide down my cheek.

Nimue stood in front of me for a moment. Her eyes were narrowed in concentration, turning over what I had just said. Her eyes then widened in realization of what I was implying. "I thought," she began . . . "I thought that perhaps you and he were in meditation—that maybe you meant he was journeying out of his body to *visit* the Otherworld. But . . . you are saying that he's dead?"

"I am *not* saying that. But if that's how you wish to understand it, then you may speak of it so," I replied.

"Speak of what so, Myrriddin?" said my friend, Baldua. He approached from behind Nimue and came to a stop next to her. His eyes looked strangely at me. "Myrriddin, there's a light coming from you!"

"I know, Baldua."

"Your Master Moscastan has di—that is, he's left this world for the Other," she said to my friend.

It took a moment for what she was saying to come to my friend's mind. "Myrriddin. Is it true?"

"It is."

"Agh. I'm so sorry. I loved him, too, but I know how close you two had been over the years. Like father and son, yes? Though I'm not too surprised, you know. He had taken on so much since arriving here. He took on everyone's glamour, or at least as much as he could. No wonder it finally got the better of him. Still, when you got here, you and the spear, I mean your staff there," he said pointing to it in my hand, "I knew we'd all be fine and I really thought that Moscastan would be too, you know. No reason for him . . . "

"Would you clamp it shut, Baldua!" said Nimue. Turning to me she asked sweetly, "What can we do, Myrriddin?" I could have kissed her just then.

"What are you talking about, Nimue? He's dead, gone. What is there to be done?" Baldua asked contemptuously.

Nimue looked at my friend with daggers coming forth from her eyes. Upon seeing the look, Baldua's eyes grew wide with fear and he actually took a step back. It was all I could do not to laugh. "You cannot be that stupid, that lame, that numb in the brain. No, no! Perhaps you really can be. I was asking what we could do for *Myrriddin*, idiot!" Nimue spat.

"I am fine," I declared, taking the attention and wrath off of my friend. "I should like to cremate Master Druid Moscastan's remains in the way of our people, in the way of the Druids. However, I don't think we should do it here. I would like to say a few more incantations and prayers of blessing the spirit, though, before I wrap his body."

"Maybe the Priest can help. They were friends, were they not?" asked Baldua.

"What say you, Baldua?" I asked, the white light around my body suddenly dissipating. At the same instant, the staff began to vibrate in my hand and an uneasy feeling washed over me.

"Father Pretorius. He's at the fire pit. He just arrived."

"Just arrived? I thought you posted guards," I said more harshly than I intended.

"I did, Myrriddin. Why do you question me thus? The priest is known, was a friend to Moscastan. The guards let him through," Baldua answered, clearly offended at my tone.

I put up a hand, palm facing my friend in a gesture of apology. "Has he said why he was in the Bishop's camp?" I asked, calmly.

"Ney. As I said, he just arrived. He simply asked for you and Moscastan," Baldua replied.

I made to step around Nimue and Baldua; to immediately go to the fire pit.

"Wait!" cried Baldua.

I stopped and turned to my friend.

Baldua pointed to the shelter. "You can't leave the dead in there," he declared nervously.

"Why?" I asked. "Do you fear he'll walk away?" I turned again and resumed my short trek to the fire pit, stifling a small laugh at my friend's obvious discomfort over leaving Moscastan's remains for the moment.

I could smell the roasted meat as I approached the fire. The people had obviously cooked most of the venison hours earlier, but more was roasting on the spit. My mouth watered. I realized I could not remember when I'd eaten last. My stomach growled. I was famished. Yet my body's needs would have to wait. Everyone around the fire pit was standing, listening to Father Pretorius and another man. The other man was Tremel.

"Here, now. Myrriddin! See who's returned," said Tremel as I approached. He turned back to the priest. "Not seen him since that night," he said to Pretorius, clearly referring to the night of All Hallow's Eve.

"Come to think of it, I don't recall seeing you that night at all, Father," I said, as several folks stepped aside so that I could come to stand before the two men.

"Myrriddin, my son. 'Tis good to see you," Pretorius said with affection, ignoring my last comment. I searched his face, looking into his eyes for any sign of what Moscastan had alluded to. All I could see, at least for the moment, was a sincere man of the Church.

He stepped forward and embraced me as a long-lost family member. I returned his embrace as far as courtesy dictated, patting him on the back with my free hand. We parted from our embrace and stood at arm's length from one another, Father Pretorius eying my Druid's staff ever so subtly.

"You look and sound well, Myrriddin," he said.

"I am," I responded.

"The good folks have been telling me of your blessed work here. You're an Angel in Druid's garb, lad," Pretorius said.

I am a Druid, Father," I said, haughtily.

"Indeed, indeed. A true Merlin, I know. You may call it what you will, but it is God working through you and your instrument said Pretorius, pointing at my staff.

"And through Moscastan," Tremel added.

"Yes, yes!" said Pretorius. "Where is my friend?!" Pretorius said this last part with such genuine love, that, for the moment at least, I brushed aside any concerns Moscastan may have harbored about him.

"He . . . he . . . " I found myself stuttering as Igraines might do, all eyes present suddenly boring into me. Perhaps I was conveying the impending news with my tone of voice or a look in my eyes. But everyone present seemed to suddenly have the posture and bearing of one about to receive a blow. "He, Master Moscastan, is no longer here. He has left his body and crossed over to the Otherside," I said.

Several of those present gasped loudly in shock. Father Pretorius looked sadly at me for a moment. Then, to my surprise, he dropped to his knees. Many others followed his lead, going to their knees as well. "Come, Myrriddin. Please join me in prayer," the priest said.

I looked at all present. Roughly half had taken to one knee or both. Baldua and Nimue had rejoined the group, standing near and behind me.

"Come, Myrriddin," Pretorius said again. "In the end, we will honor him in any way you see fit. But please allow me to, and join with me in, honoring him in my way for now. He would have liked this, I believe."

Would he? I wondered. *In the end, he suspected you of something, he did.* "Yes, Father," I found myself saying, "I believe you are right." I took a knee myself and looked back at Nimue and Baldua. They also dropped to a knee, as did the remainder of those who stood.

"Requiem aeternam donna ei, Domine; et . . . " Father Pretorius began his prayer in Latin. *Baldua must be loving this*, I thought.

We knelt in prayer for a few moments. Afterwards, several of the people came to me offering condolences, some even in tears. Tremel was one of them.

"Pretorius I've known for some time. Moscastan not as long at all," Tremel began through now controlled emotion. "But I knew his soul. I could tell, knew him for many lifetimes." He paused and turned to the priest. "Sorry, Father. Much of the old ways still live in me."

Pretorius simply smiled and waved a hand. *No apology necessary*, he seemed to be saying.

"Thank you, Tremel," I said.

"How did he pass, Myrriddin?" Pretorius asked.

"Peacefully," I replied. "He had assumed much of the evil that had been placed on these folks by Creconius," I stated flatly, looking directly into Pretorius' eyes for any sign of . . . For a brief instant, I could swear a veil behind those eyes dropped and went back up. In that same moment, the staff vibrated in my hand. Both things could have simply been tricks of my mind. But my intuition said otherwise.

"Yes. Taking the sins of another can be dangerous. It is a loving, Godly gesture, but fraught with danger," said Pretorius.

"What sins? I've not heard you talk of sins before. What so-called sins these people had were thrust upon them by another!" I was practically yelling at him.

"Myrriddin," Nimue said, as she touched my arm to calm me.

"That is all I meant, my son," said Pretorius.

An awkward silence filled the space for a moment.

"If you'll allow me, I would be honored if I could prepare his body with you," Pretorius continued. "I assume you wish him cremated in the way of your Druids."

"Yes," I said, "to both points. Come," I turned and headed to Moscastan's shelter.

NINETEEN

We cremated Moscastan's remains at dawn. We did not use the fire pit, but instead built a pyre not far from it. The burning of his corpse took the better part of the day. What bones remained, I would take with me, I decided. I would inter them in the perfect place: the Crystal Sanctuary. Many prayers were said through the day. Many condolences offered. The people had come to know my mentor and to love him.

Pretorius had insisted that it would be safe to hold the cremation there on the plateau. He had been in Bishop Rozinus' camp to secure my freedom, or so he claimed. When the Bishop discovered I had escaped – with the spear – he had, of course, insisted on giving chase. Pretorius pointed the good Bishop and his men in the wrong direction. He had evidently witnessed our escape as we headed into the forest. He'd lied to protect us: myself and those on the plateau. "'Twas a lie for the greater good and God has already forgiven me," the priest had said. The Bishop broke camp and left. I had no doubt that once his scouts confirmed there was no trail of us in the direction they were told, they would double back to find our real trail.

Pretorius' story was quite plausible. Others who were within earshot of hearing it praised Pretorius as a brave hero. I, however, had my doubts. His story did not explain where he had been for the fortnight-plus since the night of the Rite. When I asked, he dismissively said, "Why, I was there in or near the Bishop's camp. You were too injured to recall, Myrriddin." I mulled over in my head what Moscastan had said, which, in the end, was not very substantial.

That night, after Moscastan's cremation, we all communed over an evening meal. It was decided that come the following morning's light, we would leave our plateau and each head for his or her respective home. I'd not had the chance to talk to Nimue alone. The thought of parting ways with her was weighing heavily on me. I wanted to go to the Crystal Sanctuary and lay to rest the bones of my mentor, but was unsure if Nimue would go with her father to their home or come with me, were I to dare ask.

Tremel, Pretorius and several others had retired to a far end of the plateau for the night, away from the fire pit which still contained a small blaze within. Baldua, Nimue and I sat alone near the pit. I was about to ask Nimue to walk with me so that I might discern her plans when Baldua spoke with whispered urgency. "The priest Pretorius wishes to come with us, Myrriddin. He wants to see your cave of crystals." There was an edge to my friend's voice that disturbed me.

"Why?" I asked. "Why would he?" I thought for a moment.

"Obviously, he and Moscastan were close. I could see that when they both held vespers with Tremel," Nimue put in, as if it were plain to see.

"Perhaps, but I think there's more to it," I said.

"What?" asked Baldua.

"I know you don't like these men of Christ, Baldua," interjected Nimue, "but this one is open to our Old Ways unlike most of the others I've met."

"Is he? Is he really? Or is it all an act, a ruse? Is he even of the followers of Christ?" I said.

"Yes, he's a man of the Christ and yes, he's open to our ways," Nimue said defensively. "He was at the rite of All Hallow's Eve, was he not?"

"I never saw him," I countered. "Did you?"

She thought for a moment. "No, but he had to have been. He came with you, after all."

I turned to Baldua. "Did you?"

My friend shook his head indicating that he had not. "What are you saying, Myrriddin?" Baldua whispered conspiratorially.

It all struck me then exactly what Moscastan had been implying. I supposed I'd realized it when Moscastan said the words, but somewhere in my mind, deemed it impossible. Not anymore. I told them what my mentor had said in the shelter after telling him of the glam we'd witnessed at Rozinus' camp: how Creconius' glamour dropped and the Sorceress Mab stood before us, attempting to wield the sacred sword forged at the lake whose powers had been sealed into the weapon by her own sister. I then told them of the line of questioning Moscastan had convened upon me and its implication.

Baldua and Nimue sat in stunned silence for a moment.

"Impossible, Myrriddin!" Baldua finally blurted out. "Impossible!"

"And why?" asked Nimue.

"Yes, why? Why would he or she appear as an enemy's leader on a battle filed, then capture me, have his men do unspeakable things to me, then appear to you as a priest, even helping to bury the dead in the Christian way? Not to mention visiting Nimue's people here on numerous occasions as that same priest. It makes no sense! Don't you think I'd be able to look into those eyes of the priest and see the evil one behind them; the one who did those things to me?" Baldua's passion was laced with intense anger. He obviously had not completely released the tragic events that had befallen him, nor forgiven the one responsible.

"No," I said simply, gently. "That is the whole purpose of a glamour – to deceive the perceiver of a reality by creating a false one. A master at it will leave no doubt in your mind as to the truth of what you're seeing, even though it's not the truth at all. You saw Moscastan's dead face. He was in truth decades older at his death than he ever appeared to us in life every day. Death dropped his glamour of youth for good," I said.

"Yes, but we always knew it was Moscastan," he retorted. "This, what you're saying about Creconius and Pretorius, it's not possible."

"Nothing is impossible within the One. No application of Its Laws is out of bounds for someone who knows how to use them. No matter how twisted and disturbing you may think the application is, there is no judgment within the One. Its laws know only to respond," I concluded.

After a moment, Baldua rose. "No. It's not possible. I concede that you know more of these matters than ever I'll understand, Myrriddin. But this is too much," he said, leaving Nimue and me alone by the fire.

And you, Nimue?" I asked.

"My head holds with Baldua's argument. But my heart holds with what you say, Myrriddin. I've always thought Pretorius was a good man. He visited us often, never really pressuring Tremel or our people to follow his Christ," she said. "But I always sensed something else there, some other reason for him to take interest in us."

"What will you do tomorrow, Nimue?" I asked, completely changing the subject.

"Do?" she asked, confused.

"I . . . will you go with Tremel?" I asked, feeling sheepish.

She laughed. A sweet laugh, but indiscernible. "Why, Myrriddin?"

I felt myself squirm with discomfort on the inside. On the outside, though, I remained rigid, giving nothing away; nothing of my inner discomfort.

"Well, Master Myrriddin," she began, "I'm not sure I want to be married to a powerful Merlin."

Married! I thought. I'd said nothing of marriage.

"Although I would like to see your home, this Crystal Sanctuary," she said, straight of face so that I could not tell how serious she was.

"It's Moscastan's Crystal Sancturary, not mine," I said lamely.

"It is yours now, Myrriddin, and you know it," she stated flatly.

"Marriage," I said under my breath.

"Please, Myrriddin. I'm teasing you," she said. She then placed a hand on my hand, the one that was resting on my staff. "I go with Tremel. He will want to be with our people at least for a time. Then, perhaps in the spring, if you wish it still, I will come to you."

"And how will you know if I wish it still?" I asked.

She smiled seductively and leaned in toward my face. "You are the Great Merlin. Come to me in my dreams and tell me." She kissed me then, passionately. I returned her kiss equally. We embraced as our mouths continued to explore one another's, promising a future—a tender, yet solid time of oneness. I lost track of time as we slipped into the shadow of the plateau and quietly, feverently made love.

At our parting the next morning, Tremel's people treated me with the deference and respect of a High Druid and Priest, bowing low before me. Two women even tried to kiss my feet, groveling on the ground in front of me. I would have none of it. "Please," I said as I bent down to them, helping each in turn to her feet. "I can't abide being worshipped," I said.

"You are a great Merlin and are due the respect of one so connected with the gods," said one of them: a thin, wide-eyed, toothless lady of perhaps forty summers.

"Aye, or God himself," said the other woman, a doe-eyed, younger version of the first. "My mother sees through the eyes of the Old Ways, I through those of the New, True Path," she added. "You are God's servant."

"Indeed," I replied.

"We are all servants of the One," Pretorius said. He stood behind me, along with Baldua. The two women bowed their heads and retreated back to Tremel, who stood a few feet away with some others, including Nimue. I caught Nimue's eye. She smiled radiantly. We had said our farewells the previous night, but it was not goodbye. I knew in my heart, my soul, that we would not only see each other again, but be together in a more profound and permanent sense.

Baldua, Pretorius and I had hastily made—one for each of us and with the help of Nimue and a few others—a small pack from skins and woven plants in which to carry cooked venison for our journey. I had made mine slightly larger to also carry Moscastan's wrapped bones, which included his charred skull. I considered the carrying of his bones to rest in the Crystal Sanctuary a pilgrimage.

Just before we set out, I felt the staff vibrate in my hand. I realized instantly what it meant; the way we were to go. It began to pull, more of its own accord, pointing toward a specific region of the forest nearby. I asked Tremel and he confirmed what the staff was conveying. "Yes, yes!" he declared excitedly, as he watched the staff point the way. "It speaks true! You will recognize the way once you're on the other side of the forest. I know Pretorius will."

And so we parted, leaving the safety of the plateau – Tremel, Nimue and the remainder of their people going off in one direction; Baldua, Pretorius, I and the remainder of my mentor's bones going off in another.

We had been traveling down a path, walking a slow pace through the dark forest for some eight hours. The staff had been silent and still since we had entered the forest, which I interpreted as a sign that we were at least going in the right direction. But I had yet to recognize any part of the forest as being from our initial journey to the place of the All Hallow's Eve rite or my flight from Bishop Rozinus' camp. Pretorius had been leading the way when the path we were on came to a fork. He went down the left fork without even breaking stride. Though Pretorius could not see it, the staff began to vibrate the moment I set foot on the path that went left. I stopped immediately. "Wait," I said. Baldua stopped alongside me. Pretorius stopped as well, though he was some fifteen feet ahead of us on this new path. "I don't think this is the way," I declared.

"Come, Myrriddin," exclaimed Pretorius. "Do you not see the burned out crooked oak there?" he said, pointing to a huge oak up and off the path. The large tree's trunk was bent at about four feet off the ground and much of the remainder of it had grown parallel to the ground for some twenty-five yards before bending skyward again. It obviously had been there for decades if not centuries, such was its girth, length and proliferation of branches. Yet, its branches were now barren, its core-body split and blackened and charred from an ancient lightening strike by the look of it. Though its surroundings were plush with life, the tree was dead. Long dead. The sight of it made me sad, for it clearly had been something majestic to behold when alive. This feeling also made me realize that I certainly would have remembered seeing this tree previously, which was obviously what Pretorius was implying by pointing it out. Baldua and I exchanged a look. I cocked an eyebrow, silently questioning him. He shook his head and turned back to Pretorius.

"I have never seen that, beate pater (my good Father)," said Baldua, the latter part in Latin.

"Nor have I," I said. "I would have remembered it."

"Agh. No matter. I do. Follow me, lads," the priest said, as he started down the path once more.

It began as a warmth, as if I held a pole that had been placed in proximity to a blazing hearth, but not in the fire itself. It rapidly changed, though, becoming so hot that I nearly let go of it—my staff.

"Wait!" I called to Pretorius. He was already some ten feet farther down the path. He halted and walked slowly back toward us, stopping directly in front of me. For a brief instant, an uncharacteristic gleam of anger flashed in his eyes.

Before I could respond to Pretorius, however, my staff's Druid Egg began to glow, pulsating on one side only. Intuitively, I knew what it meant, for the side it glowed on was nearest the other path, the other fork in the trail we had been on. The heat of the staff became more intense and the staff began to pull me toward the other path. As I walked in that direction, the heat and the glow lessened the closer I got to the other path. Upon setting my foot on that path, the glow and heat ceased altogether.

Baldua came up behind me, Pretorius behind him. "*This* is the correct path," I declared.

Baldua turned to Pretorius. "So much for your crooked tree, Priest," he said.

Pretorius said nothing, but looked from my staff, the spear, to me.

"You can go where you will, Father," Baldua continued. "Myrriddin and I go down *this* path." He pushed past me and walked down the new path.

I stared at Pretorius for a moment. There had been a shift in his persona these past days. But I still could not fully tell what it was, which either meant that I was wrong or that he was hiding it well. I would stay vigilant and observe. For the moment, however, I followed my friend down this new path. An instant later, I heard Pretorius' footfalls behind me. He had decided to stay with us, after all.

Darkness came early. We did not make it through the forest that day as I had hoped we would. I even began to doubt the path we were on. But the spear had pulsated often, and in a beautiful green hue, conveying the fact that we were indeed on the right path, or so my intuition told me. So, I put my momentary doubts aside. What did it matter if we were not through the forest in one day?

"We need to make camp. It's too dark for trudging any farther," said Pretorius. "We might have been through by now, but such is not the way of it."

I could not tell if his comment was a slight on me or if he actually believed the other path was the one we should have taken and was simply voicing a perceived fact. I chose, for the moment, the latter, but made remembrance of the former. It would be yet another indication of his shift in persona if true. Pretorius was not one to reprimand – at least not the Pretorius I thought I knew. Perhaps I was *looking* for signs from the priest of what Moscastan had suspected. The problem with looking for signs is that we often end up seeing what we wish, regardless of what's actually there. "Pretorius is right, Myrriddin," put in Baldua.

"Yes," I agreed. A thin group of trees was off the path to our right. Odd that, for the forest to this point had been immensely thick with all kinds of oak, saplings and rowans in extreme proximity. Each tree in this thin group of trees had many feet between them, and, in fact, were spaced in apparent perfect symmetry from each other, in a circle shape. The trees in this group, some twenty odd, seemed to have grown stunted—most only fifteen feet or so high—and with branches stripped of most of their leafy foliage. Looking up, I could see that the higher branches of the taller trees which surrounded this smaller group had grown over the tops of the small group, creating a canopy, a roof over the grouping of trees. We stopped on the path, Pretorius and Baldua halting next to me on either side. I stared at the small, thin group of trees, debating with myself as to whether we should make camp in their presence. And then it came to me as to what I was looking at. At the same moment of my realization, the staff vibrated in my hand and the Druid Egg glowed bright green. And then an amazing thing happened: the ring of small trees—for that is what it was, a ring of trees, I saw that now—began to glow the same hue of green as the Druid egg, as if in empathetic harmony with my staff, my spear and the attached Druid Egg.

"Diis! (By the gods!)" exclaimed Baldua. It was a beautiful sight; the ring of trees glowed as if . . . as if . . . *Of course*! I thought. I had realized a moment before that this was a naturally formed – more or less – temple ring of standing mono-liths, like the standing stones built across the land and the one that Moscastan had brought me back to life in. This one, this Henge, however, was made of wood, of living trees. But more than that, I suddenly realized the singular power in this place: it was a portal, perhaps a focal point, for the divine energy of the Universe. I was enthralled with the prospect of spending the night in this place.

"We can't stay here, Myrriddin," said Pretorius, contemptuously. "Surely, we cannot, if you were thinking of it, that is."

Pretorius was standing on my left. When I turned to look at him, I was fac-ing away from the forest Henge. But in the darkening forest, the glow was visible in the eyes of the priest, reflecting therein. The reflected glow in his eyes helped to reveal something. There, behind Pretorius' eyes, hiding, was an Otherworldy malevolent rage. Pretorius was indeed the priest I had known for a time, but he was apparently more than that now. I cold see it, sense it. It was not that Pretorius was someone other than whom I knew, or Moscastan had known; it was that someone or something else was in his being, as well. This other *thing* looked out at me and suddenly, the staff in my hand grew hot as if also sensing the malevolence within the priest. As if knowing I could see it, the thing within Pretorius suddenly retreated. I could see it, sense it no more. The staff in my hand stilled and cooled, and the glow thereon dimmed. So, too, did the glow of the Henge.

"We will stay here tonight, Father Pretorius," I said gently. "There is nothing harmful here, save for a few creatures of the forest."

Pretorius inclined his head in acquiescence, all of his contemptuousness gone. "As you wish," he said.

"Here, now," said Baldua, "Have I no say?"

"*You* just said that we should stop and make camp, did you not?" I pointed out.

"Yes, yes I did," he said. Baldua looked at the Henge off the path. "Bonum est ('Tis good). This spot will do nicely," he declared with dramatic flair.

"Thank you. I'm glad you approve," I said, patting my friend on the shoulder as I moved past him toward the Henge.

It took us a few moments to find a suitable spot on which to settle; far enough off the path for us to be away from possible prying eyes, yet not so far away that we couldn't see the path. Though the Henge we all saw was directly off the trail, there were actually two more of the same dimensions farther in off the path just beyond the first one. It was in the center of the third one that we chose to stay the night.

"I see need of a fire. 'Tis a bit brisk tonight," said Pretorius. His demeanor was odd; nervousness seeped through his words.

"If Bishop Rozinus' men are about . . . " I started.

"I doubt that very much, Myrriddin," he said with a little more authority; even too much.

Still, there was indeed a chill in the air. "Of course," I said.

"I'll get some kindling," offered Baldua.

"Ney, lad. I will." With that, Pretorius left hastily.

"He's become a strange one at times," observed Baldua.

"You don't know the half of it," I said.

Baldua looked at me intently. "You're not on with that again, Myrriddin?"

"Aye. Only it's not what I thought."

"Good."

"It's worse," I said.

My friend sat on the ground heavily and drew a skin from his pack. He uncorked one end and drank a strong draught, satiating the days' travel with the water in the skin. I followed his lead, sitting next to him and withdrawing my own water skin. After a long pull of drink, we sat in silence for a moment, the sounds of small, nocturnal forest creatures coming to life around us.

"So tell me, Myrriddin, what is the priest about?" asked Baldua, smugly. "I don't hold with his condescending Christian ways, but he is not so bad. He's become a little strange at times, yes, but . . . " he trailed off.

"You're right," I began. "Pretorius the man is not a bad seed. I believe that. And, I also believe that he exemplifies his Christian beliefs truly and honorably, not like some of the other rules-ridden, power-devouring priests and leaders of his faith I've come across. But there is something else there, something else within him, using him."

"Ach," my friend said, disbelieving. "To what end?"

"To get the spear, most likely," I answered.

"I could think of a bushel of other ways to get the thing," he said.

The sounds of the night forest coming to life abruptly stopped. The ringing in my ears told of the utter silence that now engulfed us. Usually oblivious to such things, even Baldua noticed the change. He looked at me, questioning me with his eyes, thus echoing the preternatural quietude we were now in. The staff's Druid Egg and blade suddenly came to life, pulsating a vibrant red-green light.

"Prepare yourself," whispered a man's voice urgently. It came from the staff, the spear. "Prepare yourself."

Looking at Baldua, it was clear he had not heard the voice. It was meant for me.

The first scream came from the edge of the Henge we were in: the edge farthest from the path. It was an agonized, terror-filled female wail to freeze the blood. No sooner had that one died out, then another took its place. This one, however, seemed to come from even deeper in the forest and was clearly male, although it had the same desperate, horrified quality as the first. It subsided and the first voice screamed again, this time from a different location, some twenty feet closer to our position, though still in the tree line outside the Henge and thus its source remained unseen.

"Forest demons!" Baldua cried, jumping to his feet, brandishing from beneath his tunic a new-looking Roman gladius. It was obviously a souvenir he had kept from his borrowed legionnaire's uniform.

I too, rose to my feet, the staff in my hand, its Egg and spear's blade glowing more intensely by the moment. "Doubtful your short sword will do much good then," I said. "Against humans, maybe, but . . . "

My words were cut short by yet another scream coming from still another part of the forest. They seemed to be coming from everywhere, the screams. They were agitating Baldua, who spun toward the sound of each scream in turn apparently expecting to see some horrific sight, which was not to be seen.

I, on the other hand, became calmer with each scream. I felt myself ease into a confident centeredness wherein I could and would deal with anything that might come, and deal with it triumphantly.

"Show yourselves!" my friend yelled into the darkness.

"Peace, Baldua," I said calmly.

A red flash came from where the first scream had seemed to emanate. The flash came hurling toward us in the form of a ball of light, screaming a feral, Otherworldly sound of terror. Baldua and I both ducked as the thing swooshed violently through where we had both been standing, arching away and back into the forest. An instant later, another screaming, angry ball of red-light came flying at us. Each time, we ducked or rolled out of the way. Baldua, caught standing at the last assault, deflected the ball with the flat of his sword, sending it spinning violently out of control through nearby trees. It smashed into the trunk of a mighty oak, exploding on impact. I expected small fires to break out from all the sparks that the explosion had produced, but the sparks and remnants of the ball dissolved on the ground and in the trunk – where some had become embedded –

and disappeared entirely. With that, the assault halted, at least for the moment.

"Forest demons, I say again. They don't want us here. Maybe the priest was right," my friend said, more with anger than fear.

"I've never known you to believe in the likes of 'forest demons'", I pointed out, "let alone anything Pretorius had to say."

"Yes. Well, we all change, do we not?"

"You speak as if you're surrendering to that which you despise," I said.

"Sometimes surrender is the best option," countered Baldua.

"Surrendering your stubbornness, yes. But surrender at the sacrifice of your spirit is foolish. The latter is what I am hearing from you, my friend," I pointed.

Baldua stared at me for a moment. "I hardly think this is the moment for a Moscastan-like discourse on the advancement of one's spirit," he said.

"Moscastan-like or no, shouldn't every moment be an opportunity for learning?" I countered.

"Agh! By the gods, Merlin!"

I opened my mouth to speak, but Baldua was not through.

"I know, I know. *Myrriddin*. Not Merlin!"

"It matters not, Baldua," I said.

I then turned my attention back toward the origins of our attack. "'Tis not demons coming against us, trying to drive us out."

"Are you mad? They've thrown those . . . things at us from all over!" said Baldua, getting agitated once again and flailing his hand in the direction from whence the objects came.

"Trust me, my friend. It is not a handful of demons. It is but one individual and it is not just trying to drive us away, but to kill us," I said. I knew this to be so—in my very soul. The words from the spear came to me once again: "Prepare yourself." Indeed, I had never felt so prepared for anything as I did that moment, though I knew not exactly what was to come. All my training in the Druidic Arts; all my mentor's years of patient tutoring, and above all, the molding and connecting I now solidly felt to the Spear of Longinus, my Druid staff. All these things suddenly culminated in that moment within me. In that instant, my understanding and awareness of the All and my Self, my Spirit, transcended everything of this world. I truly knew what the Christ meant when he had said, "I am *in* this world, but not *of* this world," as I had been told by various followers of this Christ I'd met through the years. I also realized now that most of them did not fully understand the words; did not completely embody them.

"You see?" Baldua proclaimed nearly shouting and snapping me out of my moment of profundity. "You said 'it.' Is that not a demon, then?"

"Fine," I said. "She and he, if you prefer. Creconius Mab."

Then came a rumble. It started low. We could barely hear it. But we felt it beneath our feet; the earth shook. The shaking grew strong, knocking us both to the ground. The Druid Egg and spear blade grew fiery red. So bright did they become that I momentarily thought they would burst. They did not. But the mighty oak that the last ball of light had smashed into did burst. It rent asunder with such violence, such force, that its great trunk split in two, smoke and fire spewing forth. The crack and groan of timber splitting was deafening, and the booming crash of the two halves of the trunk hitting the ground shook the earth with one giant jolt. Then, all was still, save the tall figure standing in the middle of the split and now dead mighty oak.

TWENTY

"Who dares summon me?" demanded the loud, thunderous voice from the figure in the split tree: Creconius Mab in his imposing warrior form. He appeared much as he did the day I first saw him on the battle filed, save now, he was cloaked in an Otherwordly glow of red-menace.

"Shite. Him again," sighed Baldua.

"Merlin," said the figure, all but ignoring Baldua. "Your legend grows. As does the fable of your . . . wizard's staff."

"Druid's staff, is more the like," I said.

"The spear of Longinus is *more the like*," he countered. "That which pierced *His* side. Carries His power, much like this!" From the folds of his cloak, he withdrew the long sword he possessed that day in Bishop Rozinus' camp. It was magnificent, even more so this time than when first I saw it; the runes along the blade, the quality of the blade itself, the glow. It glowed green. As it did, the Druid Egg and blade of my staff, the spear of Longinus, began to glow green as well, changing from the angry red in a heartbeat. It, they, were glowing in harmony – the spear and extraordinary sword. For a moment, it had me in a trance state. The staff in my hand vibrated softly, bringing me back to the present. After a moment, the vibration ceased, but its green glow continued in harmony with the sword's. "You see? They belong together—the sword, the spear. Together, their owner would be invincible!" Creconius said, an evil glint in his eyes.

My mind began to see the truth of this moment, of what the figure before me was saying. "No one can *own* these instruments, Creconius Mab. They hold no power in themselves other than what we endow them with. One need only be in harmony with them, in mental equivalence of the desired effect. *You* do not have the proper mind to ever attune with the sword *or* the spear," I said, not quite knowing from whence the words came.

Something in what I said, however, hit this Sorcerer, (or Sorceress) hard. Anger seethed from his being, contorting his face in rigid rage.

"No one *summoned* you, Creconius Mab. No one cares that much," I said. "You came of your own accord. Now, be gone!" I yelled, glamming my voice with power beyond this world. I intoned the last word with a deep note, sustaining it with this power and thus releasing the power through it. The sound reverberated off all the trees that surrounded us, shaking their limbs. Even some of the clothes on our intruder's body jumped suddenly as if struck by a gale force. And, I saw, out of the corner of my eye, Baldua throw his hands up to his ears, so power-filled was the sound of my voice.

At the apex of the sustained sound, I raised the staff over my head. In my mind's eye, I saw a bolt of light shoot forth from the spear's blade and the Druid Egg. It was so intensely real that I felt its reality course through my entire being. Then it happened: it happened in actuality. A crisp and powerful bolt of the green light shot forth from the spear's blade and Druid Egg. The force of it nearly knocked me down. The bolt shot out and violently connected with the sword's blade, creating an arc of immense force and power.

It held fast, this arc. I held it with great intent in my mind at the exclusion of all else, and it was so in the real world. The sound of my voice faded to be replaced by the crackling and humming sound of an electrical charge in the air.

"Aghh!" yelled Creconius Mab, thus adding his voice to the sound of the charge. He agonized to break the arc, to break the hold. The effort was draining his being of vital energy, his very life spirit. Or, perhaps I should say *her*; for the glamour of Creconius, the warrior, began to drop. In a pulsating torrent of light and darkness, the true person was revealed beneath the façade: Mab. Finally, the glamour of the warrior faded completely; the arc too, the latter ceasing completely. A preternatural silence filled the forest. Next to me, Baldua rose to his feet.

The figure in the tree before us was a pitiful sight: a small, aged, haggard female figure who dropped the great sword's point into the ground and leaned on its still glowing hilt—which nearly came up to the top of her head—panting like a fatigued animal.

"Well done, Myrriddin!" exclaimed Baldua in a hushed voice.

"'Tis not over yet," I said, giving voice to the feeling of unease that had begun to crawl into my being.

Ignoring what I had just said, Baldua took a step toward the figure in the split tree. "We must take the sword!" he said, with childlike glee.

"No, Baldua!" But my warning was too late. With the speed of a coiled serpent, the crone Mab struck. The great sword came up in a burst of blinding red light, striking my friend broadside in the side of his chest – at least from what I could see. So bright was the moment of impact that for an instant, I covered my eyes. When I uncovered them, the bright light was gone. And, so was my friend. Baldua had disappeared.

A strange sound: a low-level cackle, a malevolent laugh, came from the ugly figure who now stood outside the split oak, near the spot where Baldua had been a moment earlier. Once again, she leaned on the still-glowing hilt of the great sword, whose tip was presently in the ground by some six inches. Except for the glow of the sword hilt, darkness surrounded me, and in more ways than one. The cackle sent chills through my body, but I quickly quashed the feeling, consciously replacing it with the intent of ending this absurd being's menace. I'd had enough. Baldua, my dearest friend was gone, presumably obliterated from the earth. Rage, mixed with the worst sorrow, began to rise within me.

"Be still, Myrriddin," said the voice of the spear. "Be still and know the Oneness of All. You can no more destroy the one before you than you can destroy yourself," It said.

"Sooo . . . " hissed Mab. "It speaks to you. Yes? I knew it. Your eyes betrayed you just now. It speaks to you, but you don't know its full potential or how to use it completely. Is that not so?"

"This . . . staff is a part of me, always has been. That's all you need to know," I said, flatly.

"Indeed, indeed. Which tells me volumes. The Spear of Longinus is meant for me! As was the rood, and that precious book and bowl that were so clumsily placed in that ancient Temple, which your friend so *willingly* led me to. These things hold power beyond mortal imaginings and I am the one to use them."

"You are mad, Creconius Mab. I say again: There is no power in these things but that which we endow them with."

"You lie! You hear the voice of the spear, the voice of Chr . . . of Chri . . . "

"You can't even speak it, can you?" I stated, nearly laughing. "I hear many things, Creconius Mab. Or should I call you . . . Draco?"

"Agh!" she screamed, as if the very name of Draco inflicted physical pain.

"I know it's you, Draco. Though it's been three centuries, Draco, it is you. I remember!" I said. Each time I spoke the name, Draco, Mab reacted as if being stabbed with a hot blade. I knew not why this was. Perhaps the name Draco conjured the true evil that was within Creconius Mab, reflecting it for her to see, to feel, without preamble. Whatever the reason, I cared not.

"Draco, Draco, Draco!" I chanted.

She mumbled something. It sounded like it was in Latin. For a moment, she repeated the same phrasing over and over, building in volume with each reciting.

I raised the staff, the spear, in anticipation. I was about to speak my own incantation, my own glamour, rather than wait in a defensive posture for what Mab was calling forth. But I wasn't quite fast enough.

Creconius Mab pulled the sword from the ground, pointed its sharp tip at my chest and yelled, "Id jubeo! (I command it!)"

The flutter of thousands upon thousands of wings came from within the forest, growing louder and louder by the moment. The winged creatures – whatever they were – were getting closer and closer. The trees surrounding the Henge began to shake. So, too, did the staff in my hand, the blade and crystal egg now emanating a pulsating green-red light. As one, they washed over us and the Henge like a large ocean wave, engulfing the entire area, crashing into trees and my body, knocking me to the ground in the process. Ravens. Tens of thousands of them, their cawing vocalizations all but drowned out by the deafening collective sound of their wings. I looked up from my position on the ground. Darkness pervaded now; such were their numbers. But I could see a few inches in front of my face. The ravens that now came close to me, to my face, did not crash into me, but pulled up briefly, flapping their wings and hovering in front of my face. A glazed sheen covered their eyes. They had been glammed, spelled no doubt by Creconius Mab. But after only an instant of hovering before me, these particular birds were then smashed into by their fellow ravens flying up behind them. They were thus absorbed back into the flocking hoard.

Even above the din of flapping wings and frantic cawing, I could hear Creconius Mab's cackle nearby, now madly hysterical. The initial wave of ravens had turned into a cloud, obscuring all. Though they fluttered and flapped in a frenetic cacophony so close to me that I huddled on the ground in a ball for protection, now none of them actually touched or attacked me. The initial battering I took was more likely a result of undirected headlong flight than a purposeful intent to knock me down.

"Id jubeo!" came Creconius Mab's now high-pitched command. It was laced with panic. Obviously, the birds were not performing as the crone wished. "Id jubeo!" she yelled again. This time, her voice was a shrill, out-of-control shriek.

Still huddled in a ball on the ground, I realized for the first time that my staff was no longer in my grasp. I groped around in the dirt surrounding me. Nothing. Now *I* began to panic. *Had the ravens lifted my staff, the spear? Are they even now taking it to the crone?!* I wondered. Anger quickly replaced the panic. "Draco!!" I yelled.

Then, in my mind, the din of the ravens, the cackle of Mab, receded in the distance. It was replaced by the voice, the voice of the spear; Jesus' voice. I knew it was His voice as surely as I knew I was present in my body. "Stand, Myrriddin. You need not rely on it, the spear. Just as I've told you in a past age, I am within you, because I am you. You know this, but are finally feeling it. That is the essence of True knowledge; the feeling of a Truth. Stand now, and cast out this evil in your midst," said the voice.

"I will destroy the evil Creconius Mab!" I replied in my mind.

"Ney, Myrriddin. That whom you call Creconius Mab is a fallen one, turned to the evil use of the One Law. You cannot destroy evil, only cast it from here. Balance is the nature of All," the voice of Jesus said. "Now, stand in the nakedness of your soul and cast the beast out."

The din around me came back to the fore. Still on the ground, I looked before me. It was not as dark as a moment ago. Light, a now very bright glow from the sword's hilt was illuminating the area. I stood and raised my hands. The ravens continued to swirl and dive and dart all around me, at an even more frenzied, chaotic pace than before. And, as with a moment before, none of them touched me; none swooped to attack me with their sharp talons and beaks. Another raven – or perhaps the same one as before; they all looked alike – suddenly stopped in mid-air in front of me, flapping its wings madly to keep aloft. In that instant, I knew what to do. Reaching out with my mind, my awareness, I entered the mind of the raven.

Its mind was simple. I could sense it, feel what it felt. It did not comprehend my presence in its mind. But what I found astonishing was the fact that this particular raven was but a pin-point, an individualized aspect of the collective mind of the frenzied horde of birds. There was something else there, too. I knew that this collective mind was being held together by this something else, this other presence, as surely as I could sense the evil of it. Creconius Mab. She was controlling the flock by controlling the individual minds as one.

From within this one individual raven's mind, I expanded my awareness farther and farther into the collective mind of the flock of birds by bird. I felt Mab's aggravation as my consciousness seeped in farther and farther until I broke the hold she had on them. I saw in my mind's eye what Creconius Mab had tried to get the ravens to do to me. Without thinking, I reversed the image in *my* mind and made *her* the object of the ravens' madness. Instantly in the Henge, and almost as one, the thousands of ravens around me turned and attacked the figure near the split oak.

"Agh!! Ney, Merlin! Demons be upon thee! Agh!" she screamed as beaks and talons ripped through her flesh and bone. In addition to the fluttering chaos around her, many had landed on her person, gorging themselves on her living flesh, tearing bloody chunks from her body and carrying them off in flight. Another raven would land where one had just left to take its turn at the gruesome meal. Two birds suddenly went aloft from her face, each carrying one small white orb in their sharp beak. Mab would see no more.

Still screaming, she crumpled to the ground in a bloody heap, pieces of muscle and tissue missing. Finally, her screaming ceased as one of the ravens viciously ripped her tongue from her mouth with its beak. Then more of the flock descended upon her, covering her, obscuring her from sight.

Then, I released them from my mind. The birds left, scattering away through the trees. Most flew erratically as if they had been released from a cage and knew not which way to fly. Some did not leave, however; some stayed behind, and took their turn feasting on the corpse. I stepped toward them and flapped my hands, scattering them as well. "Thank you, my friends," I said to them as I watched them fly off.

"Humph," came the sound from the corpse, as air and body gases made a final escape. I looked down at the bloodied, pecked and gouged body. The great sword lay next to it, the hilt still aglow with a green-red hue. I could see by the glow of the sword's hilt, a mist, an ethereal mist, forming just above what remained of the face of Creconius Mab. The mist began to take form; a form which I remembered from a past age: pasty-white, nearly translucent skin, black hair and ice-blue eyes—Draco! The face then changed, becoming more familiar to me in the present – Creconius Mab, the warrior. It changed once more, this time becoming the face of Creconius Mab, the hag, the crone, the dark Sorceress. The words of the spear's voice, the voice of Jesus, echoed in my head. He was right. Evil is not destroyed. It but changes form and anger, rage, hatred and fear are its tools. For all those things I felt from this misty form too.

"Enough," I said. "Be gone from this place. I command it."

Nothing. It, the misty form did not move.

"I said, be gone!" I commanded again with a violent, dismissive wave of my hand, at the same time banishing the thing in my mind's eye. Slowly, the misty face, the ethereal form, dissipated and was gone.

The corpse on the ground was now truly empty. And, the sword next to it, its hilt now only glowed a soft green, a beautiful hue. I was utterly drawn to the weapon. As if in a glamour, I approached the sword and tenderly lifted it by the handle. I held the blade before my face and closely took in the details of the runes, the quality of the craftsmanship and the powers I knew they held. I also observed the metal of the blade. I had never seen anything like it; no metal could compare—its shine, its density and quality. I could tell that one would not be able to even lay a scratch on the blade; flatten or chip its sharp edge. It must have been forged of something from the Otherworld. Or, so I wanted to believe. It shined brighter than any blade I've beheld, but it also had a reflective quality beyond mere polish and buffing. In fact, no amount of polishing and buffing could be attributed to the high reflective aspect of the metal. It was mirror-like. I could see myself, my dirt-splotched face—unshaven for a moon or so by the look of it—staring back at me. So clear was my reflection, that it seemed I was looking into the highest quality glass mirror, not the blade of a sword.

"Magnificent," I said to it. "You are truly of the highest caliber, are you not? Highest ever."

The sword responded. Its green glow began to pulsate. From pommel to blade tip, it pulsated with light. And it sang. A medium pitched tone emanated from the blade as it vibrated. It sang and its light expanded. And it pulled me. Like my Druid staff, the Spear of Longinus would do, the sword began to pull me in a particular direction, away from the Henge and deeper into the forest. I went, knowing there was a greater purpose at work here.

I walked, with the sword's guidance, perhaps twenty-five yards into the forest when I saw and heard where it was leading me. There, leaning against a whole and hail mighty oak, as if someone had gently placed it there, was my Druid's staff!

Its Druid Egg and spear's blade on top were alight with the same pulsating glow as the sword. What's more, it sang too! The spear's blade vibrated, singing a tone which was two-steps higher in pitch than the sword. Thus, each instrument was in harmony with the other. My heart leapt with joy at the sight and sound. I stepped over to the tree and grasped my staff, feeling my face stretch into a broad smile.

"Heus (Here, now)," said a voice from above. "the way yer carrin' on, you'd think that hunk of wood and metal and such was your best friend!"

I looked up to the branches of the Oak and was astonished to see a battered but living Baldua sitting sprawl-legged over a large branch some twenty-feet off the ground.

"Baldua!" I yelled, my heart now completely bursting with euphoria. "I thought . . . I thought . . . " I stammered, unable to verbalize what I was thinking.

"That I was killed?" Baldua said, verbalizing it for me. "That sword there sent me sailing through the air with a bang when the hag hit me with it," my friend said, dubiously eying the weapon in my hand for a moment. "I lost consciousness on the way. Awoke on my perch here, I did," he continued, patting the branch on which he sat. "A few bruises and cuts. Coulda been a lot worse, I suppose,"

"Well, come down from there," I said.

"Don't you think I would have by now? Woke up just as you were scattering those black birds from the corpse. Did you do that, get the birds to attack, I mean? Of course you did. But how did you get all those black birds to attack Creconius Mab? That's who it is, right? Or, was. I . . . "

"Stop, Baldua. They were ravens and, and . . . " I began.

"I know!" he declared, as if he had just uncovered a great secret. "You used both the sword *and* the spear to weave the magic to control the birds!" Before I could respond, he started in again, this time more in a counter argument with himself than addressing me. "No, you couldn't have because the spear, I mean, your staff, was here against the tree. All right then, just the sword, eh?" he said, once again focusing on me.

"If you saw me scatter the birds from the corpse, then you saw me pick up the sword from the ground," I pointed out.

I could see by the look on his face that he was thinking about what I said. His eyes grew large, then. "What say you, Myrriddin?"

"I am not 'saying' anything, Baldua," I replied.

A sound wafted to us through the trees. It was faint, from off in the distance, perhaps, but definitely not a sound of the forest. Clanging metal was the sound.

Another sound began to seep in just underneath the clanging: yelling voices – many of them.

"Do you hear that, Myrriddin?!" exclaimed Baldua.

"I do." We both listened intently, discerning what the sounds meant.

"A battle," my friend concluded.

He was right.

TWENTY-ONE

I leaned my Druid staff against my chest to free the hand holding it. Still grasping the sword with the other, I now used both hands to guide the sword over my shoulder and through the straps of my satchel. I brought the sword point down, sliding it between my back and where the straps joined together between my shoulder blades. The place where the straps joined was, I hoped, small enough to catch the crossbar of the hilt, thus preventing the sword from sliding all the way through to the ground. It was. A crude scabbard for such a wonderful sword, but one of function.

"We must . . . " A loud scraping sound cut me short of what I was about to say. Suddenly, Baldua dropped at my feet, his back to me, arms and legs wrapped around the oak's large trunk – at least, they were wrapped around as far as he could reach, so large was the trunk. He then flopped on his back, his face contorting with pain. The underside of both his arms were bloodied with fresh scrapes and cuts from his descent down the tree trunk.

"You just said you couldn't get down from there," I said in mock reprehension.

"No, I didn't. I said that I would have. That's to say . . . well, I was asleep. Couldn't do it before waking up."

"That's not what you implied," I teased.

"That's not the same as saying I can't!" he said defensively.

"All right," I said, letting the matter rest. "'Twas painful, it appears, sliding down the tree that way."

His hands went to his groin. "You don't know the all of it."

The sounds of the battle became a little louder.

"Are they coming this way?" Baldua asked.

"I'm not sure," I said. I held the staff at arm's length, looking to it for guidance. The green pulsating light was even brighter. "Let us find out."

My friend's eyes went wide. "You mean join the battle? Why would we do that?"

"Not join it, necessarily. But we must go to it," I said.

"Ah, for shite's sake, Myrriddin. I say we go the other way and get away from here altogether," he said.

There was someone I needed to find and he was nearby, at this battlefield, I felt it. "You may do as you wish," I said. "I must go." I started to walk back through the Henge toward the main trail that we'd come from, toward the clashing sounds of fighting in the distance.

Baldua scrambled to his feet. "What of the priest?" Baldua asked.

"Pretorius may be there, at the fighting," I found myself saying. Baldua caught up to me, walking along my right side. "So that's why we go?"

"I'm unsure." I said.

"Then why go?"

I simply shook my head. "As I said, you needn't come." But he did.

We made it to the trail and headed off in the direction we were originally headed in, which was the same direction from which the sounds of battle were coming. I set a brisk pace, even with the sword flopping on my back. It seemed to get heavier with each step, yet at the same time, it was no burden. If anything, its weight gave me strength and determination. It would be an integral part of the future; I sensed it.

We marched on in silence for a while, the sounds of battle nearer, but not as strong, exemplifying the ebb and flow of such things. I could see out of the corner of my eye that Baldua kept glancing at me, my Druid staff – which I was presently using as a walking staff – and the sword on my back, especially the sword. "I . . . could carry that if you'd like," he said sheepishly.

"Thank you, but no," I said.

He made no reply, but I could see disappointment in his face when I looked sidelong at him. We trudged on for another half mile or so. I must have been lost in my own thoughts for a while, for it suddenly dawned on me that silence now prevailed. I stopped, Baldua halting a step farther. "What is it?" he asked, turning to face me.

"Listen," I said.

Baldua did. "It has ceased."

Up to this point, the smells of the forest had been our constant companion: the musty dampness of the forest floor, the pungent sweet smell of the lush varieties of plant, and the putrid smells of dung and dead plant life dominated. I had become so accustomed to the odor of the moist, plush environment, that I ho longer noticed them. That is why the new smell, which began to assault our nostrils, was so obvious.

"Smoke! I smell smoke," said Baldua.

"So do I." I broke into a trot, Baldua once again by my side.

The mad battle cries rose so suddenly and from so close that it startled us both into dropping to the ground. What sounded like dozens and dozens of voices rose in a frenzied cry of bloodlust. They were answered by what seemed like another large number of voices equally mad in their desire for blood. An instant later, the clanging clash of weapons colliding rolled over us again, this time closer than ever.

"It seems it was but a lull," I said loudly, over the din of battle.

I rose but remained hunched as I made my way off the trail to our left. Light was filtering through the trees. It was not daylight. Too soon for that. Much too soon. It was firelight. I approached a large rowan and using it for cover, peered out into the area beyond the tree line. I recognized it at once; it was the meadow where the All Hollows Eve rite had been held.

"Diis! (By the gods!) It's . . . " cried Baldua over the noise.

"Yes, it is," I replied.

My attention then turned to the source of the smoke. There, in the same spot as the large fire I had been near the night of All Hallows Eve, was a huge fire casting light across the entire meadow. Light to fight by. Men engaged in violent and brutal acts on one another, hacking at each others' person and limbs. The noise was deafening, the sights were horrific. But the more and closer I watched, the more I noticed the odd behavior of those of the one faction. On the one hand, there were those who were dressed more or less as soldiers; they wore what looked like the remnants of Roman military uniforms. On the other hand, were those whom the soldiers fought. These wore little more than rags. They were undoubtedly the remainder of Creconius Mab's rabble. Brigands to a man. But in that moment, they were something else, too. The more I watched them, the more I realized that their behavior was beyond odd. It was disturbing to my very soul.

There were about one hundred men fighting hand to hand. There seemed to be one soldier for every two brigands. The brigands not only fought with Otherwordly strength, but some wielded a sword in each hand, parrying one soldier's attack while thrusting a blade into another, yet they would not die when struck by what should have been a fatal blow. They would not die! Twenty feet from me, a brigand's arm was lopped off by a soldier. This same soldier then ran the brigand in the chest with his sword. He then kicked the enemy in the stomach to remove his weapon. The one-armed brigand crumpled to the ground in a spout of blood from his arm stump and chest wound. The soldier screamed in bloodlust and obvious frustration, lunged on the body and stabbed it viciously, morbidly, repeatedly. Over and over he stabbed at the body's chest, stomach and face. So violent was his ongoing attack that chunks of bloody flesh flew, silhouetted against the fire's light. Bone fragments, too, flew from the body, scraping and chipping sounds preceding the fragments of bone. The soldier finally collapsed from exhaustion, rolling onto the ground next to the still body. After a moment, the soldier got up and looked at his work, staring at the mutilated corpse.

Then, astonishingly, it moved. Not just the twitch of the dead, sinew and tendons snapping, but purposeful movement. The corpse was trying to rise.

"Impossible!" said Baldua, watching the same drama play out as I.

"Nothing is impossible," I said.

The soldier screamed. His tone indicated naught but utter frustration. "By the Christ, why won't you die?!" he yelled at his quarry.

Now standing, holding a sword in his mangled one-armed hand, the corpse, the now faceless brigand, made no sound but lunged at the soldier with cat-like speed, stabbing the man in the center of the chest. The soldier fell in an instant and was dead. The corpse/brigand moved off, apparently to find others of the enemy.

Looking across the meadow, I saw at least thirty similar engagements as the one I'd just witnessed. One of them even resulted in the head of a brigand being lopped off, yet still the headless thing fought on until all the body's blood had spurted out. Then, and only then, did the body fall and lay still.

"'Tis madness," said Baldua. "An army of the undead. Perhaps we opened a portal at this place on All Hallows Eve. Maybe the dead are crossing back over to seek revenge through this rabble. What've we done?"

"Quiet, Baldua. *We* have done nothing," I reprimanded. I searched my spirit; reached out with my mind to find the meaning of what I was seeing on this field.

And there it was: the essence of evil that was Creconius Mab. I felt it, sensed it, and it was strong. But it was residual remnants of the thing itself. "It's not this place, Baldua. Come." I left the hiding place of our tree and headed to our left.

"Wait!" I heard his call from behind me. I kept moving in the shadows and quickly felt his presence next to me. "Where're you going?" he asked.

I scanned the darkness and found what I thought I might see: two men on horseback—one in a Roman officer's uniform, the other in the robes of a high churchman. "There," I said, pointing to the two figures.

They were approximately one hundred yards away near the tree line. We, Baldua and I, followed the tree line darting and ducking in the shadows so as not to be seen until we were near the two men on horseback.

"Wait, Merlin, Myrriddin," said Baldua. I did not wait, but kept moving, as did Baldua. "Is that who I think it is? We helped you escape his capture not long ago. You miss him that much?"

I searched my mind. Baldua had a point, but I knew I could help this situation. I searched my spirit and another answer came. "He's not what we thought he was. I'm not what he thought I was. He knows that now. I'm sure of it."

"I hope you're right," my friend said.

I hoped I was, too.

TWENTY-TWO

The men on horseback faced the large fire and the carnage taking place around it. Three foot soldiers—legionnaires—were not far away, staying close to the churchman as guards, no doubt. All of them, the men on horseback and the legionnaires, had their backs to the tree line. Thus, they had not seen Baldua and me as we made our way along the edge of the trees. Finally, we came out of the shadows and approached them.

"Darkness prevails this night," I said, startling all of them. The three legionnaires immediately ran at us, gladius' at the ready.

"Hold," Bishop Rozinus commanded of the men from atop his horse. The soldiers stopped a few feet in front of my friend and me, but kept their swords pointed at our chests. Bishop Rozinus and his companion on the other horse – the same Roman officer that was with him on the night of All Hallows Eve, I noticed – studied us, me in particular. Realization dawned on his face.

"Bishop," he said, his gaze falling to the staff in my hand.

Bishop Rozinus looked as though he was about to speak, but when he opened his mouth, what came out was a rasping cough. So violent it was that for a moment his whole body shook. He put a hand to his mouth, a dark cloth within its palm and continued to cough into the cloth, his chest rattling with each violent spasm. The coughing fit finally subsided and he pulled his hand away from his mouth. It was then I saw in the fire's light that the cloth he held was not of a dark color from a dye. It was dark from the staining of blood.

"I see you still have a *chill*," I said.

"Aye," the Bishop replied. "'Tis good to see you, Myrriddin."

"Bishop, shall I" . . . " the officer began.

"No, General Trystor, you shall not. You will leave Myrriddin and his companion be," Rozinus stated flatly. He addressed me directly. "We have much to discuss, you and I Myrriddin, should we survive this night." He said this last part in aggravation, staring back out to the insane battle taking place before us.

"This place is cursed," said the General, a scar-faced, leather-skinned man of middle years.

"'Tis not the place," I said, "but the glamour remaining from Creconius Mab that infects the souls and bodies of this rabble."

"I agree," said the Bishop. "We, too, were somewhat under Mab's spells when we fought alongside this . . . rabble as you put it, the night we captured you. We have since shaken off the effects. But Creconius Mab's men, they have not shaken the effects. What's more, they became . . . I don't know how to say it, but . . . He stopped in mid-thought, racked by another fit of coughing. It was a short one however, and he quickly regained his composure.

"They became nearly impossible to kill?" I offered.

"Yes," he replied.

A thought suddenly occurred to me. "When did they become . . . like this?" I asked.

"A very short time ago. They attacked us when we were passing here. No provocation. But they became demons only a short time ago," the General explained, clearly open to offers of any help.

"Why were you passing here?" asked Baldua.

"Later. That's not important now," said Rozinus.

"I think I can help," I said. I had been using my right hand to hold and use my Druid staff on the trail as a walking staff. I now transferred it to my left hand. With my right hand, I reached over my head and shoulder and grasped the handle of the sword still secured on my back. I pulled the thing up and free of its housing, brandishing it with dramatic flare before me. The three legionnaires holding us at gladius point took a step back almost as one, unsure of my intent. One of them even gasped audibly.

"The great sword," observed Bishop Rozinus, his tone noncommittal. His eyes, however, betrayed him. He was impressed that I had it in my possession.

"A short while ago, I killed Creconius Mab," I began.

"With a flock of savage black birds, no less!" exclaimed Baldua, proudly.

"Ravens. And that's not exactly the whole of it," I corrected. "But regardless, he or she is dead. The evil left the body . . . "

"And came here," Rozinus said.

"Perhaps. It may have followed its own essence, which had already been spent in this rabble, these men, and was still here," I concluded.

"Finding its own kind, its own likeness, you mean, instead of leaving," said the General who I now realized was in fear and awe of what he was seeing this night. His comment was not exactly what I meant. But it was as close to the mark as the General would understand.

"In a manner of speaking," I said.

The great sword, as General Trystor had called it, glowed red, pulsating from tip to pommel. So, too, did the spear's blade and Druid Egg of my staff. They pulsated in conjunction as before, then ceased, the glowing becoming normal once more.

"By Mithras!" exclaimed one of the legionnaires fearfully. His eyes grew large as he watched the two instruments glow. "You are a sorcerer?" he asked me.

"Calm yourself, man," Rozinus interjected, addressing the now terrified legionnaire. The Bishop dismounted and approached me.

I had almost forgotten the appearance of this sickly boy-man. He looked even more ill than the last time I had seen him, even more pale and thin.

He stopped before me and remained facing me while speaking to the rest.

"This is Merlin," he began, "formerly know as Myrriddin. He is a great Druid who understands the workings of all things. He is no evil sorcerer, but uses the same principles as the likes of a Creconius Mab. The difference is that Merlin here uses them to minister for the good on behalf of the most High." He paused for a moment, then spoke to me directly. "You are already becoming the thing of legends, you know. 'The great Merlin' is what some are hailing you as—simple folk, who've heard of your feats on the plateau. My own scouts told me you healed many up there, chased out the demons or the glamour placed upon them."

"I'm sure it's been exaggerated, the reports of my so-called feats, I mean," I said.

"And yet, you possess the great sword. The only way that happened is if you killed Mab, which you said you did. The only way that happened is if you were more powerful in the use of God's Law. You Druids may call It by another name, but make no mistake," Bishop Rozinus continued, becoming intensely serious, "there is One God operating through His One Law. The Law itself knows no person. It only responds. You, therefore, invoked His Law powerfully, yes, but for good, and thus also with divine grace," he concluded.

"Divine grace?" I asked, losing patience with what was beginning to sound like a sermon from this follower of Christ.

"Yes. Any use of the Law for good is by its very nature of and by God's grace," he said as if I were daft.

"That does not make a lot of sense to me. A Law responds equally to all, good or evil," I replied.

"Yes, but God is all good, you see," he said, "so any invocation for good is inherently of God."

"By good, then . . . "

A horrendous crash and a scream to boil the blood came from close by. I looked in that direction and saw that the crash was from burning timber collapsing in the fire. It was suddenly clear, however, that the timber did not collapse by the flames devouring it. Something was flopping in the flames on the timber. Or, rather, someone, which is where the horrible screams were coming from. In the next instant, it became apparent what had happened. In the middle of a cluster of fighting men, one of the rabble picked up a wounded soldier from the ground. The soldier, whose left arm dangled from the elbow down like rocks in a sock, was hitting his assailant with his right hand in a vain attempt to get free. With seemingly Otherworldly strength, the man lifted the soldier over his head like a doll of straw and threw him into the fire.

"No!" shouted the soldier as he crashed into the flaming timbers. His screams of pain and terror pierced the ears and made the soul cringe.

"Enough! I've had enough of this night!" the general yelled.

"Agreed," I said. Holding the sword and staff high in either hand, I walked toward the large fire.

"What's he doing?" I heard General Trystor ask from behind me to no one in particular.

"Just you watch," answered Baldua as he caught up to me. Side by side, we walked to meet the threat.

We stopped some twenty feet before the large fire, its heat intense upon my face. The possessed man—for that is what he was—that is what all the rabble had become: men whose minds and bodies had been taken into possession by Creconius Mab—turned to face my friend and me. His eyes had the same vacant sheen to them as did the raven's earlier. But unlike the ravens, this man, indeed all of the rabble, were under a residual glamour, not directly controlled by another, I felt it. Creconius Mab's evil spirit had been dispelled back to its source. For now. Three more of the possessed rabbles closed in on us.

"Whatever you're about to do, Merlin, now would be a good time," my friend said.

I closed my eyes and entered the state of solace within my head. Once there, I reached out in my mind to touch the mind of the men before me. As with the ravens, these men were under the glamour of a collective mind essence. But, as I suspected, this was a residual glammer. Thus, there was nothing or no one to turn it back on, as it was with the birds, and it was easy to dispel. With my mind, I touched each of the men around the fire, pulling forth their individual minds, their individual spirits to reassert themselves once more. As dirt washes from the body in water, so, too, did the evil fall away, dispelling out of their beings. I opened my eyes. The men—the rabble before me—blinked in confusion as if waking from a sleep. More and more of them gathered before me and Baldua. I could tell by the look on most of their faces that they did not comprehended what had just happened. But one of them, the man who'd been throwing soldiers into the fire, apparently did. He fell to his knees and began to weep.

I dropped my arms, resting the staff against my chest and placing the great sword back in its place on my back. General Trystor, now on foot, too, and Bishop Rozinus approached Baldua and me. They stopped alongside us, surveying the men. More of the men, the rabble, now being of right mind, began to drop to their knees as well upon seeing the Bishop. Others, I suspected, were dropping more in fear of repercussions for their barbaric actions than out of deference or respect for anyone else.

Indeed, some of the remaining soldiers, approximately thirty, began to vent their anger at the night's events. "That's right—on yer knees! Every damned one of you!" barked a legionnaire. He hit a nearby man, one of the rabble, in the back of the head. The blow sent the man sprawling on his face into the dirt.

"Cease!" bellowed Rozinus to the legionnaire. "You will control your men, General," he said to Trystor.

"This filth has committed an atrocity this night," General Trystor protested between clenched teeth. "I have lost good men, some in such a manner that even I will have nightmares about it."

"They were in the grips of an evil beyond your understanding, General," the Bishop replied.

"Then why weren't we?"

"We were for a time."

"But *we* shook it off, Bishop," Trystor pointed out.

"God was on our side, my good General," replied Rozinus.

I rolled my eyes. *Would that it be so simple*, I thought.

Bishop Rozinus must have caught my skeptical look. "Merlin? Do you not agree?"

"I do not know much of your God, I confess," I began, my use of the word 'confess' eliciting a small smile from the Bishop. "What I do know of Him is from various of His earthly representatives who seem more intent on subjugating people than freeing them with Truth. And as to God being on 'our' side, if He is truly God, then He or She or It, would be *everywhere*, in all places and thus on everyone's side," I said.

"Very well said! A bit trite, but well said," replied Rozinus.

"No one, no thing, can truly take command of you, your mind," I continued. "But the simpler one's mind, the easier it is for him to believe the opposite, and thus the easier it is for a glamour to take hold," I finished.

"Then it takes a powerful mind to free the enslaved mind, does it not? Such is how you healed those on the plateau, killed Creconius Mab and dismissed the evil here tonight," said the Bishop. That and with the help of your . . . instruments," he added eying the staff and sword on my back. "But I submit to you that it was God working through you that enabled you to do these things."

"As you wish," I said dismissively, tiring of this debate.

"Enough talk," said the General, apparently also tired of the line of dialogue. "I want justice for my men," he said, turning to Bishop Rozinus, controlled anger seeping from his very being.

Bishop Rozinus turned to face his military officer. "*I* will decide what justice is served here," he said. Though his tone was firmly kind, it was laced with deadly measure, an illicit threat contained therein. "As Master Merlin pointed out, these men," he continued, indicating the dozens of men now on their knees in front of and around us, "are of a simple mind. Their acts were not their own."

"That's not exactly what I said," I interjected.

Ignoring my remark, the Bishop pushed on. "I believe forgiveness is in order here, don't you, General?" Again, the Bishop spoke with kindness, mixed with a deadly air.

The General was silent for a moment, a long moment. *Why is he not insisting on punitive justice, but instead, standing in silence?* I wondered. The answer came to me like a bolt of lightning. Bishop Rozinus was clearly General Trystor's superior and General Trystor was obviously a Christian. A wooden crucifix dangled from the front of his armor, which I noticed for the first time. Perhaps he was even a priest as well as a soldier. Regardless, implied in the Bishop's tone was the threat of being thrown from the Church's bosom – excommunication, I believe it was called. Eternal damnation would follow if you accept that sort of thing. Obviously, the General did. His silence grew longer, his face became a mask to hide what I could see in his eyes; fear – the fear of this excommunication.

"Forgiveness is a hard thing, Father," General Trystor hissed.

Father? I supposed any higher churchman was called Father.

"It can be," Rozinus replied, "or it can be the simplest thing in the world." He turned back to those kneeling, and paused in dramatic silence, the crackling of the fire the only sound filling the air. Finally, he said, "Your sins of this night are forgiven, for you knew not what you were doing. In the name of Christ almighty, I absolve you and forgive you. Amen." He turned back to the General. "You see, Trystor. It is done. 'Tis that simple."

"As you say, Father," said the General. "I'm trying, I am. But there're times that God asks too much."

"Nothing that cannot be met, my son," replied the Bishop. He then faced the still kneeling sixty or so men. "You have been forgiven this night, given a new chance, a new life. But it comes with a price. Every one of you to a man will now swear fealty to General Trystor. You will serve in his army as he sees fit. No harm will come to you by his hand. Is that not correct, General?" he said, looking to General Trystor once more.

The General's expression softened a little, placated somewhat by the Bishop's effect on these men. "Aye," he said. "I give my word, but I tolerate no sloths!"

"So be it!" said the Bishop. "Rise, then," he commanded those kneeling.

They did as he bade, rising slowly, but surely, to a man. Most looked relieved at the turn of events. But more than a few stared at me with fear and awe in their eyes. The man that had thrown the soldiers into the flames, and who had dropped to his knees weeping, looked at me with wide eyes, his dirty face streaked with the tears he had shed. "He called you Merlin," said the man, clearly referring to the Bishop's addressing of me.

"My name is Myrriddin, but yes, I am called more by Merlin now it seems," I said, looking sidelong at my friend who still stood next to me. Baldua merely shrugged his shoulders.

"You rid us of the demons which held us," the man continued. "You are truly a powerful Druid," he said, bowing his head in respect.

"He is indeed," Bishop Rozinus added.

"Decurion," barked the General to one of the legionnaires who only a moment before had held Baldua and me at blade point. The man trotted up to the General, and stood stiff as a tree trunk upon arrival. "Take our new . . . conscripts. Have them first tend to any wounded, then have them gather the dead and bury the bodies. I don't care if it takes the rest of the night. In the morning's first light, line them up for inspection. We'll proceed from there," General Trystor finished.

The legionnaire gave a crisp salute, closed fist to chest and turned to the rabble. "All of you, follow me," he said. Almost as one, the men who only moments before had been an army of the undead, followed the Decurion as he began to walk to the other side of the fire, presumably to now organize the rabble into part of an army of men.

The rest of us stared after them in silence. "Merlin," began Bishop Rozinus, "I thank you for your service and aid. In spite of what you think, I know God worked through you this night, as He does always," he said, staring at my Druid staff, the spear. "Curious though," he continued, "that when you arrived, or shortly thereafter, the spear, for I know that's what it is – the spear of Longinus – was glowing, as was the great sword. But when you approached the men to cast out the evil, there was no glow. Oh, you held each above your head with grand flourish, but neither one was aglow."

"I had not noticed," I said, for truly I had not.

"I did. I remember, too, how the spear glowed in response to *you,* and the intent you held for us that night almost in this very spot," said the Bishop, holding out his hands to indicate where we were. "And in the next instant, it shot forth a charge that killed. Yet, just now, it did not glow. It did not seem to respond to you at all."

I said nothing.

"Perhaps you have grown beyond it, assumed your own God-given power, eh?" Rozinus said, eying the staff even more reverently.

On the night of All Hallows Eve, I had assumed that the Bishop wanted the spear for the same reasons as everyone else who sought it: for its alleged powers, to wield it for their own gain. But I saw something else in the eyes of Bishop Rozinus right now—reverent awe, bordering on worship. I realized that to him, the spear of Longinus was a Truly Holy relic. It was to be revered, respected and protected. My feelings about the man before me went from indifference to great respect.

"Do you know what has happened to the other items that were with the Spear of Longinus, the ones that were hidden with it?" I asked.

"You speak of the holiest of holies: a book of testimony in the first hand, a piece of the cross on which our Lord was hanged, and the sacred cup from which our Lord drank at his final meal, and from which he performed the first sacrament," said the Bishop. "Alas, Creconius Mab has stolen them and whisked them far, far away." He looked at my friend then.

Baldua looked away, a mixture of shame and anger washing over his features.

"I do not blame you, lad. Not at all," said Rozinus. He stepped forward and placed his hand on Baldua's shoulder. "Your name?"

"Baldua," my friend replied, looking the Bishop in the eyes.

"I know the story of what happened to you. Unspeakable things to get the sacred items. No man could have denied your tortures," Rozinus said soothingly. "And, of course, now that Mab's dead, we'll not know for sure where they have gone," he said, turning to me.

"She never would have told you anyway," I pointed out.

"I know. We have a good idea where they went, though," he said.

"Bishop Rozinus," Baldua began tentatively, "how is it that you know what happened to me?"

Rozinus paused, looking at us both, clearly considering how to answer. "I'm sure you wish to be on your way, both of you. But I think you should come to my tent for a brief respite," he said. He then turned back to Baldua. "Therein you'll find the answer to your question, Baldua."

TWENTY-THREE

Bishop Rozinus lead Baldua and me away from the fire toward the foot of the hills and a stand of trees. Within the stand of trees was a spot underneath some overhanging branches. It was perfect for a small encampment. I recognized it at once. It was the same spot where we had set up camp the night of All Hallow's Eve. In the spot now, however, was one large tent surrounded by several smaller ones. A half-dozen legionnaires were about, with more trickling in from the battle field, dirty and wounded. Two guards flanked the large tent, which I suddenly realized was the same tent I had been held in to recuperate, or held in as prisoner, depending on the way I chose to look at it. I felt myself stiffen, but held my stride behind Rozinus.

Bishop Rozinus stopped before the entrance to the large tent, Baldua and I halting, as well. The Bishop turned and faced Baldua and me. He leaned toward us, and speaking in a soft tone, he said, "Please wait here for a moment. I need to make sure my guests feel presentable." He then turned and entered the tent.

Presentable? I thought, suddenly becoming self-conscious, remembering the reflection of my unkempt face in the flat of the great sword's blade.

"Presentable?" said Baldua, in an echo of my thoughts. "Why would Pretorius need to feel presentable?"

"You think it's Father Pretorius in there?" I asked.

"Who else could it be?" he countered. "The priest certainly knew what happened to me."

"He said *guests*, Baldua."

"What?"

"Bishop Rozinus said he needed to make sure his guests . . . plural, more than one," I said.

Baldua's brow crinkled. "What of it?" he asked, perplexed. "It doesn't mean that Pretorius is not in there."

"True enough," I admitted.

The tent flap opened and Rozinus motioned for us to enter. One of the sentries held open the tent's cloth flap, and Baldua and I followed the Bishop into the shelter.

It was dimly lit, a handful of candles scattered about, providing but a scant amount of light. The area was decorated somewhat as I remembered. The large wardrobe in which the spear had been stored was still in the same place. The bed I had recuperated on, however, was not. It was pushed up against a far wall. In its place was a large round table, parchments scattered on its top. On my left, standing at the end of the table, holding a large bowl of fruit was the young lass who had salved my wounds on my last day in Rozinus' previous camp.

"Hello again," I said, truly pleased to see her.

She silently inclined her head in greeting.

I then caught sight of two other figures standing on the opposite side of the table from where I was approaching. Baldua and I stopped at the table. Bishop Rozinus, to my right, stopped at the other end of the table from where the young lass with the bowl of fruit stood. My eyes, however, were stuck on the two figures opposite Baldua and me. In the sparse light, it was difficult to discern their faces. It was clear by their figures that one was male and the other female. I noticed movement behind, and it became apparent that at least two others were in the shadows behind them. I could see the glint of metal and sameness of clothes: soldiers or guards of some kind. They came closer to the figures at the table across from my friend and me. Now I could see them better and they were indeed dressed in a uniform of some sort, though not of Rozinus' or General Trystor's ranks. They presently flanked the two figures across from me as if protecting them. My eyes focused on them. The man was clearly not Pretorius. He was not as tall, nor as broad. His face seemed rugged, but regal; his full, dark beard neatly trimmed. His hair was shoulder-length and thick. He wore a finely made leather riding tunic with gold and sliver lace. And, his bearing was that of one who gave orders, not of one who received them.

The female next to him was partly in shadow, but her scent drifted to me and I recognized it.

"Igraines?" I asked, feeling my heart thump in my chest.

For a brief moment, a silence hung in the air like a mist over a bog. It seemed to linger for an eternity. *Perhaps I was mistaken,* I thought. But that thought was suddenly dispelled when she spoke.

"Yes, M-Myrriddin. 'Tis I," she said with her lovely stammer. She moved forward an ever so small amount so that her beautiful face came into the light. "I've m-missed you."

I felt my face flush and was grateful for the dim light in the tent. "And I you," I responded, nearly stammering myself. Though it had been barely two moons and a little more, perhaps a fortnight or so more, it seemed much longer – so much had happened in that time. I suddenly had an unexpected feeling: I wanted to touch her, to hold her. However, that would have been unseemly. That and the large table between us made it all but impossible anyway.

"Igraines!" Baldua blurted out, looking as though he was about to jump out of his skin.

"Aye, Baldua," she said, without stammering. There was something in her voice. I noticed it now, but realized that it had been there when she had greeted me, as well. It was a demurity that was not of her character.

The well-dressed man next to her came forward into the light. Seeing him more clearly confirmed my initial assessment of the man's appearance and stature. The only thing that I saw now, which I did not see while he was in shadow, was that his face was lined with the crags of age, not scars. Standing next to Igraines, he could have been her father twice over. His voice also conveyed one of many years and much experience. "I am Gorlis Lot, King of Cornwalls, Merlin. It is a great pleasure to meet you," he said, his voice deep and resonate with authority.

"The pleasure is mine, King Lot," I said with a slight bow of my head. "I have heard of you through my friend and mentor, Moscastan," I added.

"Alas, M-Merlin, we have heard. I am deeply s–sorry for your loss," said Igraines.

"Indeed, man. My condolences," added Lot.

"You knew Moscastan?" I asked.

"A great man's passing is mourned by all, just as a great man's feats are admired by all." He spoke this last part directly to me.

I was not sure how to respond to the remark, so, I simply said, "Thank you."

"How come you by King Lot, Igraines?" asked Baldua in his usual tactless way.

Though it may have been tactless, it was precisely the question burning in my mind. I, however, was too concerned with decorum to ask it; or, too cowardly, might be more accurate. Lot bristled at the question, his face contorting angrily as if insulted. The two guards in the background stepped forward in a near-threatening gesture, clearly taking a stance to protect their king.

I held up my free hand, palm facing them in a gesture of peace. "Please. This is my friend Baldua. Our friend," I said, indicating Igraines and me. "His name is Baldua and he means no offense."

"I don't need you to defend me or explain me, Merlin," Baldua said angrily. He then turned to Lot. "Merlin is right when he says I mean no offense. You say you are a king and I accept that. But I do not know you, and the question has naught to do with you. It was put to my dear friend Igraines, who was taken against her will in the same attack that my friend Merlin here was left for dead! He was brought back from the Otherworld in the Henge, the Temple ring of stones near our village."

"Yes," said Lot. "We heard that too." I saw the beginnings of a smile tug at the corners of the King's mouth. It appeared he was no longer angry, but was enjoying Baldua's diatribe.

"So I ask again," Baldua rolled on, ignoring the King's remark and turning once again to Igraines: "How came you by King Lot, Igraines?"

She did not answer right away. It was apparent that she was deciding what to say. I could see it in her eyes. But I saw something else there as well, fear. Twice she looked sidelong at Lot, as if silently asking permission to tell the tale. It accentuated and confirmed the demureness in her voice I had heard a moment ago. Something was wrong. What had happened to the strong, even fierce, Igraines that I knew and loved—yes, loved? Anger began to rise in my heart. Baldua was asking himself the same question as I, for his body went rigid next to mine. But then the real blow came.

"Igraines is my wife," declared King Lot.

Stunned. I was stunned into utter silence. I kept my faced rigid, but my insides began to roil. I suddenly felt as though I would be violently ill.

"Wife?" Baldua declared, nearly shouting.

"You will keep your tone, my young friend," said Lot, a deadly edge to his voice.

"I'll speak as I wish, and again, I do not address you," spat Baldua.

The two guards flanking Igraines and Lot tensed and began to draw their swords.

Blinding light filled the space. In my mind's eye, I saw it so and at the same instant in the tent, it *was* so. Light, white and bright, exploded from the Druid Egg and spear blade *and* from the great sword on my back. I could feel a tingling sensation running near the length of my spine and knew it was energy coursing through the sword.

The girl to my left squealed in fear and dropped the bowl she had carried, the sound of it crashing to the floor, filling the tent.

"Call off your dogs, King Lot, or this will be the last moment they draw breath," I said with Otherworldly depth and authority.

"Down, boys," said the King.

I heard the distinctive sound of metal blades sliding back into their sheath and the nervous murmurs of the men. An instant later, I released the light in my mind and it was gone from the tent.

Silence and dim candle light once again were our companions. It took a moment, but our eyes finally readjusted to the sparse light.

"By the Christ," exclaimed one of Lot's men.

"What the devil was that?" the other asked nervously.

"That was impressive," said Lot.

Rozinus seemed almost giddy. "You see?" he said to Lot. "The tales are not exaggerated."

"Indeed," replied Lot. "With you on our side, Merlin, no one will oppose us."

"What are you speaking of?" I asked suspiciously.

"We, the lesser kingdoms, unite under one banner, that of the Pendragon— Uther Pendragon," said Lot proudly. "One nation, one country united to drive out foreign invaders."

"'Lesser kingdoms'? What is that? Various of our tribes and clans have occupied many regions for centuries before even the Romans came," said Baldua. "But what kingdoms?"

"The very tribes and clans and regions you speak of have been uniting under one leader as individual city-states, to use the Greek," said Lot impatiently. "You do know what I speak of, yes?"

"We were subjected to a broad education on the Isle of Mystery," I interjected. "Mathematics and philosophy and hence, a partial history of the Greeks was a part of that education. "We know of what you speak."

Baldua glanced sideways at me, his look saying, *I must have slept through that part.*

"Yes, well," Lot continued, "we also unite under one central leader, Uther Pendragon."

"Unite?" cried Baldua. "Most of the clans that I know of are only good at fighting each other. How are they to unite as one?"

"Takes a powerful leader, it does. Uther Pendragon is that man," Lot replied. "Besides, you speak of your smaller, localized clans. I speak of the larger tribes across the land." He paused for a moment before pulling his attention back to me. "What say you, Merlin? Will you join us?"

I did not answer straight away, but thought for a moment, remembering that Moscastan had mentioned this Uther Pendragon. And, I knew in my soul that part of my destiny was to help in the creation of this country under one leader. I had seen it in my visions. But in my visions, there had been a different leader; a different High King than Uther. Yet, I had been an old man in those visions. A distant future, then. Perhaps the King in my visions—Arturius was his name—was the future son of Uther Pendragon. *Yes, that was it,* I thought, and knew it to be so. I looked at Igraines then, and knew another truth; felt it in my soul: she is, or will be, the mother of this future King Arturius. The fact that she was now married to the present King of Cornwalls was irrelevant. The future of my visions would be fulfilled. I would make sure of it.

"Myrriddin. Are y-you not w-well?" asked Igraines.

It was only then that I realized my eyes had been closed and that I had been in a light trance, feeling the future and my part in it. I opened my eyes and looked into her lovely face. "Yes, Igraines. I am quite well. And yes, King Lot," I said, looking the man squarely in the eye, "I do join you. My destiny and the movement you speak of are intertwined on levels even you are unaware of."

"Indeed. Splendid," he said.

"But presently, I wish to speak with Lady Igraines in private," I said.

"Yes, we . . . " began Baldua.

"In private." I repeated, turning to Baldua. I wanted to speak to her in private, 'twas true. But denying Baldua's presence would also be a concession to Lot. My man would not be there, either.

There was hurt in Baldua's eyes, but he acquiesced. "Very well," he said.

"Yes. M-Myrriddin. We must talk,"

She then turned to Lot, placing her hand gently, but firmly, on his arm. "It will not take long, husband, and this is my long-time friend."

Lot's eyes narrowed, accusingly. *And lover*, they seemed to say in reply.

"And, he was with me the night I disappeared. I owe him the story up to now. Trust me, husband," she finished.

He considered for a moment, then smiled. "Of course, I trust you," he said. "Come, all of you. Let's give the friends some time," he said to the others. Lot walked to the tent's entrance, his guards, Rozinus and the girl following in his wake. Begrudgingly, Baldua followed a moment later.

TWENTY-FOUR

In the dimness of the tent we sat in silence. I had placed the great sword and spear on the table and pulled up two chairs for us. We sat next to each other, neither wishing to be the first to speak. But Igraines finally did.

"You are becoming quite f-famous, you know," she said, by way of small speak.

"I don't know how," I replied lamely. "I've done what anyone would have done in my place. Besides, my . . . experiences have been fairly recent. Word can't have traveled that fast."

"Words do travel fast and you kn-know they do," she said.

Again, we sat in silence. Until I realized something. "Your stammering—it's not as pronounced as it was," I observed.

She smiled sweetly. "I am comfortable with m-my station in life, Myrriddin. Perhaps for the first time, I know I'm where I belong."

I felt my brow rise. "Comfortable, but not complacent, I hope," I offered.

She simply smiled once again.

"What happened?" I asked, turning serious. "From that night, what happened?" I could not help but hear the desperate disappointment in my voice. It was caused by realizing my feeling for her on that night and sensing a possible future with her, only to have it all yanked away with her disappearance. The emptiness was then solidified permanently with the knowledge of her marriage to Lot and my own visions of a truer future. Upon reflection, however, this last point brought some comfort and perspective. I am, after all, to be an integral part of a future much larger than just myself.

"My real father, of noble birth, had come for me," she said, breaking my thoughts with the astounding statement.

"What?" was all I could manage to say.

"It was not the raiders of Creconius that attacked us, carrying me off and leaving you for dead. It was my father's men."

I was speechless.

She touched my arm with her hand, compassion flowing forth. Her eyes brimmed with tears. "I am so s-sorry for what they did to you, Myrriddin. I pray your forgiveness. Those men didn't know what you are to me. To them, you were simply in the way," she said.

I stared into her eyes, feeling the sting of bitter tears brimming my own. A question burned in my mind. But I did not speak it; dared not speak it for fear of a flood of emotions washing me away.

Yet, she must have seen the question for she answered it, nonetheless. "You are my first love, since I was a little lass. You are my dearest friend and my first lover. My first. You will always be those things to m-me, Myrriddin. I love you still," she said, her hand leaving my arm and going to her abdomen.

"Are you ill?" I asked

"Not any longer," she replied.

I remembered the visions of her being pregnant, and suddenly had to know. "Are you with child?" I asked.

"Yes," she said flatly.

"Is it Lot's?" I asked, rather indelicately.

Anger flashed in her eyes, but quickly abated. She made no reply.

"Is it mine, then?" I asked, as if grasping at air.

Igraines sat thoughtfully for a moment before answering. "Lot will be father to the child I carry, M-Myrriddin. She will be his daughter and will know n-no other," she proclaimed with the fire and conviction I had always known her by. "It is the way of it. It is the way it must be. You know of what I speak. I know you have seen a true future for us all."

"I know nothing!" I said angrily, lying. "The very least of all, you. You spent many years with us on the Isle of Mystery, then many more in our village, with our people, a stuttering peasant girl." I saw anger flash once again in her eyes, but I pressed on. "Then, one day out of nowhere, your father of nobility appears and whisks you away, nearly killing me, ney, really killing me, as Baldua said, at the time. Why? Why did this father of yours leave you with us there, and pluck you at his convenience? Why did you not tell us of your nobility?" I had become agitated. The great sword's hilt and the spear's blade and Druid Egg pulsated an angry red for a moment. Igraines looked at them with reverent awe, but no fear. I took several deep breaths to calm myself. The sword and spear's pulsating, an echo of my state of mind, ceased. "My apologies. I simply wish to know," I said.

"And deserve to know," she said, in an effort to ease my mind. "I did not tell you of my nobility because I did not know. I did not know until I met my father the day after I was taken f-from you. I suspected something am-miss, for I expected to be raped when my captors ar-rived at their camp. The opposite happened—they treated m-me like royalty. One of them was even be-be-headed by his captain for leaving a bruise on my arm during the c-c-capture. The next day, my father explained it all to me: how he had left me on the Isle for training and rearing. Paid handsomely, too. For my own safety, my lineage was kept secret, even from m-m-me." She paused for a moment. "I was n-n-never supposed to have left the Isle," she continued. "But as the years went and my father being far and away w-with no word . . . " she let the words trail off.

"After you were captured, how did you know he was really your father?" I asked.

"I was very little when he l-left me on the Isle, 'tis true. But I remember him, never forgot his face as he was ferried away, s-starring at me," she said.

There was a distance to her now, to her face. I could see it. Clearly, she was re-living the memory. I wanted to reach out, to embrace the little girl in the woman before me. But I did not. "I see," I said instead.

Another silence fell between us for a time. This silence was different, not awkward. It connoted comfort; the comfort two friends share in one-another's company when a truth has been revealed and accepted.

"A woman child," I said, looking at her abdomen. No sign of a growing life within could yet be seen beneath her traveling togs. Of course, it would only be a matter of time.

"Aye," she smiled happily. "A girl child."

"How are you so certain?" I asked. The moment the words were out of my mouth, however, I felt foolish for having asked; a woman knows.

She looked at me a bit incredulously. "How is it you are certain of something unseen?" she asked.

"I *feel* it deep in my soul and know it to be so," I replied sheepishly.

Igraines simply cocked an eyebrow as if to say, "There you have it."

"So be it," I said. I looked at her for a moment deciding how best to ask the next question. Finally, it was obvious that the best way was to simply ask it. "One last thing and then I will leave you to your life. "Marriage. Why?"

"The marriage was the reason my father came to find me. I had been betrothed to King Lot many years prior. 'Twas time."

I was surprised. "You say that with such ease, such acceptance. The girl I knew never would have put up with such an arrangement made by another."

"The girl you knew is but half the woman I am," she said. "To be sure, I did fight my father in the beginning, even had a kn-knife to him at one point, threatened to k-kill him or anyone who thought they could force this upon m-me. But I came to understand the higher purpose, the reason for the unification of people and kingdoms through marriage and fealty, and my place in this higher purpose, just as, Myrriddin, Merlin, you know yours. You've seen yours."

I could not argue the point, for I had indeed seen glimpses of things to come and my place in them. "Yes," I said.

"Come." She took my hand and stood, pulling me to stand too. "Let us leave the gloom of this tent and begin our futures."

Before I could stop myself, I felt my hand leave hers and go toward her abdomen, its palm landing ever so gently on her stomach area. I closed my eyes and could sense the new life beneath.

A soft hand lay itself gently on top of mine. "Fear not, Myrriddin. She shall be treated as the princess she will be."

"I know," I said, my voice cracking. Her hand remained on mine. I could feel her warmth, her spirit, through her hand. I closed my eyes and immersed myself in her spirit, allowing myself to be carried away to another time, another place. It was the time of the Christ in a region called Gaul. I, my spirit, was in the form of Longinus, former Centurion of Rome. And Igraines, her spirit was there; her then female form resting next to me on a sleeping pallet in a shelter. Our bodies were naked and sweating. We had just made passionate love. She raised herself on one elbow and looked into my eyes, smiling radiantly. But the face that looked at me, Longinus, was not that of Igraines. It was "Irena," I heard my Myrriddin self whisper aloud. The sound of my voice made the vision vanish and snapped me back to the present, to Rozinus' tent, to Igraines.

Igraines smiled. Her smile was not unlike that of her former self. "Irena," she repeated thoughtfully. "We have known one-another before, Myrriddin, have been together intimately and beyond. I know that. I do not know what my name has been, but Irena certainly . . . feels right," she said. After a moment, she withdrew her hand.

I dropped my hand from her abdomen and picked up the great sword, returning it to its makeshift scabbard on my back. I then picked up my Druid staff, the Spear of Longinus, *my* spear. The feel of it in my hand briefly sent me back to that life as Longinus again. In a flash, images raced before my mind's eye from that time; images of myself and lessons learned and not learned. In the next instant, I was Myrriddin once more with this life's purpose – my life's purpose as Myrriddin – affirmed in my mind and heart. I looked into Igraines' eyes. "We have different roles this time," I stated.

With a tear in one of her eyes, Igraines simply nodded, turned and headed toward the tent's entrance. With a mixture of nostalgic sadness and excitement for what lay ahead, I followed Queen Igraines out of the shelter.

TWENTY-FIVE

The next morning, I helped with the wounded as much as possible, healing those I could, praying with Rozinus for those I could not. I spoke with some of the rabble, the men that had fought for Creconius Mab. None of the men that I spoke with had any recollection of what had taken place. Some were aghast at their atrocities when it was brought to their attention. It was obvious that at least a few of them were not the mindless rabble and common thieves one might take them for, but were simply a product of their circumstances in life; circumstances that they were powerless to change. Or so that is what they truly felt and believed. I saw nothing of Igraines or her husband. No matter. I knew that it was only a matter of time before our paths would cross again in this life. Indeed, I had thought much about my visions and experiences as Myrriddin and as the eternal soul that I am. I knew with more certainty than the day before what lay ahead for me, for Britain, for all of us in the coming years. We were all connected on the level of the profound for certain, but also on the level of the mundane.

By the time the sun had reached its zenith, I was ready to leave. I still had another task before starting the rest of my life: to lay Moscastan to rest within his Crystal Sanctuary. I gathered provisions and sought Baldua, assuming he would still wish to accompany me back to our village and the not-too-distant Crystal Sanctuary. I didn't have far to look. As I approached Bishop Rozinus' tent, I could see that the Bishop and my friend were in the middle of a discussion, Baldua looking quite perplexed. I walked to the two, clapping my friend on the shoulder with my free hand upon arrival. "Pray tell me what the matter is, Baldua? Is the good Bishop confusing you with his Church's rhetoric?" I teased.

"Worse," my friend replied.

"Baldua here was asking after your priest friend, Pretorius," replied Rozinus.

"Ah," I said, noncommittally. I still had my doubts as to who, or what, Pretorius was.

"As I tried to explain to Baldua here, Pretorius was in our camp last evening," he said.

I was surprised, but dared not show it. "When?" I asked.

"Just prior to your arrival. Well, two hours prior, is more likely, to be sure," said the Bishop. "He warned us of the glamoured men who were about to attack."

"What happened? Where is he?" I asked.

"That's the rub," put in Baldua. "He seems to have disappeared."

"Once the attack began, we paid no more heed to the priest, as our attention was elsewhere. I'm sure you understand. I only now recalled Pretorius' presence when Baldua inquired of him," explained Rozinus.

I thought for a moment. "And . . . you are sure that it was the man, Pretorius?" I asked.

Now it was the Bishop's turn to look perplexed. "What is your meaning?"

"You sure he was flesh and blood and not spirit?" I clarified.

"Has something happened to him?" asked Rozinus.

"Merlin thinks . . . " Baldua began.

"It matters not what I think. What matters is what the Bishop saw," I said sternly. "I ask again—was he of the flesh or of the spirit?"

Rozinus thought for a moment. "I would wager of the flesh."

"Ha!" exclaimed Baldua, victoriously.

"If of the flesh, then why did he leave?" I asked my friend.

"I don't know," Baldua said in a way indicating that was precisely why he was confused – though, he, of course, refused to take my version of the priest into consideration.

"I, for one," Rozinus said, "am no longer surprised by anything that men do. Your friend, Pretorius, was a bit of a renegade as far as the Church was concerned on any account."

"I don't accept that," said Baldua. He would have stayed with us.

"Obviously, lad, you were mistaken," said the Bishop.

"But . . . "

"I beg of you, Baldua, enough," I said. "I came to see if you still wish to come with me. I have another task, if you'll remember."

"Aye. Of course, of course I'm with ye," he said, almost apologetically.

"You leave us then," said the Bishop, his eyes drifting to the staff in my hand. "I thought that you'd be a part of us now. What you said in the tent last evening . . . "

"I stand by what I said. I will meet you within two moons time. I must lay my mentor to rest, you understand, and see to my village."

"Ah, yes. I am sorry for your loss, truly and for my forgetfulness. I pray your forgiveness," he said sincerely.

"Naught to forgive," I replied.

"Give me but a moment to gather my things," said Baldua as he dashed off. I watched him as he ran. My eyes then drifted to something beyond my friend some distance away. Standing alone in the middle of the meadow was a figure, whose back was to me. Around the figure, in a perimeter of about ten feet, were beautiful meadow flowers. Odd, that, for it was past the winter solstice. Though it was unseasonably warm for the time of year, it was still too cold for flowers to be growing there. Then, a possible explanation became apparent. The figure turned and faced me. It was Igraines.

The afternoon was bright and brisk. Baldua and I trekked through the woods in silence for the most part. My friend was brooding. I suspected that it had something to do with the fact that Pretorius had become an enigma, one that I was apparently able to dismiss a little easier than Baldua. Ironic that, for I had assumed that my friend had never particularly cared for the priest. I no longer believed the priest to have been Creconius Mab. But there had been an evil, malevolent force within the man's being when last I looked into his eyes. I was not sure whether the dead Sorceress had been responsible for that or not, but perhaps whatever it was had finally driven the priest away from us for good. Some mysteries are better left alone.

We made camp at dark-fall near a crag of rocks at the edge of the forest. The next morning, we gathered what food the forest offered up in the way of nuts and roots and continued on our journey. The second day's travel found both Baldua and me in a lighter mood than on the previous day, and I thoroughly enjoyed my friend's company in the manner I did when we had been boys. On the third day, we began to see familiar sights, the ridge of hills and trees that surrounded our area, familiar game. The final indication that we were home came when we stepped onto the field where we had drilled with our pretend army. Then it hit us: the smells of cooking fires and food being roasted thereon. I looked at the sky, the fading light and the setting sun.

"'Tis time for the evening meal, yes?" asked Baldua, echoing my thoughts as we both stopped to savor the aroma.

"Aye," I replied. We began walking again, toward the smell. I looked up and saw the smoke from the fires billowing lazily above the trees and found my steps becoming quicker and quicker, as were Baldua's, until my friend and I were at a near run, the great sword flopping on my back. We were giddy in our excitement to have a decent meal for sure, but moreover, to be home. We found the main path leading into the center of our village and flew down it as if our lives depended on it. The closer we got, the more we could hear voices, many voices, more than would normally be at an evening's communal meal. They sounded joyful, celebratory. Before long, we were in the village and we stopped dead in our tracks, astounded at the sight before us. The whole village had been rebuilt. Not just rebuilt, but made better than ever. It was as if the murderous raid had never taken place. What's more was that there were many more buildings than had previously been in our village, large ones made of wood and stone. A throng of people hovered around the cooking fires

"How can this be?" whispered Baldua with awe. "Perhaps this isn't our home."

"Of course, it is," I insisted. "We were just on our drill field. That was our village's path we just took."

"No, I mean maybe someone else, others, have taken over and . . . "

"AGH!!" came the woman's scream. All activity ceased, all eyes turned to us.

"Merlin?" someone whispered.

"Couldn't be," said another.

"And Baldua," said a third.

Then a woman came forward, the same woman who had screamed. She came slowly toward us as if approaching two spirits. She was plump and her face smudged with soot from the cooking fires, but there was no mistaking who she was. I felt my face break into a huge grin. "Hello, Leoni," I said.

She stood blinking away disbelief.

"Hello," said Baldua.

She took us both in. Others began to gather around us.

"Well, Master Merlin, Master Baldua. Ye've come in time for the meal, haven't ya?" she said.

"We've come home," I replied.

"So ye have, so ye have."

We stood in silence for a moment, the other villagers murmuring.

"Now," Leoni began with mock perturbation, "I know ye to be a powerful Merlin and all, but does that mean yer too good to hug yer Leoni?"

"Never," I said stepping forward to embrace the woman; the only mother I had ever really known. She wrapped her arms around me with such force that I thought I would be crushed. While still hugging me, she reached out with one hand and grabbed Baldua and pulled him into the reunion embrace as well, both of us nearly suffocating in her ample bosom. A wild cheer went up from those nearby and others began clapping us on the shoulder in welcome. We were home.

TWENTY-SIX

It turns out we did indeed arrive back in our village at a time of celebration. The final structures of the village had just been completed and the neighboring village had moved in with our people to our village. They were our clansmen, after all, and for safety's sake, everyone seemed to agree that it was better for all to live together. We sat around the fire for most of the evening, gorging ourselves on the food and regaling our fellow villagers with the story of our journey. Most already knew of Moscastan's passing, but were saddened to the point of tears upon hearing my first-hand account of it. Finally, the moon's trek across the night's sky was descending, the hour was late and many began to drift to their homes. Leoni sat near me resting her head on my shoulders, Baldua on the other side of her.

"How did you get all these things built so fast, Leoni? All these new buildings, too? Did you have a master mason or the like?" asked Baldua playfully.

"Ye might say that. He's an odd sort, to be sure," she replied.

"Who," I asked, my interest peaked.

"Don't know his name. He won't give it. He helped us tremendously, you know, with the design, the building, the organizing, he was quite a carpenter, too." She said.

"Why did he do all this?" Baldua asked.

"Don't know other than he said it's his purpose. He'd talk like one of those Christian priests, but . . . " she trailed off.

Baldua and I exchanged a glance across Leoni. "What did this man look like?" I asked.

"Couldn't tell ye, nobody could. He'd show up in the mornings lookin' like he's been livin' in the forest all his life—long, matted beard and hair that covered his face. And he always looked down, not wanting to meet yer gaze like," she said, as if realizing it for the first time. "Then he'd up and disappear near night fall. Never even took a meal with us."

"Will he be back tomorrow?" asked Baldua.

"Doubtful," Leoni said sleepily, "Two days ago, he said his work here be finished. He was moving onward."

"And he never gave his name?" I asked.

"Ney. Just called 'imself, 'The Messenger'"

Save for a few of the villagers still about, we sat in solitude.

"I'd like to retire, Leoni. I have something to do in the morning," I declared.

"I know," she said. "Will ye be takin' his hovel or the Crystal Sanctuary?"

My face must've shown surprise.

"Well come, lad. Don't act so taken back. Ye've taken his place now, in more ways than one," she said. "The villagers all embrace it. And, they be proud of the fact that ye've come back to lay 'im to rest here. They're also proud of the fact that perhaps you'll be stayin'," she added.

I thought about her words for a moment. "The Crystal Sanctuary," I said.

"So be it," she replied.

By the time I arrived at the Crystal Sanctuary the night was nearly gone. I could not remember the way at first, which cost me a little time. But ultimately trusting my sense of direction and intuition, I soon found myself on the correct path through the woods. The way was much longer than I recalled, but with a near full moon's light still casting to help me and a steady gait, I came to the place near dawn. Unlike the last time I had been to this place, there was no mist near the ground outside of the opening or entrance to the cave or Sanctuary. There was a solid stone wheel in front of the hole in the side of the granite rock formation that was the cave's entrance, effectively sealing the opening. At first, I questioned whether I was in the right location, for I had never before seen or noticed a round stone door anywhere near the entrance. But I recognized the granite rock formation and surrounding area as being correct. This was Moscastan's Crystal Sanctuary, no doubt. I stepped up to the stone wheel, which was at half a man's height and approximately eight-inches thick, and shoved with one hand—my other hand held my Staff. Nothing. It would not move. I then made the attempt again, this time using my entire body weight, leaning my shoulder into the thing. Again, nothing. A momentary panic seized me. *How am I to move this thing from the entrance? I wondered. It would take three men.*

"You think as a man, not as the infinite spirit you are, aligned with the Unlimited Source of all," said the Voice of the Spear, His voice. "Do you have such little faith?"

I looked at the Druid staff in my hand, at the spear's blade and the Druid Egg thereon. I expected to see them aglow with some kind of light or to feel the staff itself vibrating slightly in my hand to correspond with the voice. Such had been the case in the past. This time, however, such was not the case. *Perhaps there's no correlation this time. Perhaps I'm just hearing it in my mind,* I thought.

"Perhaps you are," The Voice answered. "It does not matter. The thing you look to is just wood and metal. You have said so yourself. The question remains: do you have such little faith? You have fought and destroyed one who possessed a great evil, using the Infinite Power of the One, allowing it to course through your being with your understanding of the Natural Laws that govern the Power. Yet, you doubt yourself now? The thing before you is but a stone. You know how to use the Laws of the Universe. Command it to be flung into the sea and it shall be so."

I smiled. Yes. The Voice was right. I could move a mountain if I chose, or rather, the Power that coursed through me could. I closed my eyes and concentrated on the stone, on the air around it. I saw in my mind's eye the air becoming dense near the stone door, so dense that it, too, was becoming solid. I then blended with it in mind, becoming it and pushing the stone door, the wheel and rolling it to the left as I faced it. I saw this happening in my mind, saw the stone wheel, envisioned it rolling away from the Sanctuary's opening. I heard the sound of heavy stone grating on dirt and gravel; heard it with my ears in the actual world. I opened my eyes and the stone was indeed rolling gently, effortlessly to the left along the side of the granite wall. It disappeared behind a thick growth of vines and vegetation growing from the ground and cracks in the granite rock formation. Light from within the Crystal Sanctuary spilled out from the opening and onto the surrounding area. I stooped and entered the brightness.

The smell of the Sanctuary's interior hit me. I had forgotten about the wonderfully clean aroma of the place. It took a few moments for my eyes to adjust. When they did, I marveled again at the beauty of this sacred place. *Twilight of the gods*, Moscastan had called it. It was even more dazzling than when I'd been there last. After drinking in the sight and absorbing the peaceful divinity of the place,

I turned my mind back to the task at hand. I had been thinking of the best place to lay the remains of my beloved mentor in this Sanctuary and the answer had come to me during my night's trek. I made my way through the Sanctuary, down a passageway that Moscastan had led me, and entered the small hole in the side of a wall. I stood before the *Crystal Alter*, as Moscastan had called it. It was an even deeper blue in color than I recalled. It still looked like a solid piece of the ocean set in the room, but there was something more; I could see movement within the block itself, not any one thing moving, but the whole of it. There was an internal undulation to the thing, as if it were liquid inside, moving and sloshing to its own tidal forces. I blinked in disbelief as I realized I was indeed looking at a piece of an ocean set in a rectangle before me; a piece of the Otherworld's ocean or the sea between worlds. There was no leakage of any of it, it was not liquid being contained in a glass box of some sort. It was liquid being held in its shape from the Otherworld, I could sense the prescence of spirits and guardians from beyond this realm. They were waiting. And I knew what they were waiting for.

I leaned my Druid Staff against the wall near the entrance. I then removed my satchel and the Great Sword from it, leaning the latter against the wall with my Staff. Finally, I gently withdrew the wrapped remains of Moscastan from the pack. I had thought to create a niche in one of the walls of this room in which to place the wrapped remains, then close it up, sealing them into this place forever. But something now compelled me to place the remains on the solid, but undulating, liquid Altar. I did so, gently, reverently, silently saying an incantation; a prayer for peace of spirit for Moscastan. Though the inside of the Altar continued to undulate, the top of the Altar felt hard. I loosened the wrapping and opened it, allowing the ashes and bones of my mentor to be exposed. I stepped back from the Altar, head bowed, maintaining my silent vigil. And then it happened. The remains, cloth wrapping and all, began sinking into the Altar, being absorbed into the mass in front of me. For an instant, I could see the bones floating in the liquid. In the next moment, Moscastan's smiling face appeared in the middle of the Altar. It mouthed the words, "thank you," and then dissipated, as did the bones, vanishing from sight. Next, the undulation of the Altar stopped. It was once again solid: a beautiful, solid blue block. The feeling of those from the Otherworld being present left as well. Though somewhat surprised by the remains assimilating into the Altar, I smiled to myself. It had been a perfect close to Moscastan's life.

I turned, intending to retrieve the Great sword and staff. There was something else now leaning against the wall next to them. It was long and thin, approximately the height of a man and wrapped in cloth. It reminded me of what the wrapped spear had looked like when first I found it all these years past. The object had not been there when I had placed the sword and staff against the wall. Somehow, I knew Moscastan had placed it there and that it had belonged to him in this life. He was now passing it on to me. "What have you left me, Master Moscastan?" I said out loud.

I crossed to the object, picked it up and knew instantly what it was. Unwrapping it confirmed my belief. It was Moscastan's own Druid staff. But it was different than I remembered. In fact, it now looked more like my Druid staff, my disguised spear than Moscastan's Druid staff, complete with a small wicker cage atop and a Druid Egg within. Running my hand the length of the shaft, however, reconfirmed that this was indeed Moscastan's Druid staff. He had made carvings, incantations, in the wood of the shaft when first he had earned this Druid Staff. I looked from Moscastan's Druid Staff, to my Druid Staff. What he was suggesting by this gesture was clear. And, he was right. "You continue to dispense lessons even from the Otherside. "Thank you," I said out loud. Leaning my gifted Druid Staff back against the wall, I picked up mine. It took but a moment to untie the leather thongs that held the wicker cage in place. I removed the cage and crystal Druid Egg, placing both in my satchel. The thing was no longer my Druid staff. Its blade shined as if it had recently been polished, all of it save for the area where *His* stains remained. It was the Spear of Longinus once more. I wrapped the spear in the cloth that Moscastan's staff had been in, placed the sword back in its place on my back with the satchel and left the small chamber. As I walked back toward the main chamber, I could not help but sense that I was home. Perhaps Leoni had been right. This was my Crystal Sanctuary now, my home.

Voices—the sound of voices in rhythmic unison could be heard. I entered the main chamber and realized that the chanting, for that is what it was, was coming from just outside the Sanctuary. *Must be dawn,* I thought. But the sounds were close. The Sanctuary was nowhere near the place where Druids and others gathered to sing in the new day. Besides, the chant was uplifting, yet somber. Not one of the usual songs of greeting and welcome normally reserved for the rebirth of the solar disk. I stooped to exit the opening to the sanctuary and was touched by what I saw.

In the burgeoning light of the new day, standing in a semi-circle in the clearing in front of the Sanctuary's entrance, were more than two dozen sage-colored, robe-and-hood-clad Druids and worshipers; those who would normally be bringing in the new day in the traditional place near the village, were doing so here. But this gathering was more than that. Recognizing the chant they were singing, it became clear to me that this was a gathering of respect and help for Moscastan: respect for the powerful Druid that he had been and help for his crossing over to the Otherside, something I did not doubt he had done with ease. It was in no way mournful, the chant. It was a celebratory song of life and the fact that Moscastan has indeed been reborn in the Otherworld, which is a joyous thing to Celts. It means that we will all see him again. I found myself bowing my head and joining the chorus of song. It wound its way to its height and then dropped off to a single sustained note, fading in volume as the breath did of those singing, symbolizing the last exhale of the departed in this life. Then, silence. The birds of the dawn twilled and the sound of forest animals waking to break their fast were the only noises we heard for a few moments.

In utter silence, the robed figures before me began to file out of the clearing in a single row down the narrow path that leads here. One figure remained. He pulled back his hood. Baldua. I was not surprised that the others had found their way here. Druids knew of other Druids' sanctuaries, if they had one. And this place was probably the most profound of them all. But I was surprised to see Baldua. I knew he had never been here. Obviously, he had followed the others. Regardless, I was pleased to see my friend. I smiled broadly and embraced him, albeit, a bit awkwardly as I was carrying the wrapped spear and my new Druid Staff.

"I hope you don't mind that I'm here," he began, apologetically. "After you left last night, I overheard some of them," he said, indicating with his hand those who had just left, "saying that they would make the trek here for the dawn's rite and to send Moscastan to the Otherside. I simply showed up at their meeting point and joined their ranks to come here."

"Gods no, Baldua. I am glad of it. Moscastan is too, I'm sure," I assured him.

He looked over my shoulder at the cave's entrance, his eyes growing large at the light shining forth from it. "I heard tell that there's an unearthly beauty to the place," he said with a childlike tone that revealed his true meaning; he wanted to see the inside, but knew he must be invited to do so.

"I would be delighted to show it to you, but I was about to undertake another task," I replied.

"Alas, another time, then, for I am here in part on a task myself. Rozinus is here, at the village, I mean. He says he's leaving for the east. Constantinople, I think is the name of the place."

"The East?"

"Aye. Lot is here, too, with Igraines," he said.

"Do they follow Bishop Rozinus?" I asked, confused.

"No, no. But the people of the village were astonished to see her with Lot, and married no less. It was fun to watch Leoni, especially. She . . . "

"To the point, my friend," I said, before Baldua could get much further into his irrelevant tangent. "I didn't expect to see them for a time. In fact, I was going to seek Rozinus. It's time his people—his church—have something," I declared, holding up the wrapped Spear.

Baldua looked from the wrapped item to the Druid Staff in my hand. His brow crinkled with concern. I could tell by the look in his eyes that he was not fooled by the Staff I now held. "What are you doing, Merlin?" he asked.

"What is right to be done," I said, but explained no further.

To his credit, Baldua said nothing more on the subject.

"Rozinus, Lot and Igraines . . . who else is in the village?"

"Uther Pendragon," Baldua replied.

"Just the three of them?"

"Hardly. Between Lot and Uther, there looks to be a legion of their soldiers camping outside the village," said Baldua. "They wait for your council, respect-fully. They know that you are here, laying your mentor to rest. But there is ur-gency in them. Apparently, a ruthless king to the north is refusing to join Lot and Uther Pendragon and the other kings, and is, instead, threatening to have us all under *his* yoke."

"I see," I said. Images began to float before my mind's eye: images of impend-ing battles between two Dragon emblems, images of illicit encounters, one of which would be between Igraines and Pendragon, producing a King that I would rear. My mind began to drift in trance.

"Merlin. Myrriddin!" Baldua called to me, bringing me back to the present. "Stay with me. We all need your council," he said.

"Indeed," I said. "Let us go meet them." I walked past my friend and pro-ceeded down the path away from the Crystal Sanctuary, my Crystal Sanctuary.

"By the by," Baldua said tentatively as he followed me into the forest. "What did you see just now? It was obvious that you were seeing something. You always get a faraway type of look in your eyes when you go into trance and I bet it was something to do with the future this time. So, what was it? I can ask you that, yes?"

"I saw the future, yes. But, nothing is written in the sky save for what we put there," I replied.

"You're not going to tell me. Is what you're saying?" Baldua said glumly.

"Trust me, my friend. You don't need everything revealed to you. You are to make your own discoveries. And, you are going to have more excitement in the coming seasons than you'll know what to do with," I said.

"I see," said Baldua. "I forgot to mention that someone else is waiting for you at the village, as well," he said, cryptically.

"Oh?"

"Yes. She arrived late last night," Baldua said slyly, as if holding a secret.

"Well, who is it?"

"That, I'm afraid you are going to have to discover for yourself!" he said laughing.

In my heart, I knew who it was: Nimue. I would not have to wait 'til the spring solstice to call to her in my dreams, after all. "So be it!" I replied.

We walked through the forest on our way to the village, to meet our future.

EPILOGUE

The heat was oppressive; the air burned his lungs as he labored to draw breath. Lying on the ground, the man regained consciousness slowly, the deafening din of armies clashing around him aiding in bringing him back to awareness.

"Allah! Allah! Praise the One! Praise Allah!" a black- robed, sword-wielding soldier near him yelled. But the words the soldier yelled had not been in English. *What was it?* wondered the nearly conscious man. *Ah, yes. An Arabic tongue. A nonsensical language, really*, thought the man. He next wondered how he knew it, understood it, if it were nonsensical. He, as a Christian, after all, from God's country of England, and a Crusader in King Richard I's army, came to this place to rid the Holy Land of the infidel and recover the Holiest of Holy relics in Christendom.

Christianity: God's True religion, or so the man had been taught, and so he had believed. Until, that is, he had come to this land and tried to destroy these people – such as the yelling soldier – and take back Christianity's Holy Land and relics from the Muslims.

Muslims. That's what they were, thought the man. Yes, it was coming back to him more and more as he became fully aware. He was around thirty-three years of age, comely, or so he had been told, with thick brown, waving hair down to his shoulders. His eyes were green. His name was Liam Arthur Mason and he hailed from London, England. The year was . . . the year was . . . 1190 in the year of our Lord? 1192? He could not remember.

"Masoud!" someone called.

The man, almost completely conscious now, sat up. His head ached terribly. The fighting was all around. Soldiers on both sides yelled and screamed in frenzied bloodlust, fear or pain, and the clang of swords colliding in combat wrung close to his head; too close. Three sword-wielding combatants—two Arabs and one Crusader—tumbled over him, tripping and falling to the ground, one of the Arabs impaling himself on his curved-bladed sword in the fall.

"Masoud!" someone called again.

Rough hands grabbed the man's right arm, yanking him to his feet and nearly pulling his arm out of its socket in the process. "You are unharmed, Masoud, yes?" a dark-skinned man said to him, still clutching his arm. The dark-skinned man spoke in English, though his English was heavily accented with Arabic. "Sultan Salah al-Din would not be pleased if harm came to you." The dark-skinned man drew in a sharp breath as if he just realized something. "You were not thinking of escape, Masoud! Sultan Salah al-Din has been most merciful to you!"

Alhasan. The dark-skinned one's name was Alhasan, the man remembered. And though Alhasan was dressed as one of the Muslim soldiers, he was actually more Salah al-Din's servant. Alhasan was an odd sort. He was darker skinned than most Arabs, with a long hooked nose and brown eyes that were too close together, thus giving him the look of one who was perpetually cross-eyed. His black turban was always crooked and his dark beard, which had streaks of red in it, had a strange way of parting itself down the center, ending in two points at his collar bones; such was its length.

"Masoud!" Alhasan called the man again, yelling to be heard over the increasingly loud din of the battle. Two more combatants smashed into them, nearly knocking them down. "The spear! Where is the spear?"

Of course. The man's reason for living came crashing back into his mind. It was the reason Salah al-Din, or Saladin, as he was called by the Christian Crusaders, kept him alive. The spear spoke to the man. The sacred Christian relic had been in Muslim hands for some time.

"Masoud!" Alhasan yelled again, urgently, impatiently.

The man knelt down on the ground, on the very spot where he had landed when knocked unconscious. He frantically scuffled his hands through the loose dirt and sand there, searching for something that had become buried. Finally, his hand hit it. He found what he sought and pulled it free from the dirt: the ancient Roman Spear. He stood, held it before his face and reverently kissed the flat of the blade; kissed the very spot where the Lord and Savior's ancient stains remained.

Barely perceptible in the bright light of the day's sun, the blade's tip began to glow a soft white.

"Come!" shouted Alhasan as he turned and ran.

The man, Liam Arthur Mason, known by his Muslim name, Masoud, as well, also turned and followed Alhasan.

You Are What You Love
By Vaishāli

You Are What You Love is the definitive 21st century guide for Spiritual seekers of timeless wisdom who have hit a pothole on the way to enlightenment and are searching for the answers to the big questions in life: "Who am I?" and "Why am I here?" Author Vaishāli explores mystic Emanuel Swedenborg's philosophy of gratitude and love. She expands this wisdom by associating it to traditional sources including Christianity and Buddhism. Through storytelling and humor, the focal point of the book "you don't have love, you are love" is revealed. A compelling read to deepen your understanding of Oneness.

Paperback, 400 pages, ISBN 978-0-9773200-0-4, $24.95

Also available on CD an 80-minute
condensed and abridged version of the 400-page book counter part.
Read by the author.
CD, ISBN 978-0-9773200-2-8, $14.95

Also available on CD an 80-minute condensed and abridged version of the 400-page book counter part. Read by the author.

CD, ISBN 978-0-9773200-2-8, $14.95

You Are What You Love Playbook
By Vaishāli

You Are What You Love Playbook is a playtime manuel offering practical play practices to invoke play into action. Included is step-by-step guidance on dream work, a 13-month course in how to practice playful miracles, and a copy of the author's lucid dream diary. The perfect companion to You Are What You Love.

Paperback, 124 pages, ISBN 978-0-9773200-1-1, $14.95

This abridged audio version of the critically acclaimed novel, LONGINUS: BOOK I OF THE MERLIN FACTOR by Steven Maines, follows the tale of Gauis Cassius Longinus, the Roman Centurion who pierced the side of Jesus with his spear while the condemned one hung from the cross. Abridged Audio Book (3 CD). As Read By Mark Colson

CD, ISBN 978-0-9773200-7-3, $19.95

LONGINUS: BOOK I OF THE MERLIN FACTOR
by Steven Maines

Longinus follows the tale of Gauis Cassius Longinus, the Roman Centurion who pierced the side Jesus with his spear while the condemned one hung from the cross.

After that fateful day, Longinus escapes Rome and the priests who want to take the spear and its supposed power for themselves. LONGINUS follows the Centurion's life from his love for the prostitute Irena to his mystical studies with the Druids of Gaul. But it also reveals Longinus' profound spiritual awakening through his Druidic studies and the spear that speaks to him with the voice of Christ.

Paperback, 241 pages, ISBN 978-0-9773200-3-5, $14.95

Wisdom Rising
By Vaishāli

Sometimes wisdom is best served up like M&M candies, in small pieces that you can savor, enjoy and hold in your hand. So it is with Vaishali's new book, "Wisdom Rising." It is a delightful, sweet, and satisfying collection of brilliant articles and short stories, that like gem quality jewels, are a thing of beauty, and a joy to behold.

It doesn't matter what your background is there is something to appeal to everyone in this book. Vaishali's trademark "out of the box" sense of humor and wild woman perspective runs rampant throughout the book. Whether she is talking about the Nature of God or simply poking fun at our own cultural insecurities and hypocrisies, Vaishali raises the bar on laugh out loud Spiritual wisdom. The entertainment as well as the wisdom rises flawlessly together, inviting the reader to go deeper in examining and showing up for their own life.

Everything about this book from the cover to the cartoon illustrations that punctuate every story, screams playful, fun, witty, and what we have seen Vaishali dish up before . . . which is the unexpected . . . no wonder she is know as "the Spiritual Wild Child."

Paperback, ISBN: 9773200-6-6 $14.95

MYRRIDDIN: BOOK II OF THE MERLIN FACTOR
by Steven Maines

In *MYRRIDDIN: Book II Of The Merlin Factor*, it is the 4th Century A.D. A young boy has found sacred relics of the early Christians in the ruins of an ancient Druid temple on the Isle Of Mystery in Old Britain. For reasons beyond his immediate comprehension, the lad connects with one item in particular; the Spear Of Longinus, the very spear that pierced the side of Jesus and allegedly holds the power of Christ. The boy's name is Myrriddin. The world would remember him as Merlin, the greatest Druid and Wizard of all time.

Paperback, 217 pages, ISBN 978-0-9773200-4-2, $14.95

Children of the Luminaries
by Julia K. Cole

Do you Believe in the Power of Love?

Imagine everything you held dear was suddenly and viciously destroyed in one night by a power-hungry mad man, and now you find yourself being one of only thirteen survivors of a once mighty and powerful race of people.

Imagine that you have learned of another world, much like your own, with the same impending fate. Imagine being presented "the ultimate power", but not knowing what it is or how to use it. Imagine the realization that the future of a billion souls rests upon your shoulders.

How far would you go to save an entire world not your own? What would you be willing to do? How far would you be willing to go to stop the evil that now plagues a world not your own?

Journey with The Oracle and her mentor Demetrius as they race through time and dimensions to stop the dark lord Dagon and put an end to his maniacal plan to obtain the ultimate power and become ruler of all worlds. Bear witness to the quest and to the incredible transformation of The Oracle herself as she goes from naïve spiritualist to one of the most powerful champions of the Universe.

In the end . . . will Love prevail?   Do You Believe?

Paperback, ISBN 978-1-935183-00-6, $19.95

Other Inspirational Books from Purple Haze Press Publisher

Journey Through the Light and Back
by Mellen-Thomas Benedict

In 1982 Mellen-Thomas died of terminal brain cancer and survived to tell about it. While in hospice care Mellen "died" and was without vital signs for at least an hour and a half before he returned to his body.

While on the "other side" Mellen journeyed through several realms of consciousness and beyond the "Light at the end of the tunnel." He was shown in holographic detail Earth's past and a beautiful vision of mankind's future for the next 400 years. He experienced the cosmology of our soul's connection to Mother Earth (Gaia), our manifest destiny, and was gifted with access to Universal Intelligence.

Paperback, ISBN 978-1-935183-01-3 $19.95

Hitchhiker's Guide to the Other Side
(or what to do if you wake up dead)
by Mellen-Thomas Benedict

Based on his real life experience with terminal illness, loss of all hope and his own death. The story of Mellen-Thomas and his NDE has become one of the world's most popular stories about hope and eternal life.

With love and humor Mellen shares his personal insights on death as an interactive and hopeful experience. This book will enlighten and prepare you for what to expect when you or a loved one leaves this life. This is the first practical guide book to the "Other Side" by someone who has been there and returned.

Paperback, ISBN 978-1-935183-03-7 $14.95